THE
CLEANSING

THE CLEANSING

by
GEORGE RABASA

THE PERMANENT PRESS
Sag Harbor, New York 11963

Library of Congress Cataloging-in-Publication Data

Rabasa, George, 1941–
    The cleansing / by George Rabasa.
       p. cm.
    ISBN 1-57962-130-9 (alk. paper)
    1. Physicians—Fiction. 2. Lawyers—Fiction. 3. Revenge—
Fiction. 4. Mexico City (Mexico)—Fiction. 5. Triangles
(Interpersonal relations)—Fiction. I. Title.

PS3568.A213C55 2006
813'.54–dc22   2006046030

Printed in The United States of America.

For Juanita

Twenty years since he had last seen him, Dr. Paul Leander encountered Victor Aruna as a bit of speckled brown tissue which, earlier that morning, had been carved out with a Trucut biopsy needle from the liver of his one-time friend. Under the microscope, which transformed the intricate assemblage of cells into an abstraction of dappled pink, black and white, the Victor he remembered remained fragmented. He wished he could rearrange the image in order to glean Victor's features from the curious topography of ridges and craters and canyons under his lens. There was no hint of the familiar mocking smile, the soft insinuating voice, the green eyes contrasting with brown skin. No matter how intently he had stared at the magnified image, he'd been unable to conjure even a hint of his friend's face the way he would look today, at this moment, sweating out the aftermath of his biopsy in a hospital room half a mile away through the maze of corridors that crisscrossed Scripps Memorial Hospital.

The once-familiar expression remained distant and unfocused, overwhelmed by the immediacy of pulp, bile, and blood from the suspect liver. This particular sliver was not all that distinct from other ravaged samples that came under scrutiny day after day, so Leander searched for the telltale pocks and streaks of cells on a rampage, the battleground of his friend's destiny playing itself out under the lens. Technology has its limits, he thought, as he shut off the light and rolled back his chair.

He had learned of Victor's presence in the oncology wing of Scripps Memorial when his pathology tech, Beth Moreau, came in with the day's harvest of histology samples packed in paraffin inside plastic cases aligned like game pieces on a steel tray.

"Here they are, Dr. Leander. Today's heroes: three livers, two boobs, one lung, three P-glands." Her dark voice endowed their workaday language—*papilloma, melanoma, metastasis*—with a teasing ambiguity that quickened his heartbeat. She handed him a list with the names and numbers assigned by the receiving clerk. For an unnerving instant, he allowed his fingers to brush hers, then pulled his hand away to sign the roster.

He conjured the gentle contours of her body under the shapeless scrubs, only to be rattled by her gaze so that he had to look away. He was aware of the sweetness of her breath—cinnamon or clove or fennel. He'd meant to ask her what brand of toothpaste she used. After about a dozen lunchtime escapes in the past year, he marveled at the effect she still had on him. He wrapped his hand around the coffee mug to disguise the tremor that traveled to his fingertips.

He reached for the cassette identified with a white sticker as log-in *#456-L-01: Aruna, V.* He would do an immediate gross exam before asking Beth to freeze the tissue for subsequent tests.

He probed the resilient flesh with the edge of his forceps. The moist sample, olive-tinged and speckled white, was suspected of showing carcinoma, either a primary tumor or hosting blood-borne metastases. The latter would point to malignancies thriving in yet unidentified areas—lungs, colon, pancreas. The whole mess could be past the healing capabilities of medical technology.

Paul leaned back from the scope, and breathed a sigh of wonder as he rechecked the list to make sure the name matched the code on the sample. He would claim he had not given Victor much thought in the twenty years since he'd last seen him. In truth, some random image, a newspaper headline or a mention in conversation, was enough to trigger the recollection of the man that he and his wife Adele had known in Mexico back in the '80s, and who had so profoundly marked their lives. He assumed that thoughts of Victor Aruna similarly crossed his wife's mind, even if his name seldom came up.

While Leander did his examination, Victor recovered in a private room, a spot on his lower torso bandaged to cover the neat perforation from the biopsy. At the same time, in the opposite wing of

Scripps Memorial, the oncology team was having coffee and muffins on a terrace off the doctors' lounge. There was no great urgency for the pathology results. If the problem turned out to be Hepatitis B and incipient cirrhosis, then treatment would involve lifestyle changes and long-range observation. If the lab reported cancer, then, a liver being a liver, there was nothing to be done in a hurry. The patient could rest nicely sedated the better part of the day, before they would send him home after a cheerless conversation.

Leander tried calling Adele who was in New York on business. She was not in her room or picking up her cell phone. He left a message on the hotel's voice mail system. "I just ran into Victor Aruna," he said. "Into his liver, actually." It was the first time in many years that he'd mentioned their former friend. He wanted to say more, about how he was not particularly happy to encounter him. In fact, he was taking uneasy satisfaction in picturing Victor's mean life coming to an end.

As he pushed and poked the shreds of liver tissue, he pulled apart a bare dot of flesh and held it in the tiny forceps. In some dark corner of his brain he imagined placing the sample on his tongue in a kind of ritual purging of the friend who had over time become a disquieting ghost. He would put the fragment of tissue inside his mouth, force his molars to grind and mix it with his saliva, and make the swallowing action of his throat forceful enough to push the flesh of his friend down inside him. He understood what ritual cannibalism among the Anasazi, the Fiji, and the Aztecs was about. Whatever influence the man had once held over him could be masticated into nothingness, digested and excreted to overcome the power that the memory of Victor Aruna and the time they spent in Mexico City—he and Victor and Adele, all running together in those halcyon days—had cast over him for the past twenty years.

"You're going to show me stuff, doctor?" He was again distracted by Beth Moreau standing close to him.

"Take a look," he said. "Here's a good contrast between a moderately stressed drinking man's liver and one shot-to-hell with hepatocellular carcinoma." He removed the sample from under the lens and laid it on top of the cassette, ready to switch the two items back and forth, a shell game for his tech's edification. He inserted another one that Beth had prepped. This was something he enjoyed, a little mentoring lightened by collegial banter.

"Those white dots?"

"Maybe fat deposits. Potentially ugly."

He shuffled the slides; now you see it, now you don't. He leaned closer to Beth. "Look at the other one."

"It's like a mosaic," she said. "Each cell fits in with the others." He felt her breath on his face.

"Now, close your eyes while I switch them." He was able to peruse her features now, without being noticed. He so badly wanted to touch the outward curve of her chin with a tiny mole off to one side, the hollow behind her ear lobe, the rise of her cheekbone, following a line to the corner of her mouth.

"You're taking a long time juggling things around." She smiled as if she had seen through his professional demeanor.

"You can't be too careful when trying to confuse a pupil." He took the slide off the microscope, and clicked the other one into its place. "Okay." For a moment, he marveled at how successfully he had mixed up the slides.

She nodded seriously, as if more were at stake in her decision than the simple need to impress Leander. "Cancer?"

"Most likely." He beamed at her. "Poor old Señor #456-L-01. Slice off a bit and send it to Mayo for their opinion. I want to be particularly sure on this one."

He had had felt a shiver of remorse as he made the impulsive judgement that Victor Aruna suffered from advanced liver cancer; a second opinion was mandated by the momentary confusion with the samples. Double-checking the results with a respected colleague at Mayo would eventually sort things out. Victor Aruna in Room 346 was, in any case, the source of biopsy #456-L-01.

He quickly tapped out his report and e-mailed the oncologist in charge. In Leander's opinion there was little to be done for Señor Aruna, short of a transplant.

He again got no answer from Adele's cell phone. Her voice-mail message said that she had flown to New York for a presentation.

She had not mentioned her trip when they awoke on opposite sides of the bed to NPR on the clock radio. As was their custom, she pushed herself off the bed at the first glimmer of wakefulness, while he lingered, attentive to news of disasters that might have struck in the night, taking note of the weather, collecting his thoughts for the day ahead. The sound of the shower elicited an image of Adele's angular symmetry of shoulders, knees, elbows, hips. In their twenty-some years together, her body had gone from the supple and seemingly languorous to a coiled readiness toned by a lean diet and brutal yoga.

Her energy created a distance between them. Around her, he felt sluggish and dull. Even that morning, already hovering in different worlds, she dressing while he showered, she slicing a melon and toasting bread while he dressed, then for a moment, facing each other across the kitchen table, for a brief but purposeful sharing of breakfast, her actions seemed distant. Neither would acknowledge, if asked, this dulling effect their presence seemed to have on each other. Later, an unanticipated moment's tension would have them bumping into each other in the kitchen, starting conversations, changing the subject, hearing something different than what had been said, doing little to soothe a blunt word or dismissive shrug. Her not volunteering that morning that she would be spending the night in a hotel in New York wounded him, if slightly. He resented that he was not able to tell her that Victor Aruna was about to re-enter their lives.

❧ 2 ❧

Finally, at the end of the day, Leander decided to visit Victor. He took a hesitant step into room 346, already dark at five PM, its blinds shuttered, the large fluorescent lights mercifully off. He shut the door with a muted click. In contrast to the flat beige walls, the shape of the visitor's chair, the tall bed rising in the middle of the room, he could see the patient lying under a stark white sheet, only the outward curve of his belly visibly rising and falling with the long rhythms of his sleeping breath. Approaching the bed, he recognized Victor Aruna, even with twenty more pounds on him, even with the addition of a drooping moustache, thinning hair, his face bloated by dense sleep. Poor Victor, the soft curve of his lips, almost feminine in their delicacy, had been replaced by the half-open mouth, saliva welling up at one corner. He checked the chart hanging at the foot of the bed; hours after his biopsy, Victor was enjoying a nice snooze on pharmaceutical opiates.

It was unusual for Leander to visit patients. He was afraid of their pain, of their expressions of fear, of the pressure of wives and children demanding an overruling of the fates. Having little tolerance for suffering, he had chosen a depersonalized relationship with disease. It enabled him to avoid the rituals of the terminally ill, the counterpoint of harsh reality and imaginative denial: *The situation does not look good. Patients with similar conditions have been known to respond to treatment. There are options, from chemo to massive housecleaning. Bad glands and nodes and marrow can be ripped out. How about a transplant?*

Victor's long, even breaths became hesitant; a gasp was followed by a soft moan. His pale green eyes opened wide as if

11

startled; an overgrown bear of a shadow hovered massively, hugely, overwhelmingly concrete. He'd been lying in a Demerol fog after his biopsy when, after all these years, his friend Paul Leander stood by the bed, and, he could tell by the movement of his lips, began speaking to him.

"Hola, amigo," Leander said, responding to a flicker of awareness in the man's eyes. "How are you feeling?"

"Doctorcito, cabrón!" Victor rasped. "Qué pinche milagro. I thought I was going to wake up in hell. And now here you are."

"Ya ves," Leander smiled. "Miracles for those who deserve them." He hadn't been called "little doctor" since attending the medical school of the National University of Mexico. They'd all had nicknames then. He was Doctorcito. Adele, already making a name in photography, was La Fotomaniaca. Victor, because of his dabbling from tantric Buddhism to María Sabina's magic mushrooms, was El Brujo.

"I saw you staring down at me and wondered which one of us was a ghost." A small dry laugh was choked off by pain needling into his side.

"It has been a long time, Victor."

"Twenty years," the man sighed. "And now we're enjoying a reunion of sorts."

"Is that why you came to Scripps?"

"A coincidence," he shrugged. "Scripps is where rich Mexicans go when we get scared."

"You didn't know I was here?"

"How would I? You and Adele didn't even say goodbye when you left Mexico."

"That's another story."

"Yes," Victor said with a groan, as if the effort to add anything further to the conversation might be beyond him. "Are you responsible for this?" He pointed at the square bandage neatly covering a spot on his midriff.

Leander smiled. "I didn't touch you."

"Your hands are clean, then?" Victor said.

"In the matter of the piercing wound into your liver, yes."

"Just an innocent bystander."

12

"As innocent as anyone is in medicine," Leander said. "I'm the pathologist on your case."

"Ajá!"

"Yes."

"Well, I guess there's not much more we can talk about without getting to the heart of the matter," Victor said. "The liver, to be precise."

"Better that your doctor explain your options."

"He did," the man sighed. "I have none. Unless I apply for a transplant and don't die before my turn comes." Victor winced again, as if in pain from recalling the conversation, rather than from his wound. "There are always options," he said. "I am not going to die at the age of forty-five. I won't play along with that devil's joke. I assure you."

"I'm here for you, Victor." Leander was not sure he'd found the tone that would express a sincerity he did not feel. "Anything you need at Scripps, let me know."

"You are the only one," he said.

"Your family? Your wife?"

"Three wives." Victor frowned. "They all hate me. I am such a cabrón, you know," he boasted cheerfully.

"Surely, if they knew your situation . . ."

"I am not kidding," he shook his head. "These monsters would sit on my face and smother me out of my misery."

"Like I said," Leander repeated without any sense of what he could offer. "Cuentas con nosotros."

"Con Adele también?"

"Of course. She's been busy, downright frantic. But we've talked. As soon as you're out of here, we'll have a good visit, the three of us."

"Like old days."

"Better than the old days, Victor," Leander smiled. "We've all grown up, verdad?"

Victor closed his eyes and for a few moments seemed to be considering Leander's statement. He sighed and reached for the buzzer behind the headboard. "They have very nice pills here," he said. "You should try them."

"One of the perks of being a doctor," Leander smiled.

"Puro bullshit. I imagine you've cleaned up," he said. "But maybe you can use your influencias to get me extras."

"They'll give you all you need," Leander said.

Waves of lukewarm well-being lapped at the edges of Victor's consciousness, starting with a numbness in his limbs and on up to a tingling, no more than a warm tickle really, deep into the center of his belly. But then his facial muscles relaxed, his head turned to one side, and he was dozing again. He did not seem quite the scoundrel bragging about the three ex-wives who might travel a thousand miles to this hospital room, intent on killing him.

Two nurses came in to check on Victor's incision. Leander stood back and watched. They were brisk and efficient, with rounds to make in sixteen rooms for a total of twenty patients in varying states of misery. "We need some light in here." The older nurse switched on the overhead lamp. The glare solidified the mound of Victor's swaddled body.

The older nurse seemed surprised to see Leander. "Does pathology have concerns regarding this patient?"

"He's someone I know," he said. "We were visiting before he fell asleep."

"It's the pills," she said. "He sure likes his dope. I'm supposed to adjust the dosage down."

"What for?" Leander asked.

"We wouldn't want him addicted." The woman declared. "Would we?"

"What we don't want," he said, "is for this particular patient to be in any pain."

"Most insured patients are sent home after a liver biopsy," she said. "This one seems to have paid for a vacation."

"His need for medical care is not for you to judge."

"Yes, doctor," she said, her neck reddening.

Victor moaned softly, possibly feigning sleep, as the nurse pulled down the sheet, raised the threadbare cotton gown to reveal his smooth shaved belly still smeared with pink antiseptic, the bandage folded into a slender pillow, silky strips holding the padding in place. She tugged at the top of the bandage and it came off easily, the adhesive bands clinging at first, then separating neatly from the skin. Underneath, the incision was blackened and crusted over from earlier seepage. The smell of disinfectant mingling with dried blood and sweat from the body's upheaval in the past thirty-six hours made Leander queasy. Victor whimpered at the tweezers picking off tendrils of cotton from the wound and then at the vigorous swabbing of antiseptic. "It's closing up nicely," the older nurse pointed out. "But younger patients tend to heal faster."

"You ladies don't need my help to do your job." Leander tried to sound lighthearted. Stepping back to a corner of the room, he found himself panting as if the closed space had choked his breathing. He was embarrassed for Victor Aruna; there was something shameful in acknowledging that the body's intelligence had been tricked by cancer cells stupidly multiplying.

Now, as Victor lay reeling from the revelation that his days were numbered, Paul wondered if finding some explanation for life's turns would give him solace. "It's payback time, Victor," he wanted to say. Instead, he clasped his friend's hand and gave it a squeeze. Paul marveled that he could keep his lingering hostility in check.

"I have this pain pulsating deep in my guts." Victor was again awake. "That criminal surgeon left something in my liver before he sewed me up."

Paul shook his head and smiled as doctors do when dealing with patients. "It was just a needle in and out."

"Pues con mi pinche suerte," he groaned. "I would be the one in a thousand to keep a souvenir inside me. You wouldn't believe my luck, doctorcito. There are a dozen people who would like to kill me. My third wife's brothers. A particularly resentful socio in my import-export business. My eldest daughter who blames me for her latest husband. I wouldn't be the first execution by surgeons in the pay of *la eme*. You know, the Mexican mafia, the bloodiest of all."

He smiled apologetically and asked after a pause. "I need to know what *you* think."

Leander looked away for an instant. "You are very sick, Victor."

15

"What exactly did you see?"

"Your doctor must've discussed that with you."

"He did. But you and I have known each other almost half our lives. I should hear the truth from you. You don't need to communicate with me through some cabrón doctor who didn't even know my name three days ago."

"You've been told the tumor in your liver is malignant," Leander said, sounding to himself like a technician whose vision of human suffering was no larger than a microscope slide. "That's tough."

"Did you actually see them take out the piece of my liver?"

"I was not in the room, no."

"Maybe that sample didn't come from me."

"I wish," Leander said. "There are procedures to make sure there are no mix-ups. Your name was on the paperwork. That's how I found out you were in the hospital." He scolded him gently, "You should've called to say you were in town."

"What a great idea." Victor scowled. "It is entirely possible that the tumor came from someone else, that it was sent to you under my name in order to have some medical excuse for opening me up."

"Not likely." Leander felt a flush spreading from the back of his neck.

"Possible?" he insisted.

"You're better off facing reality, Victor."

"Why?"

Leander nodded. "It's what a good Buddhist would do."

"I was more of a tantric," Victor cracked a smile through the pain. "A Mexican macho tantric."

"I remember now. Tantra was whatever excess you wanted to indulge in," Leander said. "Very convenient, no?"

"You still mistrust me." Victor grimaced even as he tried to laugh away the accusation. "Which hurts my feelings."

"You never had many feelings, Victor."

The man lifted his head from the pillow with some effort and stared at Leander in mock surprise. "We must've been on different planets, then," he said. "Anyway, where am I?"

16

"You know where," Leander said impatiently. "Scripps Memorial."

"No, pendejo," Victor groaned. "This room, this bed, my head. Where are they. North? South?"

"This is the East Wing," Leander said.

"Good start. Which way is my head pointing?"

❧ 3 ❧

They left voice-mail messages on both coasts, returned calls to recorded greetings, worked out the details through the clutter of their Blackberries. Finally, Paul and Adele, husband and wife, managed to meet for dinner at a small café in Cove Beach, halfway between his hospital and her ad agency. He was already there, letting a bottle of their favorite pinot grigio chill, when she arrived, slightly irritable, complaining about the delayed flight, the traffic on I-5, the dozens of e-mails. They might have looked like a couple on a date except that they were oddly mismatched, he in shorts and batik shirt, she still in her functional blacks and grays, her blonde hair cut blunt at the collarbone, the overall severity leavened by her brooch of a Venetian carnival mask. She brushed a light kiss on his lips. "Hey, look at *you*," she exhaled as she sat opposite him. "On vacation?"

"Just happy to see you." He made himself smile.

She acknowledged his compliment with a nod. "I would've stopped to change, but I was late already."

There was an awkwardness to those first moments sitting opposite each other in the dusky room, the spattered ochre walls glowing under the setting sun. "Good meeting?" he asked as he poured wine in her glass.

She shrugged. It had been years since she enjoyed bringing him stories from the client wars.

He saw his hand tremble and quickly put the bottle down on the table. He marveled how after all this time, he was already feeling a disquieting effect from Victor's presence between them. "Flight okay?"

She nodded. "A five-hour snooze, once we finally got off."

"We should toast this," he said. "Our first dinner together in a week."

"Over a week."

"Yes. Nearly two."

"You've managed to have some fun?"

He knew what she was asking, already mocking him even before they'd had a chance to go through their elaborate renditions of how their time apart had been spent, even while living in the same house. In the past few years they had reached an unspoken accord not to inquire directly about each other's occasional infidelities, but their conversational code nevertheless managed to dig out some shadow of the truth.

"Real fun is not so easy to come by."

"Like true love."

"Harder," he said. "You can be in love and not have any fun at all."

"Well, I had no fun. Not in the least," she said.

"I didn't ask."

"In case you were wondering."

They changed the subject when the waiter arrived, a thin man named Marshall whom they knew from regular visits to the café. They liked him and gave him nice tips and he usually managed to get them seated at one of his tables by the big windows overlooking the water. Through the years he had overheard a few contentious exchanges between the two, yet always greeted them with an impassive smile. "Ah," he declared. "The doctor and the artist meet again."

"What's good, Marshall?" asked Adele.

He leaned in as if to reveal a closely held secret. "Baby squid. Inky black over white rice, red pepper flakes, much garlic."

"Okay," said Paul.

"Two?"

"Yes," said Adele. "In the spirit of togetherness."

"Like in the old days," Paul said, after Marshall had retreated with their order. "We always ate the same thing. Even during those days in Mexico, we read the same books. We agreed on Reagan, Tarantino, Madonna."

19

"The two of us, joined at the hip," Adele said.

"Except when there were three of us."

Adele took a breath as if to steel herself for the conversation, thus far avoided. "What does he want, anyway?"

Paul reached for the bottle and refilled their glasses. The pause allowed him to think up more than a rhetorical response. "Not to die alone," he said finally.

"Is he so sick?" Adele pursed her lips, keeping her other thoughts in check.

"That's what he's been told. And then I gave him the spin about how we all are dying. Some of us faster than others."

"How is he doing with it?"

"He's trying to sort the information out. Meanwhile he's happy to annoy the staff," Paul said. "He figured out that his head was pointing south, the cardinal point of rot and decay and dissolution. To be so oriented would hasten his death."

"More of his mystical mumbo jumbo."

"He made a couple of orderlies rearrange his bed with his head to the east, to better absorb the energy of the rising sun. He kept shouting that he was a morning person."

"That's a laugh. I don't have any memories of Victor in the daytime. Except him sleeping off whatever he'd ingested in the night."

"His doctor tried to tell him he was going home anyway, and that he could reposition his body any old way he wanted. Then, Victor accused all of us of leaving surgical material inside him. He's sure there's a contract out on him. That's why he came to the U.S. to have himself checked out. He claims his liver was fine until his third wife back in Mexico City bribed the cook to season his enchiladas with poison."

"He has an imagination," Adele said.

They fell silent when Marshall arrived with the two mounds of black squid drowning in inky broth. He refilled their glasses. Paul thought he was actually hovering longer than he had to, hoping, perhaps, for another installment in his customers' interesting lives. "Marshall the waiter is writing a novel, about us," Paul muttered.

"I can't wait to read it." Adele stirred the squid into the fluffy rice, staining it black with each turn of the fork.

"I can't wait to see how it ends," Paul said.

"It doesn't. It just goes on."

"Like a soap opera."

"Longer."

"Are you okay with that?"

"You mean with not getting a divorce?" She put the fork down.

"Right. Continuing until death do us part."

"Morbid," she shuddered. "That's how long we intended to be friends, you and I, and Victor Aruna. Remember the ceremony? The first three-way nuptials in history." She ate hungrily.

"Officiated by a real priest. Padre Anselmo was way ahead of the Vatican."

"He was a brave one. He married men to men, siblings to each other, old women to their cats."

"Now, our missing third is back, twenty years later."

"How did he know you were at Scripps?"

"He claims he was surprised to wake up and see me staring down at him. That it's a happy coincidence."

"Do you believe him?"

"Yes. Why would he show up now?"

"To ask forgiveness?" Adele rolled her eyes.

"I'm not happy that he's picked us two out of his past to die with. He carries more bad baggage than we may know how to deal with."

"Maybe he's changed," she said hopefully.

"He has," Paul said. "He's soft and balding and his liver has crumpled to the consistency of an old tennis shoe." Paul sighed. "He assumes he'll die in months."

"Is that what you decided?"

"I look at slides, Adele," he said.

"Really definite about this, are you?"

"There's always room for the indefinite."

"Did you ever think it would be up to you to tell him?"

"I didn't think I'd ever have to tell him anything," Paul said. "I was glad he faded out of our lives."

"He didn't fade very far back," Adele said. "Not too many days pass when I don't get an echo of his voice, a flash of his mouth or his eyes. Your message didn't surprise me. I've always expected Victor to show up."

"He's getting out of the hospital tomorrow."

"What else can you do for him, besides read out his death sentence?"

"He doesn't want to be alone, for one thing."

"Surely he has people in Mexico."

"They're not crazy about him."

"And we are?"

"We did follow him to some strange places," Paul said. "Our guide into the mysteries of the hidden city."

"Only to leave us to get lost," she said. "Now he wants to follow *us* home?"

"I haven't invited him." He shook his head in resignation rather than denial.

Adele did not see his expression. She'd been moving her fork idly through her plate; her appetite had vanished. She watched Paul bite into the last of his squid and drain half a glass of the pinot in one draught. Considering this was the first meal they'd shared in some weeks, they'd had little to say beyond mulling the reemergence of Victor Aruna. "I won't believe he's here until I see him," she said suddenly.

From the start, back in the eighties, their friendship had been an uneasy triangle. Out together, Adele enjoyed Victor's role as the worldly man-about-town. He would lead them on nightlong escapades through the rough nightlife of Mexico City, and still get Leander safely to his eight AM class at the University.

Victor did not seem to have a job or family obligations. He hung out with a group that people called Los Juniors. They were the sons of government officials and prominent businessmen. They had money, IDs from the judicial police, diplomatic passports, fake press credentials. Together, they attracted American students in summer programs at the university with a mixture of good looks, charm, and quality drugs. Victor was twenty-five and he had never worked a day. He had been a law student for a couple of years, but eventually he stopped attending class, though he remained enrolled at the university. Eventually, without taking any exams that he could recall, he was awarded a degree.

One morning, he got up around noon, just as the mail carrier was driving away from his parents' house in the Lomas. He'd left a flat brown package addressed to Victor. It was his diploma from the University, shiny black calligraphy on parchment suitable for framing and hanging on the wall of his despacho with the name of the new Licenciado Victor Aruna. He admired the certificate and thought to himself, "Ah qué la chingada, soy abogado." He assumed his father had something to do with it all; he would remember to thank him. They would trade abrazos, and Victor would promise that the title would spur him to make something of his life. Perhaps open a little office on Calle Génova, near the Zona Rosa restaurants, with a massive oak desk and green leather chairs, and a pretty secretary who would also have to be bright. He'd use his father's contacts to help people with their problems—tax problems, labor problems, immigration problems. Nothing complicated. Situations that could be resolved with a phone call or two. "Dame una manita con este asunto." Give me a hand, old buddy, he would coax his friends and his father's friends and the friends of their friends.

The first person he called with the good news was Adele Zarbo. She was working so hard at her photography that she managed to make him feel vaguely embarrassed by his idle life.

"I'll be your first client," she said, because there were many ways a good lawyer in Mexico City could be helpful.

"Adele, mi amor," he said. "You don't need a licenciado. You need an amante."

"He asked about you, of course," Paul said, feeling a familiar pang of jealousy. He folded his napkin and used it to brush a scattering of bread crumbs off the table, as if it were his job to prepare for their departure by tidying up. He looked out at the sun setting into the Pacific. Victor would appreciate a surprise visit from Adele.

23

❖ 4 ❖

They found Victor in a tan summer suit with a silk shirt open at the collar, sitting upright on the bed. His feet, still small while the rest of him had bloated, were delicately encased in a pair of basketweave loafers. A suitcase of blond, buttery leather, already zipped and latched, stood by the door.

"Adele, querida." He winced as he stood up to give her a light kiss. "Forgive me for not having the energy to give you a big abrazo. The hole in my side prevents any such displays of emotion."

"Victor," she murmured, clasping both his hands. "Cómo te sientes?"

"Miserable," he said. He turned to Leander as if asking for confirmation.

Leander ignored the look and stepped around the side of the chair to rest his hand on the man's shoulder. "I'm glad we caught you before you left," he said.

Victor seemed momentarily puzzled. "I wasn't about to go anywhere without you, was I?"

"I would hope not," Adele said. "We don't want to lose track of you again."

"No chance of that, verdad, doctorcito?" He forced out a small laugh. "Unless you have a very big house."

Adele gave her husband a quick look. "Paul didn't tell me you were visiting us."

"Maybe it's something I dreamt. But I remember you offered your old friend a room. Just a bed, and time away from anybody who might wonder where I am."

"We're hardly ever home, you know." Leander hid his surprise with a brisk nod. "There are some terrific places where you will be better taken care of."

"You prefer I go to a hotel?" He tried to sound casual about the idea, yet kept glancing from Paul to Adele for some reassurance.

"Not a hotel," Leander said cheerfully. "These B&Bs are like your own home. With a living room to hang out in, and great breakfasts, and a view of the ocean."

Victor sat back down on the edge of the bed, his knees primly together. "I don't need much," he said. "Just your company. For a very few days. Until I adjust, you know, to this news about my body. I've grown accustomed to it growing ugly on the outside. It turns out it's even uglier inside."

"I imagine we can find a way to look after you." Leander avoided Adele's gaze.

"Ay, amigos. I'm getting the feeling that you resent me still." Victor raised his eyebrows as if the thought had seemed inconceivable to him only a second before. "Twenty years is not enough time to leave the past behind?" He seemed to plead with his eyes.

"Nonsense. We want you to be comfortable." Leander raised his hands in surrender. "I hadn't thought things through. Stay with us. I insist."

"Absolutely," Adele added briskly. "It will be fun. We'll catch up. It will be like old times."

Victor stood up again, this time quietly triumphant, it seemed to the other two. "All that is true. Except for old times. Nothing is ever like old times."

"In a manner of speaking," Leander said.

"Well, yes," Victor conceded. "In a manner of speaking, anything can be true." He stood unsteadily for a few moments before Adele stepped to his side. He linked his arm in hers. Leander followed them down the hall with the suitcase.

Victor rode with Leander in his BMW, chattering about how wonderful it was that his friend had made a good life for himself. He caressed the leather seat and tweaked the various control buttons for the windows and the air conditioning and the sound system. He whistled in approval because he said it would not be as happy a meeting if it had turned out that the opposite was the case, that they had nothing to show for the passing years. One should always have a success story ready in case former friends make an appearance. He claimed he had always known that el doctorcito and la Zarbo had it in them to make a good prosperous life for themselves. It gave him satisfaction, he said, that this was true, and he would take some pride in their accomplishments. And here, as the car rolled into a gently inclined driveway, was the proof. Paul and Adele's house was positioned on the coastal road high above the ocean, a one-story of weathered siding fronted by flowering bougainvillea and thick bushes exploding with red and pink hibiscus. Green marble steps led into the foyer and the main room with a sliding glass door that opened out to the terrace jutting beyond the edge of the cliff above the surf.

Victor walked around the house, acting stronger than in his hospital room. He was fascinated by the alarm system, the code that had to be punched within seconds of entering the house. Otherwise, sirens would blare, lights would flash, and in eight minutes or less armed guards would show up. "This is wonderful," Victor said. "I could get rich selling this stuff in Mexico. But life seems so safe here. What do you have to be afraid of?"

"Drug users believe all doctors keep a stash in their bathroom cabinet."

"And you don't?"

"No," Leander shook his head emphatically. "But I've been paranoid since Mexico. It comes with a guilty conscience, you know. You think that whatever bad things you may have done in the past are somehow going to find you and bite you in the ass."

Victor gingerly lowered himself onto the plush sofa. He toyed with the glass fruit in a bowl, pretending he was about to juggle a brilliant strawberry, a golden lemon and a purple plum. He gazed around the walls and noticed the Tamayo watermelon and a couple of Cuevas ink monsters he had helped Leander buy in Mexico. Victor pushed buttons on the remote and marveled at the sound that came pouring out of speakers hidden around the living room. He turned up the volume and stood at the big window facing the wide expanse of blue ocean while the soaring Caballé as Norma came up behind him.

26

"Qué bonito," Victor exclaimed. "You are both so refined now."

"If we could only stay put long enough to enjoy it all," Adele said.

"Well, I will enjoy it for the two of you," Victor said expansively, scrunching himself deeper into the sofa. "Claro, for only a very few days."

Paul and Adele assumed a loose cheerfulness as they showed Victor to the guest room. They played at being hotel keepers, making the bed with crisp ivory sheets and stacking a set of fluffy towels in the adjacent bathroom. Adele even placed a few M&Ms on the pillow.

That night Leander marveled at how Victor Aruna had ended up sleeping just down the hall from their bedroom. His intention had been to have a parting visit with their old friend, and then set him loose, alone with the knowledge of imminent death eating at his mind. Everybody involved in his case would want to disengage themselves as soon as possible.

The next morning Victor was up early. There would be time for the three of them to enjoy breakfast before Leander and Adele headed out. Leander scrambled eggs, heated up tortillas and enhanced canned beans with cumin and oregano. Adele squeezed oranges and brewed the fragrant Chiapas coffee that they liked. They sat out on the terrace in the cool air of the morning. It felt as if they were back in Mexico, except that Victor did not seem hungry. He tasted the eggs, chewing them thoughtfully, then tried mixing them up with the beans. He sprinkled salt on his tortilla and made a taco with the beans and the eggs, and tasted that, but no combination seemed to please him.

"No hay chile?" he finally said.

"Well, sure," Adele said. There had to be some salsa around. She peered into the different corners of the fridge.

"I'm sure we have Tabasco, somewhere," Leander assured Victor. "Tabasco would be okay, wouldn't it?"

"Christ," Adele said. "Let's just eat without salsa."

"I can't believe we don't have any hot sauce in the whole house," Leander muttered, slamming cupboard doors and counter drawers. "He's used to eating with chile."

27

"I can go to a store," Victor offered. "Is there a tienda nearby?"

"A five minute drive," Leander said. "But your eggs will be cold by then."

"You shouldn't worry about me," Victor said. "I will go buy some salsa."

"Por favor, Victor," Adele said. "Stay put. I'll get the salsa. Any particular kind?"

"Gracias, querida," he said. "Habanera. La más picante."

"You got it." She gave him a tight smile. "Stay with Paul while I go on a capsicum run."

Paul ran behind Adele and stopped her as she was heading out. "Let's try not to be too cranky about this," he said. "We can work at being hospitable."

When Leander returned to the kitchen, Victor was eating hungrily, happily piling the beans on the eggs and scooping them up with the tortillas. He smacked and slurped, pausing only momentarily to shape pieces of tortilla into little makeshift spoons to gather the juice from the beans. Beside him was a jar of Herdez jalapeños.

"Where did those come from?" Leander asked.

"My suitcase," smiled Victor. "I should have remembered that we Mexicans always travel with an emergency supply of chiles, no?" He bit off half a pepper and grinned triumphantly.

"You could've waited five minutes for Adele."

"Well, you know, I didn't want the eggs to go to waste. Cold eggs are no good at all." His words were muffled as he chewed, the food in his mouth punching out his cheeks. "Qué es eso de capsicum?" he asked.

Leander laughed for the first time that morning. "It's the secret ingredient that makes chile peppers burn. Your brain discharges endorphins so that the pain will make you happy."

"Ah, I'm surprised your DEA has not made salsa illegal."

"Do you still get high, Victor?"

"Only when I hurt."

"There are a lot of good prescription pain killers you can have."

"There are worse kinds of pain than pain in the liver," he said.

"I know, Victor."

28

"You *know*, doctorcito?" Victor had wiped the plate clean with the last tortilla, and was leaning back on the chair, tilting it precariously, one foot caught in the table leg to keep from toppling over. He delicately placed his fingers on his lips to stifle a burp. "Perdón," he said.

"I'm glad you enjoyed breakfast, Victor," Leander said. "Put the jalapeños away. Adele will be pissed."

Victor screwed the lid tightly, and tucked the jar under a pile of newspapers. "So tell me how you take care of your pain, doctorcito," Victor said. "You must be like a boy in a candy store at the Scripps."

"I've been in good health." Leander rapped his knuckles on the table top.

"You don't have pain of the heart? The soul?"

"None that I feel." Leander shook his head. "You were always so melodramatic, Victor."

"And you so in control, *doc-tor-ci-to*." Victor bit off the syllables, in a kind of mocking rhythm.

Little doctor, Leander thought to himself. A Mexican endearment, which Victor had inflected with an ambiguous edge. He let the word slide past. "I didn't mean to sound smug," he said. "No question you've been dealt a rough hand."

"God as croupier," Victor said. "I see in my body the black hand of the gods."

"More than one?" he smiled. "It makes it hard to pin the blame on all of them."

"They take turns. A host of gods wouldn't be able to handle all the dirty work that needs to be done. Even with their specialized tasks, the god of livers and the god of hearts and the god of lungs and the god of blood, each must be appeased if you want to stay in one piece for the better part of your life."

"That takes care of personal responsibility."

Victor frowned as if the effort of finding the right words was taxing him. "Do we let pain live inside us? Physical, mental, spiritual, all kinds of pain. Like an unwelcome guest."

Leander heard Adele pull up to their drive, the engine shut off after a moment, the door slammed. He was glad for the interruption.

29

By the time she came into the kitchen with a shopping bag full of groceries the two men had fallen silent.

"Here are the salsas." She pulled out cans and jars out of the bag. "Tomatillo, chipotle, habanero. All super-hot." She glanced at the empty plate in front of Victor. "It looks like I'm late."

"Querida," Victor smiled sheepishly. "The eggs were getting cold."

"Well, you can make quesadillas for lunch," she said showing him a round of Oaxaca cheese and a can of Doña María stewed cactus. "With nopalitos."

"Gracias, Adele," he said. "Eres un amor."

"We want you to be happy," she said. "Paul and I, the two of us."

"El doctorcito here has just been engaging me in stimulating conversation." Victor smiled.

"Well, you two enjoy your man-to-man talk," she smiled. "I'm off to New York."

"Again?" Paul complained. He would have liked her help entertaining their unexpected guest.

"Yes, darling, for my photo film ad campaign." She seemed oddly cheerful, for Victor's benefit, he thought. "Instead of the usual babies and puppies, I'm giving them mutant frogs. Very today."

A moment later she was out the door, pulling a black suitcase behind her, a leather portfolio dangling from her shoulder. He and Victor hurried to help her carry her things out to the waiting taxi. Victor seemed particularly energetic all of a sudden, as if he'd forgotten his decaying liver. He lifted the bag and shoved it in the trunk of the car and then pulled open the door for Adele. She kissed Paul on the lips, and, quickly, Victor on the cheek. As soon as the taxi had turned the corner down Hyacinth Street and onto the Boulevard, Victor grew very pale, his legs unsteady. Leander took his arm as they shuffled up the driveway, through the front door, to a chair in the vestibule.

"I managed to look pretty strong there for a while, didn't I?" Victor spoke haltingly between breaths.

"Sí, señor. Adele was very impressed."

"I get the feeling she was glad to leave."

"She's enthusiastic about her work."

"No, relieved to get away from me."

"Nonsense. She's delighted to see you."

"Ajá, then you'd better watch me. She's beautiful, like always."

It took several minutes before Victor could stand, even if somewhat unsteadily. He jostled his way past Leander back to the living room. Steadying himself on the armrests of the sofa, he sat down stiffly. "I don't know what happened there," he sounded surprised.

"The biopsy is not a big deal, Victor. You've had hepatitis and cirrhosis for years," Leander said. "They're the start of your problems."

"Ah, sí, doctorcito. It's good of you to remind me."

"Tell me how I can help," Leander said. "Adele and I are glad you're here."

"Tu casa es mi casa?"

"That's right."

"Don't worry," Victor said. "I'm not going to sit here like meat rotting." He paused for a moment, as the effort of speaking made his breath short. "But the truth is, it will be good for me to stay with you. Because nobody knows I'm here, you see. And there are people who would like to know where I am."

Leander laughed. "You owe some money?"

"Not money exactly," he said.

"You've been up to no good. Why am I not surprised?"

"You thought I would reform?"

"Comes with age for most of us."

"There are old men out there still getting into trouble," Victor laughed.

"And you are one of them, I suppose."

"I want to die *before* I reform. I'll get the last laugh." Victor paused and gazed fixedly into Leander's eyes, as if searching out some hidden truth in their movements. The revealing blink. The brief jerk to the side. "And the longer I live, the bigger the laugh."

"Are you asking me how big a laugh you will have?"

31

"Yes, I guess I am," Victor sighed.

"Your life expectancy is your doctor's call, Victor."

"He just said I should enjoy myself."

"It's good advice."

"For the two of us, doctorcito," Victor laughed. "Your wife is out of town. We can have a good time."

"I'll call for a pizza tonight," Leander said. "Pick up a couple of bad movies."

Victor made a face like a disappointed child. "You're not going to call some putas to come and see us? I bet you have phone numbers for the best. Amigo, it has been too long since I have had sex with an American girl."

"I'm past whoring, Victor."

"But you are having a small affair, correct?" He added, "Or would like to."

"It's not the same as calling over whores while my wife is away."

"You're going to deny a little candy to a dying man?"

"I have to go to the hospital," Leander said, with exaggerated reluctance. "Behave yourself until tonight, okay?"

"Of course, doctorcito," Victor smiled. "What do you suggest I do all day?"

"You can take a nap, take a walk, take a drive in Adele's sports car. It's fun."

As an afterthought, he showed Victor how to log on to the internet with the computer he kept in his study, how to click on to Yahoo. He demonstrated e-mail and the scanner if Victor wanted to send pictures of himself to his wife and kids. He sent him on an adventure of discovery to a million porn sites. "Look Victor, this is fun," he said. "You can look at Asian girls and Latina girls and American girls, all of them having wild close-up sex."

"I didn't know computers were such fun!" Victor sighed as the screen filled with genitalia. Leander left the room, shutting the door behind him.

Google led Victor to latinasluts.com, nastylolitas.com, all-blowjobs.com. A pornographer's cornucopia, open day and night, at that very moment, in an eternal present, ready when he was. He

32

left the screen glowing and stood stiffly from his slump on the chair. He checked his body for unfamiliar pain, the knife in his side, the cramp in his lower belly, the blurring of his eyesight. He was alert to warnings now, even if, according to Leander, the twinges meant nothing. He expected his cancer to spread, a wildfire mestastizing through liver to lung to lymph glands to marrow to throat to brain. Eventually, he was told, the body eats itself in a kind of onanistic cannibalism that exceeds the most bizarre horror show.

❦ 5 ❦

In 1982, the year she met Victor Aruna, Adele Zarbo had arrived in Mexico City on a Flecha Roja bus from Ciudad Juarez determined to build a career with commercial photo assignments and gallery showings. She was tall and angular at twenty-three, taller than most Mexican men. She carried herself with fine posture, her head haughtily tilted back, her face bearing a serious expression. Mexican men were too intimidated to call out the usual *güeritas* and *mamacitas* that American women drew. She wore a wide-brimmed hat against the sun, a long peasant skirt, huarache sandals and a huipil, inspired by Frida Kahlo. There should be no doubt in anybody's mind that she was an artist.

She had sixty dollars and two good cameras—a large-format Hasselblad and a Rolleiflex. Also, a portfolio of pictures she had taken in El Paso. The images were mostly of immigrant men waiting for work, and women with children in rebozos slung on their backs simply waiting. She had business cards from guys in New York ad agencies with contacts in Mexico. She would make money shooting handsome men in cars, cute children eating cereal, even cuter dogs and cats posing next to bags of Purina. That would give her the time to get a show of her serious photography. She called herself La Zarbo.

During those years, Mexico City teemed with foreigners, mostly from the U.S. and England and Germany, many cultivating the impression that they were wildly successful someplace else. Mexico seemed ripe for the picking. Mexican clients wanted to believe that anyone from the same country as Jackson Pollock and Phillip Roth and Coppola and Caballé was blessed with the same

34

kind of genius. Adele told everyone she'd lived in New York and L.A. and San Francisco. People believed her. Prior to emerging in Mexico City as La Zarbo, with her hat and her cameras, she had gone to Dallas and shot anything that moved: strippers on smoke breaks outside Jack Ruby's old Carrousel Lounge, cowboys falling off bulls, pit crews at the Dallas speedway. Andy Warhol had shown that you could call anything a movie, whether it moved or not. She took her camera wherever she went. She pointed it at dogs doing it in the street, kids doing it in cars, and men doing it by themselves. She was hustled out of bars, restrooms, hospitals.

Then, early one morning in the parking lot outside a Winn-Dixie grocery store, she knew from the first image in her viewfinder that she had found her subject. A half-dozen men standing, squatting, leaning among the dumpsters against the back wall of the supermarket. Their brown faces showed patience and resignation that went beyond hope and prayer. They shivered in the gray cold of the morning, their feet cracked and blistered in their huaraches, hats in their hand so that the ranchers and contractors who came to hire them in pickups could get a good look. Could see that these were honest faces, belonging to men who wanted only to earn a day's wage. When asked how much they wanted for planting fence posts or digging furrows, they invariably said, "Lo que sea su voluntad." Whatever you like. A couple had their own tools, and a handwritten sign leaning against the box that might read *Plomero* or *Electricista*, because it was clear that a plumber or electrician with his own tools would be a real find in a land where such professionals earned thirty dollars an hour, instead of thirty a day.

Adele mounted her camera on a tripod and focused it on the six men who would sit or lean against the wall, with hardly any movement, no gesture beyond a tightening of their fingers around the brim of their hat, the lifting of a cigarette to their lips, or the slow expansion of their chest that came with a deep breath, perhaps a sigh of discouragement, but nothing else to show their impatience. She found their immobility compelling, with several minutes passing before there was a change of expression, a squint, a frown. Occasionally, they would stir and shift their weight from

35

one foot to the other; their bodies might shudder, arms brought to cross over their chests. Then, their eyes narrowing, they would be off at a reluctant trot to speak to a potential customer inside a car. She had asked them if they minded her photographing them. They looked at each other as if searching for some grounds on which to object, and in the end they nodded their consent. Adele kept coming back; every day there would be six or eight men, a couple of their faces familiar, but always some new ones.

Then, one of them, one that she had seen there many times before, a dark squat fellow, his unshaven face sprouting only a few sparse black whiskers, came to her. "Mucho gusto," the man said, rubbing his palm on the front of his shirt before reaching out. "Casimiro Gómez, para servirle."

She said her name, "Adele Zarbo, *estudiante de fotografia*," and gripped the man's hand. She was startled by its leathery feel. She had no conception of how those hands were used. She thought of all the hands she had touched, her father's fleshy palms, and he boys that she had allowed to touch her, their hands as smooth as hers.

"You are perhaps waiting for something to happen to us," the man said. "When the migra comes we all scatter in different directions, the cabrones going after us like they're trying to grab chickens. That's why they call us pollos. They never grab all of us. I have papers. So I run from them, then slow down so they catch me, but not my friends who are illegal. Then, we can't get work for days."

She searched for the right words. "Sometimes, I point a camera and don't really know why. The way you look grouped together, the light on your faces as the sun starts to come up, the way you stand so still. It makes a good picture." The man shook his head, as if giving up trying to understand her.

Adele realized that she was smiling, and she knew that it would look like she was flirting. And what right did she have to give an opening to someone who would not in a million years be able to take advantage of the offer, would not even allow himself the fantasy that she might allow him to touch her. Still, she was young, and the sudden onset of shame was something new in her life. In fact, she wouldn't have had a clue of the violence that her simple, reflexive behavior was causing if she had not seen, for the first time in her life, a look of anger cloud the man's eyes. Adele smiled on bravely now, no longer trying to be attractive, but as a peace offering.

"I believe you," he said seriously. "But ever since you started coming, things are not as good for us. The people who give work look at your camera and drive off. So, you see, when your camera is here, then life is not very natural for us."

"You want me to leave."

"Sí, señorita. With your forgiveness."

Of course, she went away. Later, she would drive past the wall to see who was standing and waiting, and who was missing, because she was curious as to their fate. Casimiro Gómez, she never saw again. Maybe he landed a steady job. The economy was improving; the men were getting hired early, and by nine there wouldn't be anyone waiting. The nature of the wall changed. Adele had to go back to her pictures to see the way it had been. She made some large prints, and then could see things she'd missed when she was actually standing there. On camera, their faces had a tense set, their eyes furtively looking in the direction of the lens, their bodies shifting uncomfortably, turning slightly away from her. Then she realized how angry she had made them. She would do things differently the next time. She would not introduce herself into the moment. She would be invisible. She would hide the camera.

She cropped the images and blew them up, allowing the grainy and somewhat abstract enlargement to reveal mysteries not apparent to the naked eye. She called the collection *Seis Hombres*. Years later, she had a show at the Anthropology Museum. One thing led to another. La Zarbo went on to film ritual dances in Michoacán, curandera surgery in Tepoztlán, glue-sniffing children in Ciudad Netza. When people asked her who she was, she'd tell them La Zarbo and they would nod, *Ah sí, la fotógrafa*. Important people were opening doors for her.

Adele couldn't get enough of Mexico City. Walking for hours, riding the clattering city buses, kamikaze biking through traffic,

37

she threw herself into the exploration with innocent enthusiasm. Beyond its shopping districts and wealthy neighborhoods, its boulevards and parks, a hidden community thrived outside the margins of the city, a bustling maze of rutted dirt tracks bordering industrial areas, smelly with the spills from textile dying vats, paper mills and oil refining. Outlying expanses were populated overnight. As if responding to some hidden signal, groups of families would descend on barren plains and in a matter of hours set up shacks of tar paper and tin sheeting, filching electric power from the high voltage lines along the main roads, cooking over propane burners, trucking in water. One of these settlements near the airport, behind Calzada Zaragoza, eventually became Ciudad Netzahualcoyotl, the second largest city in the country with about six million inhabitants, give or take a million to allow for erratic census canvassing. It had started out a ciudad perdida, a lost city, so closed off from the roads and surrounding streets that it was visible only from the air, as one gazed down from an airplane approaching the Mexico City airport, to discover the erratic paths and clusters of shacks in a dusty, frenzied honeycomb that stretched for acres. With an unexpected turn off the main thoroughfares, a path might open up through a crack in a wall that would lead to Ciudad Netza, a hidden parallel universe, existing simultaneously and yet apart from the safety of the public city.

In those early days, Adele got few advertising jobs. She had plenty of time for herself, to explore and dig through the mysteries of the Distrito Federal, the D.F., as the capital was known. She rode lurching buses packed with passengers standing with market bags crammed with the morning's shopping, a tradesman's tool box, suckling babies. And always the women, sighing with a kind of existential resignation through the winding routes from one end of the city to the other in journeys that seemed endless, their destinations elusive.

One particular bus had taken her out of the city to a weekly market in a village near Puebla. She'd photographed towers of oranges, dried-brown chilies, naked chickens hanging in rows, walls of rugs and blankets, mounds of herbs, snakeskins and lizard tails with healing properties. She'd eaten in the market kitchens and looked at the faces of the men and the women, daring to point her camera for only a moment, yet managing to capture their stoic expressions.

At twilight on the halting journey back to the city, she tried to keep from dozing in the bus, the packed bodies pressed around her providing a kind of pillowing, a comfort from a shared humanity. The traffic coming into the city became a slow, lurching thing, its pauses at intersections lengthening as they jammed with the evening rush. During stops, the bus was boarded by vendors of lottery tickets and newspapers, musicians armed with guitars or harmonicas, panhandlers with an explanation of their handicaps printed on cards. Weaving their way through the traffic, fire eaters, clowns and jugglers caught coins tossed from car windows.

At one stop, three acrobats stood on each other's shoulders. Adele recognized the costumes. A fourteen-year-old boy in a silvery mask and tights of El Santo, the wrestler, rattled coins in a milk can. The girl was a sugar plum fairy in a tattered tutu and rhinestone tiara. The youngest, around five, was a cupid complete with bow and arrow. They teetered outside the bus windows, receiving donations with blank expressions.

Adele placed a folded bill inside the can, and showed the kids her Minolta. The older boy nodded and the human tower stood still on the sidewalk next to the bus lane while she clicked off a couple of shots. Then, as the bus was grinding forward, she pushed her way to the front and begged the driver to be let off. She chased down the street to where the three kids were weaving their way through the traffic. This time she followed them to a traffic island in the middle of the avenue.

"Gracias por las fotos," she said breathlessly.

The younger children nodded seriously. Cupid jumped off the top of the sugar plum fairy's shoulder and then the three stood circling Adele. The older boy, his expression hidden behind the El Santo mask, rattled his change can until she took out several coins from her purse. "Cómo se llaman?" she asked their names.

"Yo soy el hijo del Santo," the boy said. He pulled his mask up to his eyebrows. He had a dark, unsmiling face. The son of El Santo himself. "She is Princesa. My brother is El Angel del Amor."

39

"Mucho gusto." Adele shook their hands in turn.

The oldest one clasped hers firmly and held his grip for several moments, until she had to jerk herself free. He smirked, and echoed her, "Mucho gusto, güerita. Como te llamas?"

"Adela," she said.

"Adelita," the girl said. "Like the song."

"Can I take more pictures?" She gestured with the camera.

"Tal vez sí." The boy rubbed his fingers together.

"Claro." Adele took another bill from her purse. The boy flattened it neatly and slipped it inside his waistband. He pulled his mask down to his chin and signaled his siblings to follow him back into the traffic.

She followed them until long past dark while they performed their stunts, caught by the headlights of the traffic along Zaragoza Avenue. The effect was of goblins and fairies scampering in the midst of the rumbling vehicles, their expressions grown animated in the dark, as if the night had energized them. She shot two rolls of their faces and their hands reaching into car windows, their mouths open and yelling insults, their hands making the occasional obscene gesture when a car sped away without giving them money. Finally, toward ten, the traffic thinned out and the trio dropped to the sidewalk, their legs splayed. El Santo lit a cigarette and exhaled long, thick plumes of smoke. He peered into the money can and his face broke into a wide grin for the first time.

"Ya se van a su casa?" Adele wanted to know if they were going home. "Con sus papás?"

"We have a house," the boy said. "But no papás."

"You don't live with your family?"

"It is a kind of family."

"Do you live far?"

"No, it's very close. Do you want to see our house and take more pictures?"

"Are you going to want more money?" Adele asked coyly.

"Si," the girl said. "Cien pesos!"

"Más," the boy corrected her seriously. "Ven con nosotros," he said, reaching for her hand. "No es lejos."

40

"Well, as long as it's not far," Adele said, wary but not wanting to lose the opportunity. They started out along Zaragoza Avenue following a high wall of concrete slabs that bordered the sidewalk. At a corner with a dark narrow street, the wall turned right, continued for a couple of blocks, and then revealed a crack barely wide enough for a body to squeeze through. The three kids easily slipped in. Adele had to turn sideways and wriggle through the opening until she emerged onto a dark field of scrub grass and rocks and prickly bushes. In the moonlight she was able to follow El Santo's silvery cape along a faint path.

After walking briskly for twenty minutes, as she stumbled in the dark, snagging her skirt on the occasional spiny branch, they reached an unpaved road, wide enough for the trucks parked along the edge. Low structures built of cinderblock and tin roofing for storage and industrial piece work, lined the road. A squat window-less building, smaller than the others, stood darkly away from the road. She followed the three children through a door of planks wired together.

It was pitch dark inside. In the closed space the smells of unwashed clothes, stale tortillas, and burnt beans mingled into a vaguely organic whole. The room was warm from the bodies huddled together against the night chill. Once inside, Adele lost track of her three guides. She found herself stumbling in the dark, stepping on someone's bare foot, then kicking against blankets and shoes and children curled up about the place. There was a soft whimper, then a startled cry as she stepped on someone's hand. Wherever she turned, some breathing obstacle blocked her way. She stood still until she grew accustomed to the dark, and could make out the figures sitting or lying around the room. And always the soughing music of long inhalations as if the air inside were scarce and thin. There must've been at least twenty children clumped in small groups, taking turns to reach for small cans of Resistol glue being handed around.

Even as she resolved to find her way back to the door, she was always within range of bare fingers gripping her skirt, grazing her skin, groping between her legs. She gasped in shock and turned

41

blindly to where she thought the exit was. She took a couple of long steps and found herself tripping over a body, and then falling, her descent softened by the children lying below. She rose to her feet quickly as if to avoid being swallowed by quicksand and stood frozen in place, her own gasps now in counterpoint with the soft keening, some kids laughing or cursing, and the hungry intakes of breath. She reached out and was relieved to feel the cold sheet metal of the door, and then as she pushed it open, the glow of moonlight and the air on her face.

She marched through the open field until she was standing at the edge of the road, empty save for the silent trucks parked along the side. She stood, indecisive, trying for several moments to recall the way out to the bus route.

Beyond the bend, the glow of headlights and the murmur of a car engine promised deliverance. The large automobile sped along the rutted track, whose driver showed no intention of slowing down or swerving as he headed toward Adele, who was signaling for help in the middle of the road. She felt relieved when, at the last moment, the car slid to a stop, its engine idling softly, the interior dark behind tinted windows. They stood like that, Adele and the unseen driver facing each other. Finally, the door swung open and out stepped a young man wearing jeans and a leather jacket. And sunglasses in the middle of the night, Adele thought. No wonder he hadn't seen her.

"Carajo, chava," he said. "I thought you were a ghost."

"I thought I was going to become one."

'What's a gringa doing here anyway?"

"Taking photographs," she said, holding up her camera bag. "There's a gang of wild children living in that building."

The man took off his glasses and squinted at her. "Ah sí, the real Mexico." He broke into a fit of laughter that went on and on until he was giggling uncontrollably.

"Are you high?" she said sharply. "I was hoping you might give me a ride to Zaragoza."

"That's just too funny," he said, finally bringing his laughter under control. "I mean this is the last place I would expect to find a tourist taking pictures."

"I'm not a tourist. I'm a professional photographer."

"Well, that's different." He opened the passenger door for her.

"And what are you?" She felt entitled to ask, boldly now that she was settled in the cushy front seat, and the car was moving.

"I'm a student," he said.

"You're too old to be a student."

"I am to be a lawyer. Law school takes many years in Mexico." He shrugged. "But tonight I am your guide out of here."

"Do you live back there?" she asked.

"Oh, no, thank God, no," he laughed again. He waited for her to ask another question, and when she didn't, he went on as if she had. "I come here to buy marijuana." He gestured at a stuffed paper bag casually tossed in the back seat. "Do you like to smoke?"

"It depends," she said.

"Yes, of course," he said almost apologetically. "My name is Victor Aruna."

"Adele Zarbo."

"I am, you know, a nice person." He sounded tentative.

"I am so very glad to hear that."

"What I mean is I can take you wherever you like to go. No problems. That you should feel safe with me."

"That's what I thought you meant," she said.

"Then maybe you will come to a party I'm giving in my house."

"When?"

"Any night," he said. "I have a party almost every night of the week."

❦ 6 ❦

From that first night when friends had taken Leander to Victor Aruna's house in Acopilco, a village in the hills above Mexico City, Victor had always taken control of even the most fluid of social situations. He'd weighed about a hundred and fifty pounds back then, an impish figure sitting cross-legged in the room's smoky gloom, watching the people around him with amused detachment. From the clay fireplace, flames formed capricious designs on the walls of unfinished stone, the light illuminating their rough surfaces and the shadowy gaps where the blocks were joined.

Leander no longer remembered by which roundabout invitation from a friend of a friend he ended up at Victor's party. In those days, he would ride the bus from the room he rented in a large apartment building on the edge of Coyoacán and head for the Zona Rosa near the center of the city, ready to enjoy the weekend away from his medical studies. He'd eat breakfast in the Juárez market, beans and eggs and chilaquiles all piled hugely under the green tomatillo salsa that he loved. He would gather a handful of coins, locate a working phone, and start calling until he found someone home. Or someone who knew where other people who hadn't been around to answer the phone would be having lunch. One name would lead to another, and he would meet up with other Americans, the journalists who hung out at the Foreign Correspondents Club at the Hilton, or advertising types who were practicing their Madison Avenue wiles on the more vulnerable Mexicans, and good-looking, opportunistic foreigners exporting pre-Columbian artifacts shopped around by villagers living near the archeological sites, or sometimes prescription drugs available over the counter at any farmacia.

They would meet at La Góndola or Fonda Santa Anita, and sit at long tables with white tablecloths and eat for hours. Over brandies and espressos they'd pass around addresses scribbled on matchbooks of where the parties were that night. Mexicans gave the best parties. Usually single guys from families with money, Los Juniors. They were generous with the invitations; if you somehow got to the party, it meant you knew someone who knew someone who had been personally invited, and you were therefore welcome. For Leander the agenda was always the search for intimacy; he felt like some throwback primate in a constant state of sexual unrest.

Paseo de la Reforma, greenly traversing Mexico City from its teeming center past nineteenth century mansions and gleaming office buildings and the museums edging Chapultepec Park on to the sudden rise into the surrounding hills on the north, was as close to the Champs Élysées as you could get and still be on this side of the Atlantic. The boulevard was divided by a tree-shaded median, a parkway for strolling, horseback riding, or whiling away the afternoon on one of the iron park benches, a book held open to give the appearance of study while one gazed idly at the flow of life. By early evening the traffic would swell to a raucous metallic river, its orderly progress degenerating into a competitive scramble around the circles of the Independencia Angel or the Petroleos Fountain. At intersections, weaving vendors of lottery tickets and toys and the evening newspapers would swarm around the cars, only to leap to safety when the light turned green. The traffic would speed onward in a polyphony of horn blasts and a roar of exhaust and gear grinding.

Leander had hitched a ride with a couple from the American Embassy, mild-mannered bureaucrats by day, and, they boasted happily, hopped-up party animals by night. They wove their way through the traffic, letting their diplomatic license plates carry them through red lights and erratic lane changes. They were heading toward a house nestled among the hills surrounding Mexico City, along where the Paseo de la Reforma became a residential boulevard and then narrowed to a two-lane road toward the nearby city of Toluca. Along the way they stopped for drinks and to pick up friends in the Polanco neighborhood, where they had to have another round of margaritas and a couple of tokes each and later maybe some tacos at the Chalupas restaurant. By then seven people were squeezed into the car, and Leander would later have no recollection of any one person, except for the happy weight of some girl sitting on his lap, and his arm pressing into the breast of another beside him, and everyone being silly. "Tokes y Tacos," one of the women laughed, "a great theme for a fast food drive-in."

It was nearly eleven by the time they got to Victor Aruna's house. Leander wondered what kind of a guy this friend of a friend was that you could drop in uninvited in the middle of the night and expect him to have a party going. There was nothing to indicate from the outside of the square stone house off a dirt road that there was anything exciting happening inside. Wrought-iron grills on the windows and a sheet-metal door barred the way. Candlelight flickered through the glass and around the edges of the entrance. Someone pressed on an intercom embedded into the wall, and a buzz signaled the lock's release. They were welcomed into the main room by a breath of sweetish smoke, murmured conversation, a coiling blues guitar line.

Coals smoldered in an open fireplace. Oaxaca rugs and straw petates were scattered on the red tile floor. A dozen shadowy figures appeared in the candlelit gloom, reclining on big red and turqouise pillows against the wall. Reflexively predatory, Leander swept the room for available women. He was not optimistic this late in the evening about his chances of finding someone unattached, preferably beautiful and not too stoned, with her own car and apartment. Nobody is that lucky, he thought.

Victor Aruna sat wrapped in a jorongo, black wool with red and white Zapotec designs. His delicate features emerged from the poncho's neck opening, silky brown hair curling almost girlishly to the top of his shoulders. He looked up and beamed at the newcomers. He appeared to be holding court over the torpid gathering, so that the right thing to do was to approach him and lean down to shake his hand.

46

"How you doing, man?" he said. "Yo soy Paul Leander."
Victor looked up at him. "Hola Pablito. Qué milagro!" he exclaimed, as if he'd known Leander half his life and had been waiting for just this moment to catch up on his latest news. In those days, he was so handsome, almost boyish, and so focused on each person he addressed, that he had gathered a coterie of friends, men and women, who were drawn to him as if to a movie star.

Leander was groping for the proper response when he noticed the young, obviously American woman sitting beside the effusive host. Victor grinned as he followed Leander's glance, "Mira, Adele, otro gringuito como tú."

Years later, Leander would recall how seeing Adele for the first time had ranked among those moments where every detail is remembered for the whole of one's life: The moon walk on a TV in the doctor's lounge at his first real hospital job. JFK announced dead during a little league game. In the first grade, staring at a page in his reading primer and finally, exultantly, seeing through the code that linked the sounds of letters into the melody of words— *The cat jumped over the moon.*

And now, on this night of half-hearted socializing, before she had breathed a word, but immediately upon her lifting her eyes to meet his, Leander fell into a tense infatuation with Adele Zarbo. She was wearing a Guatemalan huipil, white cotton with silk embroidery of tiny birds and flowers. Her hair was long and thick then, braided into a burnished rope that reflected pinpoints of gold from the candles flickering in green and red votive glasses.

Even before she acknowledged him, Leander felt disappointment. In a few seconds, before he could stake his claim for her attention, he had fallen in love, then immediately leapt to the conclusion that she was the host's girlfriend. He was mourning his loss even as they were meeting.

"There is lots to drink and eat," Victor said, nodding in the direction of the kitchen. "Also, alguna otra cosita," Victor winked. It was not a drinkers' party; the conversation was muted; the music was a bootleg Grateful Dead cut with Garcia's sweet guitar meandering a circuitous riff within an extended jam of "Cosmic Charlie;" marijuana was being handed around in generously fat

47

stubs that filled the room with a pungent haze. Distracted by a hook in the music, Victor Aruna withdrew his attention from Leander as decisively as he had first offered it.

Leander emerged from the kitchen with a bottle of Dos Equis. He stood awkwardly in the middle of the crowd until the energy that radiated from the aloof Adele Zarbo drew him to a cushion near her. As others became accustomed to his presence, one of the joints making its way around the room was insinuated into his fingers, welcoming him into the group's communion. He relished the warm complicity that surrounded the smoking, the passing of a roach, the playful, unspoken competition to see whose fingers would burn, who would receive the last hot breath of thick smoke. It was a gentle sacrament for an easygoing floating congregation complete with a priest: the clearly presiding presence of Victor Aruna. In his house, Victor was the center of every circle, the apex of any triangle.

Adele had barely glanced at Leander. Even in the belief that this beautiful woman was taken, he was enjoying a perverse pleasure from her dismissal. He went for another beer and this time found a place beside her. He felt he could claim her attention by virtue of their both being Americans in this foreign place. He was a few inches to her right, resting his back against the wall that also supported her, the warmth of her body, he imagined, seeping through her skin and her clothes and spreading along the stones to his own flesh.

Unexpectedly, he felt a surge of excitement as she shifted slightly to make room for him. Then she turned and, without a word, reached for the bottle in his hand, as if it were understood that he had brought it for her. She tipped it to her lips and swallowed thirstily. Promising, he thought, this was not a girl who drank like a lady. "You didn't get one for yourself?" she said, holding the bottle back. Her insinuating voice turned inside his head like a cat curling on a rug.

"Keep it," he said. "I'll get another." He was giddy with his small triumph.

"If we drink from the same bottle, we'll learn secrets about each other."

48

Somehow speechless, he took the beer back.

"You do have secrets from me, don't you?" she pushed.

He nodded as if giving the question profound consideration. "Dark, disturbing ones." He smiled and closed his eyes, and tilted the bottle back to drink. He couldn't get enough of the imagined taste of her mouth.

Happily sitting beside Adele, Paul was already celebrating the shift of her attention toward him. He was apprehensive of Victor's reaction. Beyond the guy's penchant for mindless partying, there was another side to his life that people speculated about. His father was supposed to be a federal judge. Victor was often seen flashing a laminated ID from the Policía Judicial. He counted drug traffickers, labor leaders and gun dealers among his friends. Everyone knew this, even though Victor tried to carry his power discretely.

Paul caught an amused glance from Victor Aruna, who seemed to anticipate how their lives would intertwine. Victor would contemplate the inevitable with a kind of innocent curiosity. Even as he manipulated everyone around him, he would not admit to any influence in his friends' lives; it was always the fates that were responsible.

"Tu pinche karma," he would say, when anyone complained. Victor collected nuggets of Hinduism and Tantra, the occasional crumb of Tarot and I Ching, and showed off his theories with abandon. He lived his life according to tossed coins, flips of the pages of the *Baghavad Gita*, the lay of the planets, and whispers of the devas while he sat in meditation. He practiced going into trances and communing with the dead. He used a pendulum to feel out winning lottery tickets and race horses. He'd dangle it over menus to detect foods that might poison his system. He was continually changing diets—one minute off pork, the next only brown rice. He learned a little Tantra from a traveling Tibetan. He knew all about María Sabina, the mushroom sage in Oaxaca. They were friends, he bragged, and dared Paul and Adele to go to Huautla with him.

The bus ride to the Huautla de Jimenez in the highlands was a jolting climb that kept them bouncing on the hard seats for ten

49

hours. When they showed up at the old woman's house, she was not there. They rented a hut for three nights, waiting for her to come back from collecting mushrooms in the hills. By the time María Sabına showed up, they were cold and dirty and Adele was ın a foul mood. The old crone smiled in recognıtion at the names that Victor dropped, but said she would not give them mushrooms because she was retired and had grown weary of tourısts takıng them so indiscriminately. The closest they got to the famous curandera was a quick look inside her special mushroom room.

Adele had brought her camera and was discretely shooting the glowıng brazier, the plate of dirty brown mushrooms, the small altar with clay effıgies of the Virgen de Guadalupe next to the goddess Tonantzin, and finally María Sabina herself, the lıned face so placid and unperturbed by the visitors. "Basta de fotos," she ordered, placing her hand in front of the lens. She waited for Adele to put the camera away and then sent them across town to a niece of hers who had taken on some of her practice. It was apparent that the close relationship that Victor claimed to have with the famous healer was exaggerated. Yet, it was typical of him to ımply that it had been his plan all along that they should now consult the new number-one curandera in the village.

La sobrina Felipa, a placid woman with a round, shiny face and a radiant smile punctuated by a gold tooth, chanted some prayers ın the Zapotec language and threw copal resın on the burning embers. Then, taking the hongos from their banana-leaf wrapping, she delıcately placed a dirt-crusted button in their outstretched hands. She called Victor endearments such as mi hijito and Victorcito and güerito. For his part, Paul stared at his hands and arms and was sure the jungle of downy hair and the swampy marshes of his skin cells were a port of entry into God's creation. Adele couldn't keep them down. Every time she tried to chew off and swallow bites of mushroom she would vomit. She remembers throwing up the most beautiful green frogs. Frogs the color of emeralds. God had visited her in the shape of a frog, Felipa had explained. She had not been pure enough to hold Him inside her.

When Paul and Victor returned the following night for another session, Adele stayed in their rented hut. She tried to tell Paul that

Victor had no idea how to handle the poisons they were swallowing. She was relieved to know Felipa sent the two men away, saying that obviously they were too sick for her kind of therapy. The mushrooms were not for fun, but to unburden the mind and strengthen the spirit.

Two weeks after they got back to the city, Paul discovered a tangle of thin white worms in his stool from the dirt around the mushrooms. He was proud he knew enough about local remedies to treat himself with a mixture of arsenic and iodine.

❖ 7 ❖

Once in New York, away from Victor and Paul rattling around the big house overlooking the ocean, settling their odd scores, Adele was able to breathe easy and concentrate on her presentation. Work was a welcome distraction. She shut down her iBook around two AM and took a long hot soak in the tub. Within easy reach was a tray from room service: thin French crackers, artichoke dip, soft brie, white grapes, M&Ms. Sustenance for the woman on the road, lonely in her Concierge Floor suite. She did her best thinking while floating in a fragrant bath in the middle of the night. She'd been brought up in a family with five siblings, then went to college where she lived in a dorm with thirty other students, and then a house shared with six other women. A long soak, whenever she wanted, was a gift. She drew the water so hot it flushed her skin pink when she lowered herself in with a shiver. Her hands on the side of the tub, she slowly submerged herself to the waist, sweat beading up under her lower lip and rolling down her neck and gathering along the tops of her breasts. Scented candles from the lobby gift shop suffused the bathroom with a golden light. She breathed in lavender and bergamot, reliable aromas for serenity.

She leaned back and let the water cover her up to the chin. Her eyes stung from the hours of staring at the screen, juggling pictures and text for her client Artofilm's new ads. Print-outs of a dozen layouts were taped on the walls. Through the steam and flickering flames, she gazed at her evening's work, the images blurring through the soft light, reflecting themselves in the mirrors. With ordinary family photography going digital, only die-hard enthusiasts were left to use traditional 35 mm film. Kodak was still showing doddering grandpas and burbling babies and pubescent lovers on TV. It was up to the upstarts like Artofilm to come up with a different language to open new possibilities for the serious amateur photographer.

Dare to See read Adele's headline. Everywhere, there was nothing but frogs—big warty closeups of buggy-eyed, goitered swamp monsters in muddy greens and browns. There was a frog with one back leg stumped to a length of three millimeters and a lump on its back. Adele called him Quasifrogo. Another frog with knobs coming out of its head: Frankenfrogo. A blind frog in full frontal closeup stared out, the milky orbs of its eyes glowing with a sort of inner, swallowed light. Adele called him Tiresias. All the ads showed frogs, and together Adele thought they made a weird kind of truth. All you had to do was see them. Really see them, not as pathetic little mutants, victims of toxic runoffs and dirty rain, but as angelic creatures announcing an overdue apocalypse.

She soaked and gazed at her frogs. The longer she stared at their deformities, the less she was repelled. The sight of an extra limb jutting out of a swollen frog belly had initially revolted her. The fluorescent green cast of frog skin, as tough as leather under the photographer's lights, had elicited disgust. But as she grew familiar with them, she began to think of them as the weird children that a mother loves best. These particular frogs were long dead, their bodies donated to science, their images on the way to becoming myths. She felt a kind of empathy with their freakishness. She envied them their visible badges of misfortune. They awakened new levels of understanding. She celebrated their horror. No question, this was her own little gang of mutants. The frogs would make her famous and happy. Each one a prince. They would gain market share for the client and garner awards for the designer.

Adele would have to explain all this on Monday morning. Trying to look as credible as a nun, she would wear the charcoal suit with the short jacket and long but strategically slit skirt. Brushed-silver choker, pearl earrings. No color except for her eyes and her lips, little magnets drawing attention to her utter sincerity, the forthright gaze, the mouth speaking with conviction.

Meanwhile, with the coast time difference, she thought her husband would be awake. When she called him, she got his voice mail.

"I can't believe Victor Aruna has shown up out of the blue," she spoke hurriedly into Leander's machine. "I'll be at the Plaza all day Sunday, but leaving early Monday morning for my presentation." She asked as an afterthought, "Has he told you what he wants?"

Around seven, which was four in the morning back in San Diego, Leander called her back, and was transferred, in turn, to her voice mail. "I think Victor has decided to die in our house," he said. "I'll have a talk with him as soon as he gets over learning he's terminal. He's not handling it well. But then who does? Hope you are having fun."

At eight, in the lobby of their hotel, Adele met Bundt and Farley, the account executive and the media planner from her advertising agency. They were presenting the Artofilm campaign with her. Bundt had dashed off a jargon-filled rationale on *Dare to See*, without knowing what the client would actually see. Adele had told him to talk about being unconventional, unexpected, unKodak—no babies, puppies, grandparents, couples at sunset. The two executives kept asking to see the ads. The layouts were secure inside her portfolio, she said. They would see them in due time. They had surely learned to trust her by now. Could they get a peek? A hint?

"Frogs," she said.

"Anything else? Girls, maybe? The client likes girls."

"More frogs," she dismissed their question with a small wave.

"You are being self-indulgent," Farley said.

"You're right, guys," she said, striding down Fifth Avenue between the men. "This is a small account, remember? I work on it so I can have some fun." She couldn't wait to flash her frogs at Bundt and Farley and watch their faces pale. Good ideas were scary.

It was not hard to scare Bundt and Farley. The person she wanted to shake was the head of marketing for Artofilm, Blanton LeMay, a darkly arrogant man in perpetual need of a shave and a comb, looking like he'd slept in his black linen suits and sockless loafers. He would stare at her breasts through the course of a meeting as if some magical truth about the fortunes of his company could be liberated by unbuttoning her blouse. In this latest creative effort, she had toyed with the idea of giving the client nothing but breasts—pendulous breasts, flat breasts, old breasts, pubescent breasts, mastectomized breasts. Like frogs, also unKodak.

They were ushered into a cozy meeting room with big leather chairs around a table, cork walls with pushpins and track lights that she could adjust to show her work to best advantage. Her presentation would take about a minute. Then she would sit down at the far end of the table to get out of the way of Blanton LeMay's seeing her work.

While they waited, she thought the conference room, with the door closed and the AC on the blink, was starting to smell a little like a swamp, either because of the frogs, or her nerves. She was sweating under the fine silk blouse and snappy jacket. Chew on these frog legs, the ads would scream from the pages of the *New Yorker* or *Modern Parenting*. LeMay would understand that, even if it wasn't his normal style. *Dare to See* meant finding beauty in the grotesque, the prince waiting to be released. Warts and all, but still, you know, a prince. She paged through the layouts on the table.

"Are you fucking crazy?" said Farley, blinking rapidly as if to drive away the images before him.

"I'm just going to sit back here and watch," said Bundt, crossing his arms over his belly.

"Could you at least turn the damn things over?" Farley pleaded. "We don't want LeMay to walk into this frog zoo without a modicum of set-up."

When Le May showed up about thirty minutes late, trailed by four associates, he was impatient with Farley setting him up.

"All you are doing," he reminded him, "is regurgitating what *I* told *you*. Why do agency people do that? Of course we don't want a sentimental campaign. Heart-warming will not make me tumescent. If your campaign doesn't engorge me with blood, no sale. Can we get on with it?"

"We're there already," Adele broke in.

"That's right," Farley said pulling out a flat piece of card with the words in bold type: *Dare to See.*

"Hey, I get it," LeMay said. "Do you *dare* show me the ads?" He laughed boisterously, and his group sniggered.

"What our theme aims to communicate to the target consumer," Farley began undaunted, "is . . ."

"I know what it's trying to say. Artofilm is for the bold, the curious, the original seer in all of us."

"I couldn't have put it better myself," Farley nodded eagerly.

"Ads," LeMay pressed on. "We're here to see ads."

Up went the frogs. One by one, Adele revealed Quasifrogo, Frankenfrogo, Cyclopfrogo and the rest of the mutant menagerie. She didn't say a word. Bundt and Farley didn't speak. After all the setting up and the banter, you showed the work, and then you shut up. You let its impact resonate throughout the room. Silence forced the client to make the first statement. If the client said, "I hate this," you still didn't say anything. You let him think things out in his own mind so that he had to tell you *why* he hated the work. That was the worst case. Usually, there was a question. "Why green frogs and not purple ones?" That meant that the frogs as such had been accepted; details were left to quibble about. The worst reaction was "I don't get it," because that lay on Adele the burdens of explanation, clarification, justification.

The room was silent for several moments. LeMay knew better than to be drawn into any hint of approval. "Froggy went a-courtin', he did go," he sang under his breath.

The group stirred for the first time, as if a collective breath had been suddenly exhaled.

"What does everybody think?" LeMay asked, taking a look around the room. There was no answer. "Surely one of you has an opinion. You can't look at the work on these walls and not have some kind of a visceral reaction. No time to be shy."

Adele looked around at the blank faces that had previously been grinning along with their boss. She breathed a sigh of relief. LeMay liked the frogs; he hadn't yawned or picked lint off his coat or stuck an unlit cigar in his mouth. He was using the frogs now to play with his marketing team. For an instant her eyes met LeMay's, a knowing glance was exchanged. She relaxed into her chair.

"Well, it's certainly provocative," said a woman. "The frogs dare you to look at them, you know."

"That's very insightful, Trish," said LeMay.

"The frogs are visually powerful, no doubt about it," said a frat-boy type in a Polo shirt and khakis. He glanced quickly at LeMay for some sign as to how he might conclude his statement.

"And?" LeMay encouraged him with a paternal smile.

The man took a breath, as if steeling himself to fire a gun aimed at his own foot. "I was just wondering," he said trying to affect a breezy tone, "just how much of our market is into nature photography."

"So you think we're saying that Artofilm is the best product for photographing frogs. And other amphibian wildlife, of course."

The man struggled to minimize the damage. "Some people might interpret the ads that way."

"Not you, of course," LeMay coaxed him.

"No, I would say that I'm capable of seeing the larger picture."

"The larger frog," LeMay nodded. Without waiting for a response he stood up from his chair, and lifted the layouts from the wall. "Thank you for your presentation, Ms Zarbo. I apologize for the insipid discussion my friends here have conducted. It's interesting work. I hope you weren't planning to fly back to California today. Let's meet again at six this evening. My office. Since our chat will be about creative matters, your cohorts can go home whenever they want. I will try to have a decision by then."

When Adele showed up at Artofilm for her six o'clock appointment with Blanton LeMay, she was asked to wait in the lobby. He appeared twenty minutes later, after most of the office staff had gone home; he took her by the arm and steered her inside his office, closing the door behind him. "We've finally got some peace around here," he said.

"Did you have comments about the layouts?" she asked.

"Yeah, make yourself comfortable." He pointed at the small sofa to one corner. "Kick back, Adele. You're always so uptight."

"I'm not uptight," she said. "I'll relax after you tell me what you think of the ads."

"The frogs have made me tumescent," he said. "You're a genius. Now would you like to have a drink with me?"

"Here?" she said.

"It's my home away from home," he said as he drew open the curtains on the large windows facing the glittering skyline. There was a leather sofa and a wing-backed armchair. A marble-topped coffee table. Persian rugs. A big TV on rolling casters. Stereo components on a vertical rack. Big speakers faced each other diagonally from opposite ends of the room. Recessed lights glowed from the ceiling.

"Okay," she said. Certainly, she would not sleep with him in order to sell a campaign, but she would enjoy watching him maneuver the situation from the professional to the personal. She would wriggle out of his reach at the last minute.

"This is my favorite possession." He indicated the large aquarium behind the sofa. Hidden lights gave the sea shells and coral formations an ethereal iridescence. Three flat, brown fish clung to the tank's glass wall, their eyes staring out with a kind of muted intensity. "My babies are hungry," he explained. "Piranha are always hungry. If this was a river in the Amazon and a cow fell in, they would eat the whole cow. I buy ground chuck for them. Lean stuff. We'll feed them in a while. An absolutely thrilling ten seconds, you'll see."

He walked across the office to a cabinet at one end. "I'll get us some wine. Red okay? The first duty of a wine is to be red. You heard that before?" She sank into the sofa's soft leather. Behind her, the three toothy piranha stared out, their eyes made large and bulbous by the magnifying effect of the tank's wall.

They sipped wine and she waited for him to make a move. She was good at waiting; she could sit still and be silent, allowing for the possibilities to gel around her. Stillness provided subtle resistance. Let the man overcome his own inertia. They sat on the opposite ends of the couch with a wide expanse of slippery black leather between them.

Suddenly he stood up, as if he'd just remembered something urgent. He opened a little refrigerator behind the desk and held up, like an offering, a raw meatball the size of a grapefruit.

"Watch this," he said. "I'm training them to be competitive. The last thing captive piranha need is a human keeper who makes survival too easy. I could just drop meatballs, and they would deal with them in an instant, and they would all get fat and forget how to kill. Life needs to be hard for people, too. The constant scramble keeps us from forgetting that we are human. Not Gods and Godlettes."

He pinched out a chunk of meat and let it dangle from his fingers. The three fish gathered under him, hungrily jerking up and down. He flicked off a couple of pieces into the water.

"Go to it, my darlings," he whispered as the fish gathered, their jagged mouths forming the points of a perfect triangle, staring up at LeMay who stared back as he licked bits of red hamburger from his fingers.

A new twist in the old come-and-see-my etchings ploy, thought Adele. "Can you tell them apart?" she asked. "Do they have names?" She couldn't tell if the question pleased him.

"They have names, just like your frogs," he said. "The small one is Caligula. The fat one is Torquemada. The mean one is Cleopatra. Cali, Torqui, and Cleo for short."

"I expected all three to be males," she said. "The girl fish is apparently the most assertive one."

"Well, isn't that how life is?" he said. "As above, so below."

She sat back on the sofa and sipped her wine. In the past few minutes she'd grown certain she would not sleep with Blanton LeMay. Not because of his fascination with killer guppies, but because of his eating raw meat from his fingers.

"Did you want to talk about the Artofilm campaign?" she asked.

"Well, sure," he said, inching toward her.

"Do you have any questions about the layouts?"

"No. Can't say that I do," he said after a long pause.

"Any comments?"

59

"I don't have much to say about the frogs," he sighed. "Except that, of course, I can't really run those ads."

She was shaken off-balance. "I thought you liked the layouts."

"Oh, honey, I love them. I think they're brilliant. You're brilliant. I mean *Dare to See*. Wow!" He did a little wave with his hand as if words were insufficient to express his admiration. "I get tumescent again just thinking about them."

"So what's wrong?"

"People buy film to take pictures of their grandkids, not of sick frogs."

She took a deep breath and tried to keep her voice from quavering. "I'd better be going, then. It looks like I have some work to do back at the office."

"I'll get you another glass of wine," he said. "That pesky issue is out of the way. Let's enjoy ourselves."

"I'm going, thank you."

"No," he said simply. He took her by the arm, raised her from the couch, and pulled her to the aquarium. He clasped her hand between both of his and dipped her fingers into the water. She noticed how warm he kept the tank; these, after all, were tropical fish and had to be kept at a cozy level. There was a brown blur as the fish quickened from a corner of the tank. She thought of her blood flowing in silky warm ribbons so that the open flesh bites on her hand would not feel any difference in temperature, just a soft tepid flow into the tank's salt water, the imitation Caribbean sea, providing the basis for a broth of her own blood. After a second, he let go of her fingers. She jerked out her hand with a gasp just as the toothy predators darted to the spot, eager for whatever their keeper was putting in.

"I can't believe you would do that," Adele said. A knot started at the center of her chest and moved up her throat with a sharp acid taste.

"Believe," he said. He pinched off some pieces from the meatball and dropped them at different spots on the surface of the water, teasing the little monsters, making them rush from one spot to another.

⚜ 8 ⚜

On his way home from work, Leander picked up a pizza piled high with everything on the menu, and, for Victor, a couple of the recent Mexican movies getting good press. He found the house empty. He called Victor, peered into the guest room, the shady patio in back of the house. Around nine, just as he resolved to start *Amores Perros* and finish the bottle of wine, he grew suddenly afraid for Victor Aruna. His first intention had been to let the man go through whatever gyrations and medical fantasies suited him. After twenty years, he could argue that Victor's reappearance did not obligate him in any way.

He discovered a note on the kitchen table in Victor's ornate handwriting:

Dear amigos del alma, he wrote. *I decided I do not want to wait and take my death lying down. In fact, I do not want to take death in any form. Since gringo medicine shows little hope beyond getting high on prescription narcotics, I've gone across the border. Clínica La Esperanza offers enough alternative therapies to give a man hope that something will work. I'll call soon. Abrazos, Victor.*

Terminal diseases were a growth industry on both sides of the border. Wealthy Mexicans checked into Scripps; desperate Americans flocked to Tijuana for their last-ditch cures. A search on Google for alternative medicine/tijuana yielded pages of bright color graphics on La Esperanza's variety of miracle therapies:

A dozen elderly Americans were pictured lounging on rattan chairs in a bright spacious solarium filled with plants. Their arms were plugged to an IV pumping them up with their own blood, which had been previously "chelated" overnight in the clinic's special chelation chamber. Chelation being, as everyone should know, the enrichment of the blood through forced oxygenation.

In the ozone cylinder, patients were bathed in the invisible, nearly weightless gas that would reverse the body's destructive polarity, which would affect only the patient's checking account.

Past-life regression through hypnosis was known to neutralize bad karma at its source. Eliminate the sin, and the debt will spontaneously pay itself under the light of, well, under the light of its own light.

A Filipino psychic surgeon was always on call. La Esperanza's own curandera, Doña Panchita, was ready at a moment's notice to call on the help of her spiritual brother Cuahutémoc for the egg rubs that sucked evil and the herb wraps that stewed healing. There was a Cuban santero and a Haitian Voodoo guy and a Huichol shaman. The emphasis was on magic. Esperanza, in Spanish, means hope. Victor could get his blood reconstituted, his organs bombarded with virtual gases, his pancreas shocked with insulin, his colon filled with a coffee enema. He would swallow ground apricot seeds and desiccated monkey pituitaries, and get shot up with placenta tissue from calf birthings. Leander imagined them all together hovering around the bed where Victor might be lying in a sweet fog of Demerol, not knowing whether he was dreaming or in fact opening up the biopsy incision to the charms of the assembled team.

Leander breathed out a sigh and sat cross-legged on the rug at a low table. He let the video begin and took a pizza slice out of the carton. He poured himself a glass of thirty-dollar cabernet. The lonely-boy special, he called it.

He was glad to be by himself. He was not up to Adele's edgy companionship, the delicate equilibrium of their negotiated marriage, subject to polite evasions and sporadic lust. Beth Moreau demanded a measure of tenderness he could act out, but not make himself feel. And he was grateful, at first, that Victor had chosen to go to Tijuana. Victor knew he was dying, and so every moment was loaded with odd possibilities that the past might be revisited, that mutual transgressions be confronted. He could not begin to imagine how Victor remembered their time in Mexico City. So

62

Leander was wary of old conflicts being revived, alert to the subject of Victor's impending death.

"Don't worry about pain," Leander had told him with gentle authority. "Morphine is nice. You'll have your finger on the drip and get as wooly as you like; you'll practically levitate from the bed, drift off and die of pneumonia."

Leander accepted the responsibility of being the bearer of bad news, obtaining, not coincidentally, power and status. You're fucked, my friend. Say your prayers. Get your affairs in order. Prepare your goodbyes. Settle accounts. Make apologies. Repair, repair, repair. The cruel part comes from knowing the inevitable is emphatically close, rather than distant enough for the event to be an abstraction. Distant objects are closer than they appear. The looming deadline, the mortgage payment, the dreary meeting are there, ready to sap our energy and drain our happiness. Then the violence of fear and denial crawl in a creepy shiver up the spine.

It was only after Leander had pushed away the cold pizza crusts and drained the third glass of wine, that he ventured into the room where Victor was staying. He had hoped that Victor had taken his things to the clinic in Tijuana. Instead, his clothes were hanging in the closet and a package wrapped in brown paper sat on top of the bed. He untied the string to reveal a two-kilo box of Sanborn's famous chocolate tortugas, the pecan and caramel turtles, at once sweet and darkly bitter, that he and Adele had loved in Mexico.

It wouldn't do any harm to open the box and sneak a couple of pieces. He lifted the lid. Instead of the anticipated sweets, the box was filled with hundreds of snapshots. There were pictures from family vacations, kids on the beach, groups of men sitting at restaurant tables and raising their glasses toward whoever was pointing the camera, a young mother with a new baby. There were some pictures of Victor himself. In one, he was standing in front of the black 1980 Ford Galaxy he used to tool around Mexico City. In another he had his arm around a tiny, stooped woman, perhaps a grandmother. It was as if Victor had left Mexico for good and had wanted to take some of his past with him. Then, as Leander was about to stuff the pictures back in the box, he saw one of Victor

63

standing between him and Adele, his arms protectively around their shoulders. The three wore matching pink t-shirts. Though the two Americans towered over him, his hold on them gave him a proprietary air. Leander tried to remember the occasion. He switched on the reading lamp beside the bed and scattered the snapshots like playing cards over the blue bedspread. He sifted through them, sweeping away the ones he didn't recognize, looking for shots of Adele or himself, some with Victor, but quite a few of the two of them together when they were clearly in love, beaming their joy at Victor behind the camera.

Another picture made him pause. He was standing with a group of classmates on the steps of the medical school building. They were all in their first year, looking earnest and determined to become doctors. Leander's face stuck out, pale and somehow bewildered from the back row where, being the tallest, he had been positioned.

His B-minus average from the University of Minnesota was all it took to get admitted. Unlike other foreign med schools, Mexico's Universidad Autónoma had a fine reputation in the U.S. It graduated over a thousand doctors every year, and sent them off to practice two years of social service in the jungles and deserts and slums before allowing them to make their living. The most challenging aspect of studying medicine in Mexico was learning the language. Lectures were held in Spanish. Calling a liver an hígado or a heart a corazón made the whole process somehow poetic and more mysterious. He remembered his first cadaver. The sound of his partner's voice, a dark-eyed girl from Culiacán, was like the incantation of a priestess: *Vesícula, riñón, pulmón, vejiga.*

Leander became infatuated with intestinal parasites. Amoebas and shigella and trichinae were downright bizarre in their evil opportunism. They latched onto the body with rapacious determination. In the case of amoebae it would take massive doses of arsenic to kill them and flush them out. Tapeworm and screworm were like alien invaders that could get quite comfortable before their presence became so much of a crowd that in remote villages children's bellies swelled, and in time the things started crawling out of their mouths and noses. There was something

64

science-fictiony about the whole thing. He liked throwing his knowledge around for the tourist girls from the U.S. and Canada who would listen to his advice about drinking beer instead of water and eating tripe stew instead of salads. He would offer medical advice in restaurants and bars to anyone who would listen. Stay away from margaritas and other vehicles for crushed ice. Keep your lips tightly sealed in the shower. When Victor Aruna called him "doctorcito," he didn't mind it much.

Well into his third year, he liked wearing his white coat carelessly unbuttoned as if he had momentarily stepped away from the consulting room for a snack, too busy with the drama of medicine to change costume. He kept close at hand a sort of emergency kit consisting of a stethoscope, a blood pressure gauge, a hypodermic, scissors, a sterile scalpel, suture kit, bandages, vials of adrenaline, thorazine, some ibuprofen and a couple of joints, all neatly packed inside a Big Bird lunchbox.

He lived in a cramped apartment near Coyoacán, and the neighbors all knew he was a doctor. Sometimes they came to him with minor complaints—the flu, bacterial infections, measles, a missed period. It made him feel important. He was not above the occasional opportunistic exam, palpating a breast, pushing a panty's elastic below a tummy to the sweet downy mound. He was called upon to lance boils, give shots, stitch cuts. All on his own, outside of school. He wouldn't accept payment, but was always happy for home-cooked meals with a neighbor or a few beers in the corner cantina with a relieved father.

Occasionally, he was asked if he could do something for the woman pregnant with her sixth child or the unmarried girl with a sleaze for a boyfriend. He believed in a woman's right to rule her body, but he wouldn't venture beyond his ability. There were pharmacists and OB nurses willing to terminate pregnancies for a modest fee.

Leander sifted through the remainder of the photos in the candy box. Many of the pictures were close-ups of men he didn't know. They looked helpless, staring passively ahead as if for a license or a passport, and there was nothing to set the time and context for the shots. There were dozens of these, impassive faces under the same fluorescent glare, the barely visible back of a straight chair, a similar plaster wall in the background.

A couple of shots seemed to have been taken from a staircase above a living room and showed several men lying on the floor as if they had all decided to curl up at the same time and take a nap. It took only moments before Leander remembered the image of the men, all in their absurdly cheerful parrot and monkey shirts. Then with a start Leander saw himself in a rumpled medical coat, oblivious of the camera aimed at him, standing next to one man whose face was swollen, eyes bewildered, hair plastered onto his skull as if he'd been caught in the rain. He was confused that the photo had ended up with Victor Aruna. He stifled a rising nausea and hastily pushed the whole bunch back in the box. He would steel himself for another look later.

Leander could not show much enthusiasm upon Victor's return from La Esperanza a week later. He had been sitting alone in his house that evening, wanting to talk to Adele who was back in New York. He heard the cab come up the driveway and, from the living room window, he watched Victor emerge from the taxi looking wan and slightly embarrassed as if he had panicked and run off in a cloud of fear and now was ready to face his mortality.

"It's the most depressing place in the world down there," he announced. "All these really sick people clinging to their last shred of hope. They sit around with IVs in their arms reading the large-type *Reader's Digest*. It's like a waiting room in purgatory. The doctor will see you now? Hah, there is no doctor, only these Mexican witches blowing you up with enemas, handing out capsules the size of small eggs, taking your blood. Taking your money."

"What did they do to you?" Leander was genuinely amused.

"They kept coming back to collect blood. Every day I'm convinced that they put more back in than they took out. They were pumping me up with blood. I don't know where it was all coming from."

"Hopefully it was your own blood. It's called blood doping, Victor. It gives a surge of energy. It won't do anything for you in the long run. And you don't want just anybody's blood in you these days, especially not at a place specializing in last-ditch cures."

Victor fell back on the couch, legs splayed, arms akimbo. "Those people down there all know they're going to die. They don't really believe there's a miracle cure. But doing nothing is more frightening than doing something. Even if it's something ridiculous."

"Everyone has their way of coping," Leander nodded. "You're doing fine."

"I don't really believe I'm dying, you know. I look down at my belly and see that little hole they made, and what's the big deal anyway? I feel fine."

"You're a strong guy, Victor."

"The fuck I am," he burst out laughing. "Anyway, if you think there was some chance that I don't have what they say I have, you would tell me. Verdad, amigo?"

"Of course, Victor."

"Meanwhile, we can talk about old times."

"Of course, Victor," Leander had said, but the attempts at conversation would soon dissipate. He would not yet ask about the photos, but the knowledge of their existence nagged at him.

There was much about those months in Mexico that remained silent and buried between them. He resolved to watch his friend closely, as if his sudden reappearance after twenty years had been somehow premeditated and ominously purposeful.

❖ 9 ❖

As Victor made himself at home, while Adele and Leander were off at work, he would wander throughout the silent house. It looked almost unlived in, a cool semi-whiteness permeating everything, the blank sheen of eggshell walls, the nubby berber weave of sandstone carpet. He peered into the musky darkness of closets. He turned on lights to reveal a hierarchy of suits, slacks, sports jackets, and pressed shirts hanging in rigid order. He opened drawers, touching the mounds of soft sweaters in pastel colors, knit shirts, Hawaiian shirts, t-shirts. Finally, a feast of lingerie, his hand swimming through a quicksand of silk and crisp lace, from which a fragrance rose like an exhalation, this signature from Adele's skin stirring his thoughts.

He went into the bathroom adjacent to their bedroom and boldly now rummaged through drawers and cabinets, old medicine bottles storing capsules past their expiration dates, for viral attacks and bacterial infections, for migraines and toothaches, for flaking scalps and itchy skin. Menstrual paraphernalia neatly arranged in one drawer, next to the jewel case of a diaphragm, the tubes of KY and Gynol. He felt the quickening heartbeat of the intruder, the voyager into other people's nights, peering through keyholes and listening through walls for the thump of passion, the moan of release, the cry of the nightmare. These were no longer his friends; he hardly recognized them. Victor was hungry for the renewed intimacy that the truly revealing object would award him. He searched actively now, for dangerous pills, the sleeping potions and mood massagers that signal the soul's unrest.

One Sunday after Victor had arrived, Leander and Adele lingered in bed. She had slept fitfully, waking often in the night, feeling strange being home after days in and out of New York hotel rooms. Sometime near dawn, she had gotten up and locked the door, then drawn the curtains shut against the approaching light.

Once they awoke they were quiet, eager to prolong the easy snooze of an unhurried morning. They lay on their backs with a duvet for cover and turned the radio on to Saint Paul Sunday, Satie piano pieces.

Adele had taken great care with their bedroom. Tulip shaped lamps on either nightstand could be dimmed to a tender light tinged purple by the glass shades. The heavy plum curtains, drawn to filter out the morning sun, gave the room a dusky glow. They had discarded the orthopedically earnest mattress that was the vogue when they married and replaced it with one that cradled their bodies in a pillowy embrace.

Adele grew restless and kicked off her share of the cover. She stood on the tips of her toes and reached her hands toward the ceiling, then bent forward straight from the waist, her arms out in a swan dive, finally reaching to grip her toes. She held the pose until she felt the muscles in her legs and back relax their morning stiffness. Her skin glowed in the room's gentle light. She was aware of Leander's gaze on the graceful line of her back narrowing into a tight waist and flaring to her hips and toned buttocks. His interest made her stand up straighter and walk with easy graceful steps toward the dresser.

Leander felt a stirring between his legs and gradually the idle nub uncoiled into the first erection he'd experienced in Adele's presence in over a month. He felt a pang of disappointment as she leaned down, so seductively, he thought, to pull plain cotton panties and a bra from a drawer.

"So, are you getting dressed already?" he asked.

"You should get up too," she said. "We have a guest to take care of."

"I wish I had as much money as I'm up," he said, glancing at the obvious tenting in the sheet.

"I can see that."

He tried to discern some kind of promise in her voice, a softening of her resistance. For even now, after some twenty years of marriage, Adele wanted to be wooed and seduced. "So come back to bed," he said. "It's nice in here."

"I'm not sure I'm in the mood," she said, even as she felt desire gather within her.

"I have enough mood for the two of us," he said. "You can just lie back and see what happens."

"Okay, Paul." She quickly slipped back under the sheet. "We'll make believe we're alone in the house," she said, as the sound of a toilet flushing and faucet splashing came from the adjoining bathroom. A moment later a door slammed, footsteps rang out over the terrazzo floor, plates and pots clanged in the kitchen.

"We're alone in the room," he said.

"He's trying to tell us he's up and about."

"He can manage without us," he said.

He heard her murmur, "Can we manage without him?" Paul had buried his face between Adele's breasts and words would not form in his mind under the smell of her skin and the pressure of her fingers.

They made brisk, efficient love that elicited an unusual, early orgasm from Adele. She had not wanted Paul, and suspected she had, instead, felt stimulated by Victor's presence within the house. She had tried to muffle a surprised cry by turning her head and pressing her face to the pillow. She gently pushed Leander off her. He lay on his back, breathing heavily, his erection undiminished. "What was that all about?" he said. "I thought you weren't in the mood."

"Alert the media!" she laughed. "Girl gets off before boy." She then added softly that she was sorry. She put her hand around his cock. After a moment, he slipped his hand under hers and brought himself to a cheerless climax.

"I owe you one," she said.

He found the kindness in her voice oddly irritating. "I didn't think I had such an effect on you anymore."

She kicked off the sheet and rose quickly. The underclothes she'd left on the dresser were within easy reach. She bunched them in her hand and slipped into the bathroom, shutting the door behind her.

Leander stayed in bed, finding it difficult to break the inertia and muster the energy to get out of bed and face the intruder beyond the door. A dark knowledge weighed over them, even if its nature was contradictory, like two sides of one coin, two answers to a single question. Leander had found the effort of listening to Victor's constant chatter about his rotting liver tiresome, even knowing he could alleviate Victor's fears with a few expert words, from the senior pathologist at Scripps Memorial no less.

Adele came out of the shower, her head wrapped in a towel and a robe belted under her breasts. The scent of soaps and lotions of sage and bergamot followed in a cloud of steam. "We need Victor to move on," she said.

"He's not that much of a bother to you," Leander said. "You've hardly been here."

"What if he dies in our house? It would be like him to lay that trip on us."

"Don't worry. He won't."

"I thought you said he was terminal."

"We're all terminal cases in the world according to Leander."

"Garp," she mumbled.

"What?"

"It's Garp. Remember?"

"Right. Anyway. We're all terminal cases." Leander felt at a disadvantage trying to have a discussion with Adele while naked. He slipped on a pair of sweatpants and a t-shirt. "It is a kind of test," said Leander. "Victor, day after day."

"He knows more about us than we know about him."

"Is that what aroused you this morning?" Leander said. "Victor Aruna waiting and perhaps listening just outside our bedroom." He sat heavily on the bed as if deciding that a conversation would, after all, take place.

"I didn't say anything aroused me."

"That's right, you didn't." Leander sighed. "But you could say it now."

71

"I still can't get over the feeling that he knows our every move," she said. "You know he had an uncanny ability to see right through people."

"What people?"

"Me, for one. There was a weird moment, years ago, during those weeks when you were away," she said with a hint of complaint, "that I thought he had seen into my every thought."

"You knew where I was. I couldn't quite help being away."

"Not for a while."

"You and Victor saw each other much, then?"

"I went to his house in the hills one night," she said, trying to toss off the revelation as some nearly forgotten incident. "He wanted to cook dinner for me, and we were sitting in front of the fire, inside that big room with all the masks on the wall."

"So, what happened?"

"He offered to guide a meditation for me. Did you ever meditate with him, in his odd mixture of esoteric mumbo jumbo?"

"Can't say I did," Paul said.

"Sometimes we meditate without knowing it," Victor had said to her.

She had been leaning against the wall, and mirrored his posture, sitting erect, cross legged. "Now what do I do?" she asked.

"You don't do anything."

"Do I have to close my eyes?"

"Some people do, some don't."

"Your eyes are closed," she said.

"So they are."

"Are you stoned, Victor?"

"I haven't smoked in days."

"Do I think about anything?"

"You can think about your clothes."

"What about my clothes?"

His voice seemed to come to her from a great distance, softer with every exhalation. "Are they you? Are you the clothes you're wearing?"

She thought about the clothes she had chosen for that particular night. "Of course not," she snapped.

"Fine. You are not your skirt, your blouse, your underwear."
He spoke so slowly, his words were sinking into the vacuum
of each long pause. "Feel yourself naked inside your clothes," he
said finally.

She felt the fabric unraveling around her, the weave returning
to its web of weft and warp, then to a single thread thickening into
coils and tufts of cotton, finally dissolving into a cloud of fuzz.

"Are you anything less than Adele by being naked?"

And she knew herself to be naked, feeling the air on her skin,
the rough stones of the wall on her back. She had the sense that
Victor was staring at her, but when she opened her eyes the room
had fallen into such a gloom that he was only a shadowy form in
front of her.

"No. I'm still me."

"Who would you be if you shaved your head? If you went
through the whole of your body with a razor and removed all the
hair from under your arms, your pubis, your legs and arms and
eyebrows."

Adele was more naked than she had ever been in her life. She
lost her eyebrows and her eyelashes and the tiny hairs inside her
nostrils. She glistened from head to toe, from the smooth pinkiness
of her bald pate to the hairless folds of her vagina.

"Your fingernails," he whispered. "Your toenails all painted a
pretty red. They have to go."

She expected pain. The soft translucent coverings fell gently
off her fingers and toes, dropping soundlessly on the floor like dry
flower petals.

"Your teeth."

"Yes," she was barely able to whisper in a pained rasp.

One by one, first a molar or two, then her front incisors dis-
lodged themselves from their gums into her waiting mouth. They
rolled around on her tongue and she spat the dead teeth out. There
was a wet silken feel to her bare gums now, as innocent and helpless as a baby's.

Her organism seemed to hold together. Heart would keep on
beating; lungs expand and compress in spongy rhythm; ovaries
and tubes dripping ancient blood; stomach churning an acid storm;
bowels intertwined and coiled in place; blood fountaining.

"You are not your skin," Victor murmured. "Are you your flesh, your blood?"

She was staring at her own bare-bones head, as if she were hovering above it. It was a grinning fool of a skull, hairless, eyeless, lipless, tongueless. Then, in an instant, the skeleton holding up the head collapsed into a heap of chalky bones. A hot wind blew through them bearing a sweep of dead leaves, bugs' wings and ancient sand, finally scattering the fine white powder of the piled-up bones.

Victor's voice seemed to emerge disembodied from thin air. "Are you your bones?"

"I am not my bones." Her thoughts swirled like dust.

Victor's voice was a faint murmur. "That's really the question, isn't it? Not what I am. Or what I do. But who."

She heard a song. *Who are you? Who, who? I really, really wanna know.*

"If not flesh and bones, maybe you are nothing."

"I am not nothing." She was filled with a sense of her own being that expanded to fill the whole of the room, the cracks between the stones that made up the walls, within the beams and eaves and hollows in the roof tiles. She was inside closed drawers and locked boxes and covered pots. She slid within the pages of books, nestled inside records' grooves, fused into the dyes in the wool rugs and the glazes in the pottery. She was the marrow before the bone, the cell before the blood, a running river untouched as yet by oxygen. Was there memory before thought? Breath before air? Sight before light?

"Show me the face you had before you were born." She was surrounded by faces everywhere she looked, eyes staring, mouths opening to speak, bats and frogs about to spring toward her. The assembled masks were a chorus that watched in judgement.

"There was something dangerous about Victor," she said. "It made him attractive, the places were he could take you. He's kind of pathetic, now. But you never know. Victor can surprise you."

"Has anyone ever gotten to you in that same way?" Paul asked sadly.

Adele shifted her gaze to Leander's hands laced primly over his crossed knee. He was waiting for her to answer when she was saved by sudden, insistent door chimes, then footsteps racing down the hall as Victor rushed to open the door. There were men's voices followed by Victor's familiar greeting. Then more heavy steps through the hallway and the living room, and Victor's muffled words.

"Sounds like our guest has guests," Leander said, accepting that the opportunity for talk had passed.

"Just ask him how long he's planning to stay," she said abruptly. "But nicely."

Adele opened the door and led the way down the hall. The house was silent again after the last steps had faded, and Adele caught her breath. The entrance foyer and living room had been nearly filled with flowers. There were arrangements of orchids and irises and roses in vases and pots on every possible surface, on the window ledges, the mantel, on end tables. Several vases were lined up along the hallways, and more were on the dining table. The effect was one of such passionate beauty and excess of celebration that Adele had to grasp Paul's hand. Then, appearing dramatically from inside the kitchen where he'd been spying on their reaction, Victor Aruna grinned at them sheepishly. He held out two roses toward them. "Para mis amigos del alma," he said. "Because it means so much to me that you are here for me, when I did not expect to see you again. You didn't expect me, and yet we have managed to reawaken the friendship we felt for each other at one time, so many years ago." And with that little speech, he took a small bow, and pressed the roses into their hands.

❧ 10 ❧

One time, during the heady days in Mexico when they were inseparable friends, Victor invited Paul and Adele to a party in Puerto Vallarta. He wouldn't tell them the host's name; he kept giggling as if anticipating their eventual surprise. It was just another party, he said, only this guy was unbelievably wealthy, and his house had been featured in *Architectural Digest*. He had it built brick by brick to reconstruct some famous villa in the south of France. Anyway, it was a party and there would be some good dope there. Like going to the tree itself and shaking down all the apples you could want.

He convinced them that he had been very lucky to get the address to this particular event, and that because the host was a proud guy, it would be considered very offensive to turn down his invitation. "So, please," he cajoled Paul and Adele. "It's just for Saturday night. We party all night, then we sleep. There will be a room for us there so we don't have to go shit-faced trying to find a hotel in PV, and then the next afternoon, we say goodbye to my amigo and off we go."

"I'm not sure I want to meet some of these friends," Paul said.

Of the three, only Victor truly enjoyed drugs. Adele and Paul would smoke dope now and then, but ever since Victor had introduced them to each other, what they really wanted was time alone. Wedging himself between them, Victor had become unshakeable.

"Really," he insisted, "he's not like a gangster at all. You will like him."

Adele and Paul found it hard to wriggle out of the invitation. Paul had skipped out of a Saturday morning lab to have lunch with her. It was only going to be lunch, he said, then back to work. To show the seriousness of his intent, he had worn the white jacket with the stethoscope in the breast pocket. He looked oddly antiseptic in the cheap taquería they favored for its cold beer and soft tacos rolled up to order with fragrant tortillas hot from the comal. Once he'd ducked out of class, it was easy to have another beer and forget the patently unfair schedule that kept him shackled to his microscope every Saturday. He loved watching Adele lose herself eating. She had a lustful appreciation for the fine guisados lined up in pots before the women that rolled the tacos—green and red moles, stewed tripe, frijoles borrachos cooked in beer, slices of poblano pepper that would make the back of her neck moist to his touch.

By the time Victor had coaxed him into a third beer, it was past expectations that Paul would return to finish his assignment. There would be time Monday. That's when Victor urged that they all go to Puerto Vallarta for the party, an hour's flight straight west to the coast. Adele's eyes glistened with excitement. She would tuck her tiny Minolta in a string bag and take sneaky shots of the rich juniors and the whores and the models, the young transvestites, the old guys with more money than sense, their bellies bound in girdles, their feet encased in buckled loafers, rings on half their fingers.

"I can't afford to fly to PV," Paul complained.

"I have a friend at the Mexicana de Aviación counter," Victor said. "He will give us special stand-by fares."

Victor had friends everywhere. He was not a friend of the gangster giving the party, but his father was a colleague of his lawyer, and that was how the invitation had come. In a world run by friends, wealth was measured in names, not cash.

Paul didn't like the narco class that seemed to dominate the night scene in Puerto Vallarta, the thuggish squat men, always in pairs, like Mormons. They were unpredictable. They picked fights and came on to the foreign women as if to rightfully claim them away from husbands and boyfriends. Usually, the anticipated violence remained quietly submerged, thwarted at the last moment by someone from their group exercising unspoken authority. The idea

77

of going with Adele to a party hosted by Victor's nameless gangster intimidated him.

"Come on, Paul," Adele said. "It will be interesting. Maybe fun." He looked at this woman that he had just fallen in love with, and knew that he would follow her almost anywhere. If Adele wanted to go dancing with drug dealers, then that's what they would do.

"If you want," Victor said slyly. "I can go to PV with Adele, and you can stay here to practice medicine on dead people." He burst out laughing at his own joke, which he thought was wonderful and therefore bore repeating, "Doctorcito especialista en muertitos."

"I need to change," Paul said.

"No time," Victor said. "We're going straight to the airport."

Paul rolled his white coat inside a beach bag that Adele had brought along, and the three of them squeezed into the back seat of a taxi. In an airport gift shop, Victor bought matching *I Love Mexico* t-shirts, bright pink, the shade of slutty lipstick, said Adele. The three of them looked like the stragglers of some odd tour group. Adele handed the little Minolta to the clerk at the souvenir shop so he could take a picture of the three of them. "Now we look like we're going to a party," Victor said.

"More like lost tourists," Adele laughed.

"That's the look we want," Victor said. "Gangsters don't trust other Mexicans. They like tourists."

They sat in the back of the plane in the last row available by the lavatories, the three friends in their pink t-shirts. Paul said they looked like the three no-evil monkeys. He got Adele to cover her ears with her hands and Victor to cover his eyes and he covered his mouth, and people in the aisle would see them and burst out laughing. Paul felt pleased with himself. Adele handed her camera to a passenger to take another picture.

At Victor's urging they drank rum and cokes during the short flight. Paul didn't want to get drunk before the party, but he didn't want to arrive too sober either. The three beers he'd had at lunch and the cuba libres fended off the sensation of dread that had started to creep into his awareness since he'd agreed to go to the party.

The airplane lurched into some turbulence and, in spite of the drinks, Leander felt a shiver of fear rise up his back. The thin fuselage shell groaned after each bounce. He was aware suddenly of the torn seam of the seat's upholstery, the burnt-out bulb in the reading lamp, the dangling tray table, the chemical smell coming through the creaking partitions that separated their last-row seats from the lavatories. Surely, these small details were a sign that major mechanical systems were apt to be similarly frayed.

It would be his bad luck for the plane to crash, for the toilet to spill over behind them, for him to throw up his tacos. He was sure that some bolt of the fates would seek him out of the millions of people living in the world and strike him with all the accuracy of a sniper's bullet.

As a teenager Leander had backed out of riding with some friends in a more-or-less borrowed car, changing his mind at the last minute, only to learn that the group had sideswiped into a semi which had slammed into the passenger side door and killed the boy riding shotgun. Since then, he tried to be particularly prudent. Bullets and blood clots were ticking away, biding their time, following him through life just so they could strike when he least expected it. He suspected there was not much he could do to escape his fate. He nevertheless tried not to take risks. From the age of fifteen, the dark hours before dawn were filled with dread. He would wake up with dreams of falling or drowning or burning, and cling in a panic to a girlfriend for comfort. As long as tender arms were wrapped around him, his ear pressed against a loving heartbeat, then death would be held at bay.

Thoughts of Adele during those first days of their friendship depressed him, because he could not admit his misery to her. He expected her to intuit his need to cling to her, to be enveloped by her as the hours crept on.

On some anxious nights, he would take a taxi to the hidden hotels on the dark side of the centro, where the city lost itself in a tangle of nameless streets and blunt alleys. There was the Conga, El Club Starlight, El Hollywood. He had spent Saturday nights at all of them. He felt protected in the company of Estelita or La Gordis or Marla because he was a regular and they would make

79

sure he was not bothered. He could go to any of them, and the man behind the caged office would slide him a room key. A favorite girl would be knocking softly within minutes. Or if she was with someone, a message would be delivered under his door: Estelita says, Don't go anywhere, querido. She's on her way.

He liked Estela, with her dangerous look of a pandillera from an East LA girl gang, but who was sweet and eerily understanding of his reluctance to face the night alone. She would hug him and call him Pablo. She'd tease his erection with a rhyme, Pablito clavó un clavito. And when he came, she'd follow up with another one, Allá en la fuente había un chorrito . . . se hacía grandote, se hacía chiquito. When he asked her what the song meant, she said it was a children's game. It meant that there was a fountain with a spurt that got big and got little. He said he didn't understand. And she said, I told you Pablito, it doesn't mean anything. It means we have fun together.

She was never in a hurry to leave because he was so grateful to her that he'd pay her twice her normal rate. He made sure she understood how to divide her money. He would lay the bills on the dresser. First a thousand pesos, he'd explain, for the man who sends you. That leaves five hundred for you, he would say, and she would nod that yes, that's how it worked. Then he would put five hundred next to it and say it was for her alone. Then whatever he had left, some small bills, he would say, This is for the Pill, checkups, tus condones. Make the men use them. She would nod seriously, and he would be happy even though in the back of his mind he knew that more than half of the whole stash would go to a pimp, and that the rest would end up on diapers, baby formula, the sitter, and something to smoke. None of that mattered as long as he could feel like he was doing right for someone who was still in a position to use his help. And she knew what his conscience needed, because she would neatly fold the money and say, You are a good man, Pablito. Gracias. She helped him rejoice in his high goals: the drive to study medicine and do good.

In the face of his dread, the fine details of life glimmered like jewels: He relished the exhausted satisfaction of a completed lab assignment. The city's crowded cafes energized him. In the early mornings, he ran through the sleeping neighborhood streets and marveled at the feel of the road under his rhythmic steps, every small bump in pavement sending a pleasurable sensation, snaky anatomical tremors up his legs and thighs and buttocks, settling finally with reassuring solidity at the base of his spine. He was making the city more his own every year.

Minor miracles in his life had also happened when he least expected them. He'd had sex with Adele for the first time on such a night, only days after meeting her at Victor's. He felt that if he was going to die on that particular Saturday, it would be a happy death from having loved and thrilled beyond his expectations. He'd first fallen in love with her neck, leading from her collarbone down to the gentle outswell of her breasts, a sprinkling of light freckles on white skin. That first Saturday afternoon she had stood gazing down from her third floor window at the busy tree-lined street, and in the distance, Popo and Ixta's snowy peaks glistening under the luminous expanse of blueness pressing down, miraculously clear of smog on that singular, memorable day.

He'd been on the sill in front of her, his hands on her hips, his face pressed against her midriff, breathing in fragrant waves, first of laundry soap on her dress, and then skin moist under the crisp fabric. It was the first time he had really touched her, and he tried to sense resistance on her part. But then she edged her knee between his thighs, forcing his legs apart, and the assertive gesture startled him; he never learned to fully read what Adele was thinking.

An erection strained within the bind of his underwear as she parted his legs. She was wearing a wispy cotton blouse and her skin was warm through the fabric. She watched him undo each button in turn, starting with the collar and then to the middle of her collarbone, to the soft freckled nudity of chest, to the clinical whiteness of her bra. He knew she was watching him, and he felt like some parody of the adolescent lover, who thinks that going slowly down the middle of a cotton blouse is some kind of required foreplay. He did not dare look up at her expression of bemusement. So he unbuttoned away, the buttons themselves tight

81

inside their buttonholes, unable to flip down the line—*pop-pop-pop*—as he wanted to.

She leaned back and slipped off her blouse; then quickly released the brassiere catch, letting the two straps fall off her shoulders and dangle under her arms, the cups slowly inching down, empty now, and her breasts so white and tender that he had to palm them as if they were fragile things needing his protection.

He was so gingerly and delicate about the whole thing; she thought perhaps he'd never held a breast before. She pulled his hand hard, so that he could feel her nipple stiffening in the tender junction between his index and middle finger. He was lost in a maze of Vs, the V between his legs, pushed open by her own legs, and the V between his fingers to allow the penetration of her rubbery nipple, and finally the V of her thighs, culminating at her flowering labia. How he loved that word, both the majora and the menora, soft and untechnical, yet resonant with the gravity of Latin. You could kiss lips, could be drunk by lips, could be allowed into the vestibule and beyond, by parted labia.

That first time with Adele he'd felt profound relief. In the past he had often gone limp with a new partner, especially if there was any shadow of unease which his mind could blow up into guilt. The possibility of surrender to pure lust was frightening to him. He had been inept at infidelity, opportunistic couplings, friendly relations. He liked prostitutes because it was easy to satisfy their only demand on him.

As the plane landed with several hard bounces, Leander felt a knot in his stomach in anticipation of the impending socializing. He would attend the big party, but he and Adele would remain detached tourists depending on their expert guide, Victor Aruna, to shield them from too much excitement.

Leander's queasiness increased as the taxi, a '70s Chevy Impala swaying on soft shocks, rumbled away from the airport. The main thoroughfare leading past the town was clogged with honking cars, backfiring buses and clattering trucks, all in a race that was at once numbingly slow and anxiously frantic. Eventually, the traffic thinned, the road narrowed to a rutted track. Victor and Paul with Adele in the middle sat together in the back; Paul was aware of her body swaying from one to the other, her skin moist against his in the tight confines of the steamy car. They headed north for a few miles, skirting the edge of the palisades bordering the coast, the impossible blueness of the Pacific stretching out below them until the road turned abruptly inland and then began climbing into the cool hills, leaving below the sweltering streets of Puerto Vallarta.

"How much farther?" Leander asked.

"I don't know," Victor yelled against the roar of the road.

"You don't know where you're taking us?" Leander said, his voice also rising to a shout.

"I gave the driver the address," he insisted. "He says he knows where it is."

"Cuánto falta para llegar?" Leander said, tapping the driver's shoulder.

The man had been intently hunched forward with both fists gripping the wheel. He raised one hand to indicate a vague distance. "Pues un trecho," he said. A good way still.

"Van a la casa de Reginio, verdad?" The driver turned around to face the three of them as if finally giving in to curiosity about his passengers. The car started to drift toward the edge of the jungle; he turned and got it back on the asphalt with a jerk of the wheel.

"Is that who's giving the party?" asked Adele. "Reginio Aguilar?"

"Who is he?" Leander asked.

"Should be interesting," she said. "Ask Victor."

Leander turned to Victor, who pretended to be absorbed in the passing landscape out the window. "So, where are you taking us?"

"Adele is right," he said. "It will be an unusual experience for American tourists."

"Reginio Aguilar is the top drug lord in the country," she said.

"Just on the West Coast," Victor said. "He's like a general of his own army. The real violence happens several levels below him. Little wars among the narco troops."

"Two gringos in his house?" Leander shook his head in disbelief. "He's going to think we're DEA."

"No, he knows who you are," Victor said.

"You told him about us?" Leander said.

"He likes Americans. He lived in Boston for three years. He learned to make acid at MIT."

"You gave the gangsters our names?"

"Pues, for the guest list," Victor said, as if it were an obvious thing.

Adele spoke quietly in Paul's ear. "Calm down, dear. These guys give parties all the time. They're careful about who they invite."

"When did you get to be such an expert?" He had started to resent the occasional collusion he perceived between her and Victor.

"If we're going to have a spat about this, let's just stop for a pinche minute," Victor said. "Deténgase aquí." He slapped the hot vinyl seat cover behind the driver's shoulder. The car crunched to a halt at an intersection where an unmarked drive, shiny with new paving, split off from the main road and cut straight into the jungle.

The driver nodded down the smaller road. "La casa de Reginio está a dos kilómetros."

"We're almost there," Victor said. "Anybody who doesn't want to go to the party can ride the cab back to town."

"I wouldn't miss it for anything," Adele grinned. "It must be the social event of the season."

Paul shrugged unhappily. He would go along with Adele. He was not about to leave her in a house full of delinquents.

"Vamos, pues," Victor said to the driver.

The road sliced through the thick foliage forming in places a dense green tunnel, blocking the sunlight, moist and sweltering as if under a greenhouse. Even in the shade, the effect was one of dense humid heat, an airless passage that dove deeper into the jungle. The scent of stagnant marshes and the whir of crickets from deep in the brush came through the windows. It was mid afternoon but a growing darkness dampened the friends' earlier chatter.

Leander felt two slight bumps as the tires rolled over a cable barely visible across the road. "What was that?"

"Motion detector," Victor said. "They knew we were coming from the moment we turned into their road. They've been following our progress with trip wires and photo-electric cells. They don't mind us driving in. But if we had stopped for any reason, they'd be suspicious."

"They'll be shooting any minute," Leander murmured.

"Nobody's about to shoot at us. Could we please not get paranoid?" Victor said. "We're their guests. They know we're just here to enjoy ourselves."

"On my cue, we start having fun," Adele said. "Ready?"

A three-story house rose dreamlike out of the jungle, a regal chateau with a soft cakey look, heavily slathered in pink paint with white trim that gleamed like sugar. The cab stopped at a barrier where the blacktop turned into a graveled drive circling to the massive front door. A guard in a shirt with parrots and monkeys raised the pole. Moving sluggishly as if he had just been roused from a deep siesta, he scarcely glanced at them. Approaching the house, they could see that it was frilled with white cornices and wrought iron filigree protecting every window and balcony door. A low parapet along the crest of the upper story provided a view of the grounds surrounding the house.

"It's lovely," said Adele, "in a really silly way."

"More of a cake than a gangster's lair," said Leander.

"Reginio is proud of his cosmopolitan taste," Victor said. "He is rumored to have seen this exact house on the road outside Aix-en-Provence. He copied it brick by brick. Except for the color."

"Does anybody else agree that pink really screws up the image of nasty gangsters?" asked Adele.

"Reginio is a romantic," Victor said. "He built the house for Rosa Ferrán, the love of his life. He thought she would like pink. Like her name."

"Is she going to be at the party?" Leander asked.

"Actually, no," Victor said. "She drowned last year while cruising to Baja in his yacht."

"He probably pushed her overboard," ventured Adele.

"Quién sabe? There are always rumors." Victor raised his eyebrows in mock ignorance. "It is known that he had refused to marry her. She'd gotten pregnant. She had an abortion without his permission."

The car stopped in front of the door, and the three emerged into the waning light of the afternoon. Adele pulled out the

Minolta from her beach bag and snapped a shot of the big white entrance, carved with angel heads and open roses.

"Maybe this is not the best time for photography," Victor said, taking the camera from her hand and stuffing it inside her bag.

"I'm just being a cute little tourist," she laughed.

"If this is a party," Leander said. "Where are all the cars?"

"Reginio is discrete. His parties never look like parties from the outside." The guard, watching them from his post by the gate, motioned them inside with a flutter of his fingers. A yawning hall of pink marble and white iron trim opened before them. Cumbia music with its insistent organ lead echoed from hidden speakers, doggedly festive in the nearly empty room.

A leather sofa and matching chairs had been pushed out of the way to make room for an improvised dance floor. Three couples shuffled about listlessly, oblivious of the new arrivals. The women, small and plump in miniskirts and beaded tops, danced bravely, their short legs unsteady in their high-heel shoes. The squat, thick-necked men in the recurring parrot and monkey shirts, cupped their hands under the women's buttocks.

A buffet table stretched along one wall; of the once-generous spread there remained a scattering of crusty enchiladas in a cold chafing dish, and tossed about the table, picked-over chicken bones and fruit rinds. Empty glasses and full ashtrays lay everywhere. A red high-heeled sandal had been kicked into a corner; a black brassiere hung like a pennant on the banister spiraling along the staircase.

"Let's get out of here." Leander raised his voice above the muffled beat. "This party is long over." He stepped toward the open door just as the taxi was disappearing down the drive.

Victor shrugged. "Reginio's fiestas go on for days," he said. "The rest of the guests are in their rooms taking siestas."

"Then *we* should take a siesta." Adele sat down on a nearby sofa, sinking into the soft leather cushions, her legs stretched out before her. "Might as well make the best of this." She patted the couch for Paul to join her.

He shook his head. "This feels too weird."

Adele sounded irritated. "Say what you need to say, won't you?"

"I'm trying to tell you that I don't know what we're doing here. And neither does anyone else."

"You're just being antisocial again."

"Yes, that too."

Victor went back out to talk to the guard. They spoke for a minute, Victor gesturing impatiently, the man reaching out to clasp the hand that Victor was waving about. All the while, he kept nodding and smiling and murmuring assurances. Finally, they shook hands.

"It's like I said," Victor came back smiling. "They're all sleeping. We're supposed to take the two rooms with the open doors at the end of the corridor. He says not to go into rooms with closed doors," he laughed. "You never know what we'll interrupt."

He led the way into a small bedroom, its walls papered in a motif of pink hibiscus and seashells, weirdly girlish in comparison to the hard-edged glass and leather of the main room below. There was something homey about the twin beds such as siblings might share, covered with spreads of the same flowery pattern as the wallpaper. The beds were separated by a simple nightstand which held a glass ashtray and a lamp with the shade repeating yet again the flower and seashell motif. There was a narrow window above the beds, too high to provide a view of more than a blue sky.

"What a sweet room," Adele said. "So ungangsterlike."

"Reginio is particularly fond of his girl children," Victor explained. "He has several daughters from different wives." He added expansively, "I leave you now. Enjoy."

"Buenas noches, Victor," Leander said, even though it was early evening. "Knock when the party starts up again." With the door closed, the cumbia from downstairs had receded to a drone.

He removed his medical coat from inside Adele's beach bag and hung it on a wire hanger. He tugged at the wrinkles on the back and smoothed the lapels. The ceremonial white jacket was visible proof of his privileged status. It allowed him entry into intimate spaces, dark nooks and slippery crevices of the human body, a glimpse into automatic functions undisturbed and unseen by most. When Victor Aruna sarcastically called him doctorcito, it was still an acknowledgement of his special status.

87

Adele sat crosslegged on the bed. She took out the Minolta and a roll of film, slipped in a new cartridge, then clicked it shut with an air of resolve.

"You plan to take pictures?" Paul said.

"I earned my photography merit badge," she said. "Being Prepared."

"I don't think Reginio and his troops would appreciate having their photo taken."

"It's a party. Everybody likes pictures of the party."

"Adele, please don't go pissing people off."

"I like it when you get serious and protective," she laughed.

"Am I the only one who thinks this is all very strange?" he said. "Victor thinks it's normal for the party to get interrupted in the middle of the afternoon. Most parties haven't even started by this time. This one is winding down."

"We have no way of leaving," she inhaled deeply. "It's exciting, actually."

"If this thing doesn't get normal soon, you and I are walking out the door and down the road."

"All the way to PV," she nodded agreeably.

"We'll get to the main road and hitch a ride."

"I'm certainly dressed for it. Mexican guys always stop for blondes in short skirts."

The house shook out of its siesta with a sudden eruption of the music, the driving organ and the insistent cumbia beat thudding against the walls, rattling the doors and window panes, the musical mess screaming out as if the amp had been accidentally nudged to its full power. Heavy footsteps tramped past their room, scattered shouts echoed in the hallways, a door slammed with a sound like gunshot, a woman shrieked with a kind of manic laughter. "Sounds like the party is picking up," Paul said.

What had at first sounded like a burst of hysterical laughter had with repetition evolved into a series of cries and anguished shouts finally quieting down and blending into a soft keening chorus. A man shouted at the women to be quiet. "Cállense, cabronas putas."

Adele leaned back from the door, stepping away gingerly as if it might suddenly burst open under the pressure of violence building just beyond it. "Some people out there are not enjoying themselves," she said.

Victor burst into the room, followed by the whine of the blaring music. He slammed the door shut as if to block the chaos behind him. "There's nothing to worry about." He couldn't steady the shaking in his voice.

"Sounds like someone crashed the party," Leander said.

Victor frowned. "What does that word mean, 'crash'?"

"Uninvited guests," Leander said. "Rowdy, drunk freeloaders out to steal the silver and other people's girls."

"Yes. That is the absolute truth. Fortunately, it is not our party. We will stay out of sight until the trouble is over."

"Oh boy! Did I hear the word trouble?" said Adele with mock enthusiasm.

"Yes, the Policía Judicial," Victor nodded.

"It's a raid?" Adele said. "That could be exciting." She reached for her beach bag and held it protectively against her midriff.

"Yes, a redada. There must be twenty judiciales running around the house."

"We're probably in trouble just for being here," Leander said.

"Trouble for Reginio. But not for us. Anybody wants to know, we are not in the drug business. We are not even users of drugs. We are a medical student and an artistic photographer."

"And a lawyer. Right, Victor?" Leander said. "It is good to have a lawyer around during these things, I'm sure."

Victor nodded seriously.

"I was joking, Victor," Leander smiled. "We couldn't really be in need of a lawyer yet."

"No matter, I can help." He put his hand protectively on Leander's shoulder. "I talked to the Capitán. He said we have nothing to worry about as long as we stay inside the room."

"They were mistreating women, weren't they?" Adele said. "They should have stayed in their rooms like good girls."

Victor nodded unhappily. "They are actually whores from the bars downtown brought to entertain Reginio's men. They are not being hurt. They are being put on a truck and taken back to Puerto Vallarta."

"Women are being transported in a truck?" Adele repeated.

"That is not so important right now," Victor mumbled.

"Adele," Paul said, taking her by the shoulders. "Let's not worry about the niceties of the situation."

She twisted away from him and reached for the camera inside her bag. "There are pictures out there." She pushed the lamp and the ashtray off the nightstand and climbed up to see out. "My God." She held the lens against the window and clicked off a half dozen shots. "They really are herding them like cattle," she said. "About a dozen women. Marching in a row like obedient schoolgirls, holding on to their dresses, their shoes, their little purses, up the loading ramp of this flatbed truck."

"They're not students, I told you. They're prostitutes," Victor said.

"I'll make a note of that when I print the pictures." She stepped down from the table onto the bed, nearly losing her balance, then almost slipping on the floor as she went for the door.

Paul tried to hold her back. "I'm going for a closer look," she said, shaking off his grip. She swept past Victor, who was trying to stand in her way. "See you boys later."

"We're not following her, okay?" Victor shut the door after her. "Adele can talk her way out of situations, in case you hadn't noticed."

"I think it's time *we* talked our way out of here," Leander said.

"That will not be possible yet," Victor said. "The judiciales must investigate everyone that is here, before they decide who they let go."

"Like the whores."

"Of course," Victor said. "They've been investigated and found to be innocent."

"Innocent of what?"

"Drug trafficking."

"Of course."

"Yes. They were just here to party."

"Like us."

"They're not so sure about us," Victor said unhappily. "They wonder if we're friends of Reginio."

"Fine," Leander said impatiently. "Let them ask Reginio whether he knows us or not."

"They would like to do that, of course," Victor said. "Only Reginio is gone. They find this frustrating."

"Frustration all around," Leander sighed. "Can't we explain things to the head guy and leave?"

"I've already talked with him," Victor said. "We're to wait in our rooms until he's ready to listen."

"It would be good to leave before nightfall."

"I can't do anything more," Victor sighed. "The capitán said, wait. We wait. He said we stay in our room. We stay. He said don't fuck around with him. We don't."

"He said 'fuck around' in Spanish?"

"He said, 'no estén chingando.' You know what that means, no?"

Leander nodded unhappily. "Chingar means whatever anybody wants it to mean."

Victor stood up; he buried his hands in his pockets and paced about with his head down, as if searching the floor for answers. "I'm going to get Adele." He finally looked up. "They won't like that she's clicking away."

Later, as the night deepened, Leander climbed onto the nightstand to look out the window; he steadied himself by hanging on to the curtain rod. The truck taking the women back to Puerto Vallarta was gone and had left behind only faint tracks across the lawn which was now deserted under the overlapping circles made by floodlights. For a moment Leander marveled at the vivid colors, the inner lawn a luminous green, and around it, the pearly glow of the pebbled driveway.

Then, as if someone had spied him looking through the narrow window, the lights were extinguished, plunging the space below into a dense darkness. Eventually, the house had grown silent; the music was turned off, the shouting and running along the corridors ceased. Outside, from the central garden to the massed rows of palms at the edge of the road and into the jungle, the still air vibrated with the din of crickets and bird squawks.

For a moment, Leander harbored the illusion that perhaps the house was empty, that the police had arrested everyone and left. It was clearly time to go home. He would find Adele and Victor and then, one way or another, they would make it to the road and get a ride back to town. He opened the door and was startled to face a man sitting on a chair tilted against the wall.

The guard wore a pleated guayabera shirt over black trousers. He was about twenty years old with an incipient mustache and dark hair slicked back. He raised a thin leg to block Leander's path. "Ajá! Where are you going, my friend?" he asked.

His first impulse was to simply walk around the small foot in a highly polished ankle boot. Then he saw the glinting barrel of an automatic rifle resting on the man's lap, the fingers of his right hand lazily curled around the trigger guard. "Voy a buscar a mi novia y a mi amigo," Leander explained that he wanted to find his girlfriend and his buddy.

"No es posible," the guard shook his head. "For now, everyone is in their rooms. There is no more party."

"I don't want to party," Leander said. "I'll get my friends so that we can go back to Puerto Vallarta. We can do that, can't we?" Unable to resist his sense of the irony surrounding this night, he added, "Now that the fun is over. It is over, verdad?"

"Claro que sí." The man was grinning as Leander stepped to the railing and looked down toward the main room. The scene below had the look of a party gone oppressively silent, its whirl frozen in mid-motion. The fury must have lasted only a few seconds, too sudden and shocking for even surprised cries and angry curses to rise above the staccato gunfire blending into the blaring music. Men's bodies lay on the floor, over a table, over the back of a chair, supine on a couch as if caught in a nap, positioned as if the men dancing had only paused to take a break, before seeking out new partners. It was a massacre of bleeding parrots, monkeys with powder burns, a scattering of torn feathers and split fur. His gaze froze on details: a bullet hole the size of a poker chip partially hidden by matted hair, a bloom of blood still red and wet on crisp cotton fabric, and then, reluctantly, a glimpse of skin, a dropped shoe, a pair of eyes open and unblinking.

Even as he took in the scene as a whole, he was envisioning a makeshift triage. There were five men that he could see. Uno, dos, tres, cuatro, cinco. They were dressed as if they had all shopped at the same store, in the beach shirts with designs of palm trees and monkeys and parrots. "Uno" was positioned at the foot of the sofa and seemed to have dozed off and rolled onto the floor, his shirt hiked up to reveal a large brown belly. "Dos" had slid down a chair slouching like molten wax, only to be stopped by his butt finding a perch on the chair's edge, head slumped forward so that his chin touched his chest. His white linen pants were caught midcalf, the skin on his leg hairless and shiny brown. "Tres" had been stopped on his way out the door. He'd fallen to his knees and then tipped back so that his legs were unnaturally bent beneath him as if in some acrobatic jitterbug. "Cuatro" was partially hidden behind a rubber tree in a corner as if he had tried to find protection behind its big waxy leaves. "Cinco" had been shot while trying to run up the stairs and was hanging on the balustrade, eyes staring out in surprise. The floor was littered with shell casings, shards of glass, broken plaster; shreds of greenery lay tossed about like wilted salad.

The guard calmly rocked the chair forward and stood up to block Leander's view, firmly crowding him back from the railing. His breath smelled of spearmint and it momentarily masked the stink of gun powder. "Orders of my capitán," the man insisted. "You go back to your room. Same as everybody." He poked his fingers against Leander's chest, causing him to stumble over the threshold, then reached after him to jerk the door shut.

Feeling that his legs were about to give way, Leander sat heavily on the bed. He remained still for several moments as if waiting for his mind to settle; finally, surrendering to a numbing confusion, he lay back. He tried to calm the images that crowded his mind by directing his attention to the sliver of light between the floor and the bottom of the door. Occasionally, the light would darken when someone stepped close, then reappear when the person outside walked away. He prayed that the next sign of movement would be Adele returning safely.

As he grew accustomed to the surrounding gloom, his eyes surveyed the pattern of flowers spread throughout the room. The flowers that arched over the doorway were connected by some invisible root system to the flowers on the bedspread, on the curtains, on the wallpaper. What one single petunia knew, all the room's petunias knew. Under the building's veneer, its walls were as thin as plywood. Reginio's unhappy castle was a place of restless sleepers. When Leander held his breath he could hear the labored breathing of the uneasy dreamer, the back-and-forth refrain of oblivious snoring, gasping apnea, percussive shouts and cries. Toilets flushed and doors slammed from one end of the building to the other. Footsteps creaked above the ceiling, so close he felt he could reach through the plaster and trip someone. Meanwhile, as if everything around him were settling into a weird kind of normalcy, distant voices became whispers. Slow, measured footsteps made their way up and down the hall. An occasional pause would give way to absent-minded whistling. Vaughn Williams' "Lark Ascending." The serpentine development of the main theme, with its curious unfolding of flight and freedom, seeped into the room. Then the music stopped in mid-phrase. Leander sensed a presence just beyond the door. He tried to pull it open, but it had been jammed from the outside.

He strained to hear the other's breath or the rustle of clothes. He rapped a light four-beat pattern. He did it twice, and waited. Then he slammed his palm against the door several times in rhythmic succession. He paused to rub his stinging hand.

"Estate tranquilo," the same man's voice spoke softly just outside the door.

"Please, what is happening to my friends?" Leander said.

There was no answer. The voice had appeared in some disembodied form, spoken, and then vanished. After that, the house settled once more into its edgy silence. He would wait out the night, and hope for Adele's safe return. He'd kicked off his shoes, but made sure they were by the bed in case he had to put them on quickly. The bed was firm and narrow. Sheets smooth under his back. The pillow was fragrant with the scent of a ubiquitous Mexican perfume. Reluctant to surrender to the inviting fabric, he clung in a fetal position to the edge of the bed.

He felt his breaths lengthen, his heartbeat settle down to an even, slow beat. The last few hours had left him with a deeply rooted exhaustion that chilled his bones and weighed into the base of his stomach. There was mainly a formless dread. He was beyond being afraid of the young guard outside the door, but still anxious about Adele running around with her camera. The urge to flee or physically resist danger was replaced with a kind of passivity, a sense that if he could only sleep through the following hours, the situation would revert to normal on its own.

Sometime later, while the night was still dark outside, he opened his eyes at the sound of the door opening and saw Victor slip into the room.

"Where is Adele?" Leander asked.

"They didn't want her running around shooting photos," he said. "They took away her camera. They put her someplace to have her tantrum."

"They are worried about her shooting pictures?"

"Cops and criminals shoot each other," Victor said. "They're none of our business."

"So why are we still here?"

"It's the middle of the night. We'll get a ride in the morning."

❖ 11 ❖

Adele had leaned over the balustrade, snapping pictures of the mayhem in the living room, then quickly tucking the camera into her beach bag. She was spun around by the shoulders, her face pushed to the wall. "Quieta, mi amor," a man murmured in her ear. Then, once he felt her be still, he softened his grip on her.

She turned to see the man's face. In his iridescent blue shirt and white tie, creased black pants, and ankle boots polished to a high gloss, he was different from the ones who'd been dancing and drinking and having a good time in their party shirts. He kept the hold on her arm, and with practiced grace guided her down the hallway. He introduced himself as Neto, a sus órdenes, and familiarly called her Adelita. He acted as if there were no doubt that she would do whatever he said. He led her quickly past the main room, holding her head down so that she could only see the floor. Out of her peripheral vision she was aware of the still faces down below, the words caught in mid-breath, the eyes now staring longingly toward some final vision of hope, perhaps seeing a momentary hesitation in the executioner's eyes.

She was steered to the opposite end of the house into a bedroom with a chintz loveseat, lace curtains and a king-size, four-poster bed. A purple velvet bedspread was bunched up at the foot, pink satin sheets rumpled as if from a restless night, the pillows punched into shapeless lumps. Adele stood back, lingering at the door until the man shut it behind her. When he offered to take her bag, she said gracias, and held it close to her body. He slouched down on the loveseat and watched her with an expression of amusement. "I think that it's nicer here than in your other room," he said.

96

"Yes, quite the place," she said uncertainly.

"This is Reginio's private bedroom," he explained proudly. "It's where the great ugly lord sleeps like a baby. Nobody is allowed in here except the woman he is spending the night with." He ran his hand through the smooth sheets and picked out a single wiry pubic hair. He looked at it intently. "I can go anywhere in his house now, because we have him on the run." He flicked the hair to one side of the bed with an expression of distaste. "You can look around if you like." He pulled out a drawer and scooped out soft bunches of silk and lace that filled the air with a feminine fragrance. "You could put on his wife's nightgowns," he invited. "They are like what a princess would wear. Verdad?"

"No," she shuddered.

"Tranquila, por favor." He indicated for her to sit on the edge of the bed. "Estás en tu casa," he grinned, pleased at his own little joke. "You should make yourself comfortable. We can have ourselves a little relax." He smiled a tight-lipped grin.

"I need to use the bathroom," Adele said.

"Claro." He indicated a path for her to walk between the bed and the chair where he was sitting. As she moved past she felt his hand lightly graze the back of her thigh. "Ay, perdón," he exclaimed as if he had caught himself doing something naughty in spite of his better judgment. "It was without intention."

She felt him reach for the bag but she clutched it close to her. "I must have this," she said firmly. "I am in my time of the month. Problemas femeninos."

She was safely in the bathroom when she heard him tell her not to lock the door. She turned both gold plated faucets and ran the water hard. She didn't hear him protest when she turned the lock anyway. Mexican men were horrified of menstruation. A friend of a friend was reputed to have avoided rape by holding up a used tampon at her assailant like a cross against a vampire.

While Neto waited outside, Adele rewound the roll of film and removed it from the camera. The coiled ribbon seemed so light and insubstantial in contrast to the images it contained. She wrapped the roll in a ragged Kleenex and buried it deep in the bag. She reloaded the camera and tossed it casually on top. Finally, she sat on the toilet seat and broke into a sudden shaking spasm.

97

There was insistent knocking. Adele flushed and splashed her cheeks with cold water. When she swung the door open, Neto's face was an inch or two from hers. He stared at her hard, his small eyes squinting as if to drill into her head. Adele blinked and avoided his gaze. His expression had changed from good-natured tolerance to suspicion. He brushed past her and emptied the beach bag on the floor, kicking aside the camera, suntan lotion, sun glasses, a straw hat. He felt around with his fingers, even picked out the crumpled wad of tissue and dropped it back in the bag. "You are not in your time of bleeding, verdad?"

She felt her throat squeeze shut with anxiety. "I thought it had started," she said. "Because I'm under stress."

He shook his head as if in amazement that she could be so stupid as to lie to him. "Mentirosa," he scolded playfully, with a smile, as if he had decided to forgive her.

"I was afraid," she tried to explain.

"Of me?" He opened his eyes wide in disbelief.

He took the stuff that had spilled out of the beach bag and threw it back inside. He was about to put the camera away but changed his mind. He held it to his eyes, and pointed it at her. "Me regalas la camarita," he said.

She nodded. "You can have the camera. I'll trade it for the film inside."

He shook his head sadly. "These are very provocative pictures, no?" he grinned. "I will develop them for my collection. Now, I would like to take a sexy picture of you," he said. She sat rigidly on the edge of the bed while he aimed the lens at her and told her to smile. He made a big deal out of finding the proper angle and clicked off a couple of shots. He put the camera aside. "Do you mind if we have a cigarette?" he said.

"You can smoke as much as you like," Adele muttered.

"The two of us, that is. To smoke and have a conversation. No es un problema, verdad?" He reached for the pack in his shirt pocket and offered her one. "Just to hold it, you know. We can be two people having a chat." He kept pointing the pack at her until she took one. He struck a match and offered to light her cigarette. When she pulled back, he shrugged and lit his own.

He took a few puffs in silence as if he were weighing a decision. Then, with quick resolve, clenching the cigarette between his
teeth, he took his shirt off, taking care not to wrinkle it, and carefully laid it on the back of a nearby chair. He stepped out of his
pants and stood in front of her in his black socks and white briefs.
In contrast to his brown face with its wispy moustache and side-
burns, his chest and legs were pale and hairless, wiry muscles
dancing just under the skin.

"Would you like to undress?"

"Is that what you want me to do?" she asked dully.

"Well, yes. But you have to want to, verdad?" He climbed up
on the bed and walked on the soft mattress. He took long drags on
the cigarette, all the time staring at Adele through the smoke,
looking down on her with something like curiosity, and also with
a vague expression of disapproval.

Adele tried to look away from him standing before her. She
hoped that if she sat still and did what he wanted, he might not hurt
her. She was intimidated by his nearly ritualistic smoking,
drawing deeply on the cigarette to get the end burning brightly,
scattering the ashes about him with nervous flicks of his thumb.

"I sense you have questions in your mind," he said.

"I'd like to know what you are up to," she said flatly.

He shook his head in wonder that she could be too thick to
understand. He sat next to her and ground out the stub on top of
the dresser. "That is no way to have a conversation," he sighed.
"It should happen naturally. We would tell each other about
ourselves. The movies we've seen. The music we listen to. We
could be friends and I could come and visit you when you go back
to the D.F."

His vaguely ingratiating tone did not ease the fear that he
could at any time unleash a kind of casual violence. "I'm sorry,"
she said in a near whisper. "This has been too strange a night
for me."

"Yes," he nodded unhappily. "Perhaps under other circumstances . . ."

He stepped down from the bed and put his clothes back on
hurriedly, as if embarrassed at having revealed some weakness in

his character. He opened the door and stood aside, indicating with a jerky little bow that she was to go first. He led her back down the hall, his fingers barely grazing her arm. She kept her eyes on the floor, but then, unable to ignore the main room below, she stole a glance over the balcony. She felt no empathy with the dark, anonymous bodies lying about, bloody wounds crusted already, their faces ashen and oddly peaceful. The shock was more about aesthetics and abstract drama than personal pain.

Leander had been lying on the bed quite still, his eyes shut, his breath attempting to ease itself into the rhythm of slumber. He heard the door swing on its hinges, a rectangle of light shone on the ceiling, and then quickly closed with the snap of the latch. He was relieved that it was Adele; the motion of her body, the soft brush of her steps were all familiar. He felt like a coward for feigning sleep. He couldn't own up to the possibility that she might have been harmed.

Adele dropped her clothes, went into the bathroom and turned on the hot water full-strength. She stepped into the tub, and soon her muscles softened and relaxed their tension. She felt a vague gratitude that the night had come and gone and she had suffered nothing more serious than the loss of her camera.

A crisp white towel felt pleasantly rough on her skin, as if whatever taint had lingered after the long soak still needed to be rubbed off. She wished she had clean clothes. She rinsed her panties and laid them near a vent. She searched through the bag and was reassured to touch the film cartridge safely wadded up in Kleenex. In the dark she found Paul's shirt hanging on the back of a chair and buttoned it all the way up to her neck. Its familiar smell pushed away the memory of the Mexican man.

She lay down gingerly, sensing that Paul was feigning sleep. She wanted to tell him that he would feel better after taking a shower, but then, as if relieved by her return, she heard his breath ease into sleep. Outside, a soft gray light illuminated the palms and the flowering clumps of wisteria and hibiscus. It was five and with the light there was the call of a rooster that seemed to be just outside the window. How Mexican, she thought; whether in city neighborhoods or in country villages, every backyard or rooftop seemed to coop up a few straggly chickens and a rooster.

When she awoke a couple of hours later, she could hear Paul in the shower, the ordinary sounds of an ordinary morning. The room was oddly cheerful with sunlight and a breeze, musky from the nearby ocean, blowing through the window. Outside, the rooster's call had been replaced by the frenzied squawking of gulls rushing seaward. She was struck by how normal the day felt. She had never been close to violent death before.

The shower went silent and a moment later Paul was in the middle of the room toweling himself dry. She couldn't help comparing his naked body to that of the cop's wiry frame. Paul's was soft and somehow undeveloped, as if used for little more than pleasure and recreation. The Mexican's body was built for physical labor, and for violence.

"God, I was glad to see you," he finally said. "You're fine, right?" He put on his jeans and t-shirt. He looked like a high school boy in his Nikes and tube socks.

Adele nodded. She wanted to say that she was afraid to cross beyond the door. Whatever violence had swept through in the night had been somehow pushed back and shut outside. She steeled herself with a deep breath. "I'll be ready in a second," she said.

She went into the bathroom and reflexively locked the door. She rubbed a little soap on her teeth and ran a comb through her hair. "I can't wait to get out of here," she called.

"I'm not sure we can just walk away," he said.

"Yes, we can." She stepped out of the bathroom. "We will walk through the main gates and on to the highway. We won't stop unless someone points a gun at us."

"Funny," he said. "What about Victor?"

"We can call him later to thank him for a very nice time."

Paul felt they had to be rational. "It will not do to make anyone angry."

"No, we wouldn't want a repeat of last night."

"That had nothing to do with us. It was a problem between natural enemies—cops and robbers."

"Except that we saw it all."

"I'm not sure what we saw," he said blandly.

"You can look at my pictures."

By the time they emerged into the hallway and cautiously made their way down the winding stairway, there was nobody left in the house, except for a couple of housekeepers, placid square women standing smiling by the door to the kitchen. They seemed to take pride that everything was now in order. They wore white blouses and flowing, ankle-length skirts under their aprons. They had cleaned the great room, emptied the ashtrays, picked up glasses and beer bottles. The marble floor gleamed, without a body in sight. A glass table on a granite pedestal was loaded with platters of red papaya, slices of cantaloupe, a gleaming urn with strong coffee, pitchers of orange juice and foamy piña colada. Chafing dishes held simmering huevos a la mexicana, beans, chilaquiles. There were stacks of traditional blue and white talavera crockery and massive silver utensils. From the kitchen came the sounds of other women's voices, chattering and giggling, pots banging, oil sizzling. The smaller of the two Indian women stepped forward to greet them, hastily drying her hands on her apron. She beamed a smile and said, "Buenos días, señores."

"Dónde está nuestro amigo?" Leander asked for Victor.

The woman indicated her ignorance with an exaggerated raising of her shoulders. "Quién sabe?"

"I'm here, doctorcito." Victor was standing by the window as if he'd been watching for someone's arrival. He looked fresh and well rested in crisp beige slacks and pressed guayabera shirt, dainty feet sockless inside his loafers. "Everyone's gone," he indicated with a small wave.

"A long time ago," the woman nodded. "Los señores judiciales left very early. They said to let you sleep."

Adele looked uncomfortably at Paul. "I think we should go too."

"You will eat first, verdad?" the woman insisted.

She took a couple of plates from the table and handed them to them. "Serve yourselves of everything. Me llamo Josefina. I'm in the kitchen for whatever you need."

"Gracias." Victor took the plates from the woman and put his arm around her hunched shoulders. "You are as kind as you are beautiful." The woman stifled a giggle with her hand and hurried away.

"Those women act as if it were a normal day," Paul said.

"They do what Reginio tells them. He sent word for them to take care of us."

Anxious to get out of the house, they ate quickly. Adele picked at the papaya, diced up into coral-red cubes, sweet and yielding to the inside of the mouth. The eggs were laced with green chunks of raw serrano peppers which brought a flush to Paul's face. The freshly made tortillas had that perfect chewy texture that lasts only a few minutes after they've been made.

Adele had settled into a glum silence. From the sofa, she watched Paul eat hungrily and marveled that he could keep the food down. "Please," she said. "Can we go soon?"

Victor shook his head. "I cannot believe you Americans," he said finally.

"I don't know what you're talking about," Adele said.

"You must," he insisted. "You both act as if Josefina does not exist. She said buenos días, and you said nothing. After eating, you do not go into the kitchen to say thank you. All the time, it's as if she's invisible."

"After last night, you worry about me being polite?" Leander said.

"We all have to do things we don't want. We got off easy. We didn't get hurt in someone else's business dispute."

"It wasn't all about business last night," Adele said. "I made a friend. He got down to his white underwear and black socks."

"What are you talking about?" Leander looked up from the plate before him.

"Not a big deal. I'll tell you some other time." Adele wished she had a friend she could entertain with her tale of the lonely policeman. There was some humor in the situation. Paul was not the one to get it.

"Okay. You want to leave now? Let's go," Victor sighed.

Adele stepped out of the house as a taxi came crunching down the gravel road and stopped in front of her. Victor reached for her bag, but she pulled it back . He was suddenly insistent. "Dame la bolsa, Adele."

"Yo la llevo," she said. I can carry it.

"You act as if you were hiding something," he said with a new, terse authority. "Maybe you have some souvenirs in there."

"What are you talking about, Victor?" Leander snapped. "They took her camera."

"You know what I'm looking for, verdad, Adele?" He gestured for her to hand over the beach bag.

"You're with them," she said.

Victor shook his head as if the issue were too complex for words. "You have to understand that somebody is doing us a favor. I promised that we would not embarrass anyone."

He reached inside the bag and felt with his fingers until he found the roll. "I have to give them this, Adelita," he said unhappily as he tucked it into his pocket. "You have no other film?"

"You're an asshole," she said.

"Let's just go," Leander said.

Victor nodded to the driver.

The driver said buenos días, and shut the doors once the three friends were in the back seat, Adele between the two men. She thought they looked again like the three blind, deaf and mute monkeys. Not even remembering evil. From that time, things would not be entirely right among them.

❧ 12 ❧

In the days following the night in Puerto Vallarta, Leander had fallen into a numb inertia. There was no such thing as an innocent bystander. The thought of facing Victor filled him with vague anxiety. He kept putting off calling Adele because he was sure she viewed his earlier passivity with contempt. The next several days found him plunging into his studies, spending long hours at the university lab, then riding the circuitous bus route to his new apartment in a noisy, congested neighborhood, far from the tree-shaded boulevards and residential streets that even budget-conscious students could afford. He put off telling his friends about the move.

Leander's new place was in a traditional vecindad, two stories of apartments arranged around a courtyard. The high wall facing the street gave him a feeling of invisibility. The place was crowded and noisy with the squeals of children, mothers scolding, ongoing squabbles. At the center of the patio was a cistern with fresh water that was a blessing during the hot dry season from March through May, and there was barely enough pressure to keep the flow going through the pipes. At the far end was a playground with a swing set, the chalk markings of an ongoing game of hopscotch, a couple of chairs for mothers to keep an eye on the younger kids. Leander was soon a familiar figure as he wound his way through the courtyard, his Spanish fluent enough for brief neighborly chats, occasionally stopping to watch the children play, and smiling at the mothers. Within days of settling into his new apartment, the joven doctor in room 14 was being greeted with deference.

One afternoon there was the sudden blaring of a car horn, followed by a screech of brakes locking and tires sliding down the street in front of the building. A moment later, Leander was startled by anxious rapping at his door. He put down his chemistry textbook and tried to ease the queasy cramping in his stomach with some deep breaths. It was the first time anyone had knocked since he had moved in. He wasn't expecting guests, and reflexively he made sure the way to the balcony was clear, that the doors were unlatched. He waited, hoping the visitor would assume there was nobody home.

"Ayúdeme, doctor," a woman's voice called from the other side of the door.

"Qué pasa?" Leander answered hoarsely, as if his ability to speak had fallen into disuse.

"Mi hijito tuvo un accidente."

Leander would be glad to help a child who might have suffered a fall. "Ah, señora Loreto!" he exclaimed, wondering if she could hear the relief in his voice. She owned the building and lived in a suite of apartments with her three kids and no sign of a husband.

"Mire, doctor. Mi hijo Fito se cayó de la bicicleta." She was leading her eight-year old by the hand. He knew the boy as a bully who terrorized the younger kids. He was already a thuggish fellow with a round head and a plug of a neck. Instead of his habitual scowl, the boy's eyes were tightly shut. His head from the crown to the eyebrows showed the bloody evidence of the contusions and scrapes of a fall on the street. The woman launched into a breathless account of how the boy had ridden his bike into the path of an approaching car and fallen to the ground.

"Tranquilo," Leander murmured, reaching out for the boy's hand and leading him to a chair near the open balcony. He was lucky not to have been run over. Leander positioned the head so that it caught the waning sunlight. He worked his fingers into the sticky hair to reveal the scalp.

"No es nada serio," he said to the woman who stood gripping her son's shoulders. "But it will hurt when I clean out the scrapes and asphalt. You're going to be a machito?" he said to the boy.

"Tell the doctor que sí," the woman ordered her son.

"Sí, doctor," Fito muttered.

Leander placed a floor lamp near the chair. He removed the paper shade so that the bulb cast a bright light on Fito's head. The boy whined as Leander scissored off his hair and cleaned his scalp with alcohol, and then with a pair of tweezers and a fine scalpel, dug out one by one the embedded bits of gravel. He methodically made his way from right to left, uncovering the scalp in rows, the red scrapes glinting though the black hair. He felt the boy stiffen at every touch.

Leander got so that he could predict the amount of pain he would cause with every motion of the swab. He thought that the pain was dependent on the amount of asphalt rubbed into the wound. But then he realized that the pain had more to do with how he handled the boy's head, how roughly he rubbed into the skin to clean out the tar. He marveled at his willingness to inflict varying degrees of pain because of a vague dislike of the boy. He took the kid's cries as censure and lack of gratitude. He breathed deeply and jerked his hands from the kid's head. He waited as the sudden impulse to punish Fito for his whimpering faded.

Señora Loreto tightened her fingers around her son's shoulders to hold him still and nagged him to be quiet or she would tell his father that he'd acted like a crybaby. When Señora Loreto tried to pay Leander, he pressed the money back into her hand. He said he'd been glad to be of help. "Bueno," she said. "In that case we will be friends, no?"

The next day his landlady brought him a serving of flan, then another day, a pot of pozole that he could heat up on the room's two-burner stove. She lingered at his door and kept on chatting until he realized he was having a hard time looking away from the bright dark eyes and acknowledging an urgent sensuality behind her placid features. "Is everything satisfactory with your apartment?" she wanted to know. She could send someone to clean for him. Or perhaps a lamp that he could read by, because she had noticed him studying late into the night. He was after all a third-year student of medicine, and the building was very lucky to have him as a resident. With her husband, Licenciado Loreto, gone on

107

business for months at a time, it was a relief to have a person of some culture for occasional chats.

"And what is señor Loreto's business?" he asked diplomatically.

"Business with guns and bad people," she said pensively. "He does not want my son and me to be affected."

"He's in the army?" Leander said weakly.

"Procuraduría, the district attorney's office. He's always after the narcos. They all hate him and would like him dead. Sometimes he doesn't come home for many weeks. To protect us."

"That must be difficult for you."

She smiled weakly. "Sometimes I feel very much alone."

Later that week, one night after ten, Señora Loreto knocked softly. "Tonight I have a surprise for you," she said. She smiled nervously, challenging him to guess what she was holding with both hands behind her back. Her face looked paler than usual under a base of makeup, her eyes heavily lined, her lips freshly painted in a dark shade of red. She looked ready for a night on the town, in a short black dress that revealed her pudgy legs and clung tightly to her rear. Two buttons had been undone to reveal the tops of her breasts rising above the fringe.

"Señora Loreto, you are too kind a landlady."

"Me llamo Lourdes," she said. "Señora-this and Señora-that is very tiring, don't you think so, doctor?"

"Lourdes," he repeated.

"And you are Paul, verdad?"

"Yes, Paul Leander." He was nervous about inviting her in across the threshold.

"Pablito," she said. "In Spanish you are Pablo. But because you are so young, I can call you Pablito. Do you know the children's game? *Pablito clavó un clavito.* It is a trabalenguas. If you can say it fast it means you can now speak Spanish very well. Try it for me, please," she smiled.

Leander nodded amiably. Yes, he had heard the rhyme before. He said the words and then she told him to say them faster. She laughed when he got all tangled up in the syllables.

"Maybe I should give you this surprise to help you loosen your tongue." She presented him with the bottle she'd been holding behind her back. "Do you like the tequila?"

"Claro," Leander said, still trying to sort out what was happening.

"Well, take it," she said, holding the bottle out for him.

"Thank you."

"Maybe we can have a little taste together."

"Yes, that would be nice," Leander said.

"But not out here for all to see, verdad? You could invite me in."

"Of course," Leander murmured, standing out of the way and opening the door wider for her. She stepped into the middle of the room and looked around curiously as if she were unfamiliar with the apartment.

"You take nice care of your room," she nodded approvingly. "You would be surprised how messy men who live alone can be."

"I wasn't expecting visitors," he said, hanging up a shirt and pushing his shoes under the bed.

She sat in the chair and watched him shuffle about. She had crossed her legs, idly swinging one foot until her thin-strapped shoe dangled from her toes. "Perhaps it would be better to close the door now," she said.

He pushed the door shut with a soft click. In the closed room, her perfume was an intense mixture of citrus and gardenias. He rinsed two glasses in the bathroom, all the time thinking up a plausible excuse that would shorten the visit. He didn't think señora Loreto would be persuaded by a pressing need to study.

He served a little tequila into each glass and sat opposite her on the edge of the bed.

"Salud." He took a sip.

"Salud y valor," she added as she downed the contents in one pull.

"Courage?"

"Yes, don't you know tequila gives courage?" she said, extending her glass for him to serve her again. "But you have to drink it all at once."

He poured a shot.

"Don't tell me you don't need courage. I have seen you stay in your room all day and all night, except for a little walk to the store and the café. What are you afraid of?"

"I have exams to get ready for."

She shook off his reply. "Why do you read all these newspapers?" She pointed to a stack by the door. "Are you waiting for some news of importance, perhaps?"

"I read them to improve my Spanish." He was pleased by his reasonable explanation.

"Do you like to practice your medicine by looking at pictures of murders and accidents?" She shook her head as if to dismiss the subject. "I think it will be better if we do not lie. We hardly know each other and it is no good to begin by telling lies. I think we should start our friendship by telling each other some important true things that will reveal us in the eyes of the other. I will start. Then you will tell me a true thing, and then I will speak, and we will do this three times. And you will see. We will know each other very well in a few minutes. Do you agree?"

Leander finished off the tequila and refilled his glass. Then, noticing that hers was empty, he poured some for her too. "Do I start by asking you something?"

"No es necesario. We know what are the questions in the other's mind, no? That is part of the fun. You go first."

"Your being here, Lourdes," he began. "I don't think it is a good thing for you. Or for me."

"Excelente," she said, clapping her hands. "Now that was not so very hard, verdad? My turn now." She took a breath. "I feel very alone, and very bored, and very inquieta, you know?"

"That is three truths," Leander smiled.

"It is three aspects of one truth."

"I go again?"

"Yes."

"I am alone because I let my girlfriend down, and I'm somewhat ashamed."

"Shame is not good," she said. "It is unnecessary. I am here because I have a desire for you. See?" She held her palms out. "Sin vergüenza."

110

"I am worried about that," he said. "I think I should be somewhat afraid of Capitán Loreto."

"Naturalmente." She smiled sadly. "I am also afraid of my husband."

"So you should go."

"Para qué? The harm is already done." She glanced toward the closed door, the bottle between them, the shoe that had slipped off her foot. "Do you have a desire for me too, even just a little?"

"You're breaking your own rules, Lourdes. No questions. Three truths only."

"You are right," she said. "Now we know each other well enough to trust our actions." In the end, he marveled at how simply she rose off the chair and yanked the string under the bulb. She stood a couple of feet from where he sat on the bed. The room was suffused in the pale glow from the street lamp outside. She kicked off her other shoe. Then she turned her back toward him, and almost inaudibly whispered "Por favorcito." His hands shook as they found the zipper at the collar of the dress and his fingers stumbled onto her moist feverish skin. She pulled the dress over her head and laid it on the chair. Then briskly, pulled off her bra and rolled down her stockings, and then she was this white placid body topped by a face painted like a mask, and long black hair that she loosened so that it fell to her shoulders. Almost casually, she stepped around him and slid into the bed. "Qué esperas?" she asked, as she modestly pulled her panties off under the sheets.

It was good that she did not ask him whether he found her attractive. He had been lonely the past weeks, so that the closeness of her soft, yielding body was a pleasure not quite yet sexual, but a comfort nevertheless, and he clung to her with a long sigh of something like relief. After a few minutes, as his mind shut off the apprehension of the moment, he felt himself grow hard against her. He liked that she did not seem to be in a hurry for him to perform, as if it were understood that the greatest reward was in finding refuge in each other. Excitement would follow from the shared recklessness.

For now, he buried his face in her hair, breathing in its oily fragrance, lavender and roses, and the perfume of the pink Pétalo

111

soap. He shut his eyes against the light in the room, sinking his brain into an inky gloom that might stifle the thoughts of jealous violence and vengeful mayhem that flashed in his mind. While he could easily remove himself from danger, Lourdes would be stuck in here to face the certain wrath of her Licenciado.

Leander's penis was a conduit through which its dose of bad luck and pain would surge. He pushed back on either side of her shoulders and started to pull out. But her legs clasped his hips, followed by a tightening spasm inside her. With a long exhalation he gave up the attempt to withdraw.

She dressed quickly, turning away again, so he could pull up the zipper. She slipped into her shoes and gave him a quick brushing kiss on the lips. Her makeup had rubbed off and her expression now was young and somewhat sad.

"Aquí no pasó nada," she said. Nothing happened here tonight.

"Whatever you say, Lourdes."

"If I come again, and I'm not saying I ever will, it will be as if it were the first time."

She did return two nights later. And the night after that. And then not again until a whole week had passed and he was stewing in worry and fear for her. He grew more sensitive to the sounds outside his room. Even during the day, he was sharply attentive to the murmur of traffic, the occasional truck roaring its explosive exhaust along the street, the percussion of hammer and chisel chipping away at cement. It seemed as if that was the official sound of the D.F., a city continually in the throes of destruction and reconstruction.

Now, whenever he ran into Lourdes' son, the boy would scowl and look the other way, as if he did not know him. When Leander asked him how his cuts were doing, the boy simply stared at him blankly, pretending he didn't understand his halting Spanish. Leander pointed to his head. "Tu cabeza," he said. The boy walked away with a shrug.

One day he offered to check her son's scalp. He was confident that the scrapes were healing under the scabs, but it was still a good idea to make sure there was no infection.

"Gracias, doctor," she said blandly. "I will bring him to you after school."

He had Fito sit in the same chair where his mother had first sat crosslegged, sipping tequila and swinging her dainty sandal on her toes. He pulled the kid's head down, separating hanks of his hair to reveal the wounds. "Everything looks good," he said. "Just a little cleaning to make sure no infection comes." The satisfaction Leander derived in causing the boy fear made him uneasy. The white coat gave him a sense of power and righteousness; it was an efficient way to establish his authority. He felt an ambiguous pleasure in his ability to both cause and ease pain. He poured alcohol on a cotton ball and roughly swabbed a particularly reddened scab, eliciting a startled cry. Leander found himself eager again to hurt the boy, as if to convey some vague retribution. He saw in him the easy embrace of power and petty cruelty that he perceived in Mexican men, the influence of the father in the kid's playground bullying.

"Dile gracias al doctor," Lourdes ordered Fito. "Ya sabes, en inglés."

"Thank you very much," the boy muttered.

"De nada, amigo." Leander felt himself smiling for the mother's benefit.

❖ 13 ❖

Adele waited several days after their return from Puerto Vallarta before she decided that if she was going to see Paul again, it would have to be on her initiative. Victor Aruna had called a couple of times. He had insisted on chatting even though she had not felt like talking to him; he asked her if she had heard from Paul.

"I thought you guys went out for beers all the time," she said.

"Not in the past weeks."

"He is in the middle of exams," she ventured.

"School has never hindered Paul's ability to have fun."

"I suppose the party at your drug lord's house gave him all the fun he needed for a while."

"You are being sarcastic."

"How perceptive of you, pinche Victor."

"What happened there was not my fault," he insisted. "We were lucky, you know. Not very much affected by the whole mess."

"I'll let Paul know you asked about him." She hung up abruptly. All along she had assumed the two men were out together, drinking more disgustingly sweet rum-and-cokes than were good for them. The two liked to hang out at the clubs around colonia Cuahutémoc, buying drinks, asking the women to dance the raucous danzones, getting close and grinding away at their bellies. Adele had gone along one night, but had stayed less than an hour, during which time she had fended off the advances of at least a dozen guys who figured she was the establishment's new gringa acquisition. She announced she was going home. Paul could stay with his buddy.

"Don't worry," Leander laughed. "I'm just here for the dancing"

"Let's go home then," she pleaded.

"I want to make sure Victor doesn't get into any trouble."

"How about me getting into trouble?"

He put his hands on her shoulders and kissed her on the cheek. "You're too much in control to get into trouble."

She drained the last of her drink and marched out quite regally, she thought, weaving through the crowded dance floor, down the narrow passageway that led out of the bar. She would not be humiliated by the sight of women selling themselves to ugly, smarmy men. It was at times like this that she enjoyed her height, enabling her to look down at the men in her path. "Fuck off, the lot of you," she muttered as she walked straight to a waiting taxi.

Paul finally showed up at her apartment around three, knocking shyly on the door as if afraid to wake her, but persistently enough that she sensed she was not going to be able to ignore him away. He reeked of cigarette smoke and spilled beer, and inevitably, the cloying scent of Mexican prostitutes.

"No, Adele," he replied to her quizzing. "Not sex like you imagine."

"What kind of sex?"

"Sex of the eye, of the brain."

"You're full of shit," she said.

"Yes, what the hell, but I did not get laid."

"Okay," she offered, "let's go to bed."

But first she made him stand under the shower for vigorous scrubbing, until his skin was wrinkled and rubbed pink and all traces of his night on the town had been washed off. She'd felt slightly sickened by the possibility that he was lying. They made love, more to derail the possibility of a rift than out of desire on her part.

For days she had expected that even if Paul did not call, she would run into him in one of the cafés or in the park near his apartment where on sunny afternoons he liked to sit and read the English-language newspaper. On the morning she resolved to find

115

him, she went directly to Café La Estrella. She packed her dictionary, sunglasses, a sweater, and the nifty Pentax she had bought to replace the confiscated Minolta. She chose a sidewalk table with a clear view of the street and ordered a café con leche, pan dulce and a plate of papaya. The pudgy waiter with the shiny pompadour recognized her. He asked where the joven doctor was, and said that he had missed them both, their having been such regular customers.

"He hasn't been here?" she asked.

"No, señorita," he said. "It's been at least three weeks. I think maybe he moved away." He paused, as if realizing that possibly his opinions were not particularly cheering to the señorita. "Maybe he has been very busy with his studies."

"Yes, that must be the reason."

"The papaya is very good today, very red," he said as he hurried off to get her breakfast.

It was Paul's habitual breakfast. The steaming glass of milky coffee and the sugary rolls and the bright coral fruit would be a kind of magnet. Even though she found the wishful thinking dippy and inane, for this one pressing circumstance, she would make an exception and turn on the powers of prayer and telepathy. The exploding sugar crystals of the bread and the smooth texture of the papaya would focus her mind on Paul's. He would awaken or look up from a book or stop in the middle of a conversation and think of her. Meanwhile, she would enjoy a leisurely breakfast, and they would meet as if by chance, without him getting an inkling of her anxiety.

The walkway between the café and the plaza bustled as the morning ripened. Lottery vendors, girls selling trinkets, and boys offering shoeshines alighted from table to table. There was one girl, maybe ten years old, who Adele and Paul had befriended. Her name was Inés and she sold Chiclets in two-tablet boxes.

This morning Inés was weaving her way around the café when she spotted Adele; her face broke into a grin. She was thin and light skinned with tawny hair. She looked out of place among the brown children. Adele suspected that they had, in fact, been attracted to the girl because of her fair skin. She was just as poor and dirty as the other children, just as obnoxious, clinging to their table until a purchase was made. Her hair, which would have been lovely if clean, was matted and twisted into pigtails. She'd had a persistent case of the sniffles and Adele had asked Paul if he couldn't do something for her.

"Not until she starts washing her hands and stops hanging out with other sick kids," he said. "They keep catching the same germs from each other." Then he pulled out a handful of paper napkins from the dispenser and made her blow her nose. He soaked one inside the water glass and used it to wipe the crusted mucus above her lip. "There," he said to Adele. "First aid in the age of nuclear medicine."

"You're meant to be a doctor, you know," she said to him.

"Sometimes I wonder," he said with a shrug. Then, as if to change the subject, he gave the girl a coin. She offered the box of Chiclets for him to take one, but he kept insisting that he didn't want any. It wasn't until Adele picked out a couple that the girl was satisfied. "She's not begging," Adele said. "She sells Chiclets. When you give her money, you buy what she's selling."

Paul sighed. "She needs to sell a hundred of them a day, just to buy herself a meal. It's fucking depressing."

"Is it more depressing because she's white?"

Paul frowned. "Probably."

"We can't help our biases, can we," Adele said.

"I have a great idea," he announced as he watched the girl wend her way out of the café. "We'll get married and adopt her. After we give her a bath she'll look like any regular American kid. And if her mother objects, then we'll kidnap her, and smuggle her into the U.S. We'll teach her English, total immersion twenty-four hours a day. Once she's fluent we'll send her to school. She'll become a cheerleader and homecoming queen and she'll go off to college to study drama, and then she'll go to Hollywood where she'll become a star and take care of us in our old age, out of gratitude that we rescued her from the slums of Mexico City."

"Aren't we nice," Adele agreed.

"In any case, she'll thank us for making her blow her nose," he said. "I bet she sells a hell of a lot more Chiclets."

117

After that, whenever the girl came around, they wouldn't even look at her, making believe they didn't see or hear her until she got the idea and blew her nose. At first, she'd continue on her way once a couple of boxes of Chiclets had been sold. With time, she took to hanging around their table whether she made a sale or not. Eventually, the waiter would send her away, but before she went, Adele would let her pick out a sweet roll from their basket.

Now, the girl stood expectantly by Adele's table, waiting for her treat. Her cold had cleared up.

"Hola Inés," Adele said. "Cómo has estado?"

She gestured her ambivalence. "Mucha hambre, mucho frío, pero bien."

"Toma un pan," she gestured at the rolls.

After long deliberation, she picked out the roll with the stickiest frosting. "Gracias," she said. "Quiere chicles?"

Adele gave her a coin and picked out a couple of green boxes—spearmint, her favorite. Inés had started to leave when Adele called her back. "Espera. Have you seen my friend? Sabes quién, el doctor?"

The girl hesitated as if considering what she would say. "Pues sí," she finally admitted with a decisive nod.

Adele took her by the arm. "Dónde?" Adele sounded breathless. She realized that she was hurting Inés with her fingers. "Lo siento," she whispered, letting go. The girl rubbed her arm.

"Siéntate," Adele pulled out a chair. Inés, not quite sitting at the table, perched herself on the edge, taking frugal nibbles from the sweet roll. "I want you to tell me all about your seeing the doctor."

The girl nodded seriously.

"Estaba aquí, en el café?"

"No, en el jardín," she glanced at the park across the street.

Adele lifted her eyes and pictured Paul sitting on a bench, maybe reading. Sometimes, he'd smoke Victor's sinsemilla in his room, and then go sit outside, staring into the trees, watching the dappled sunlight filtering through the leaves, warming his face and drawing patterns on the inside of his lids. He might buy a package of plain María cookies to share, a few crumbs at a time, with the birds.

"Was he with someone?"

"No, estaba solito."

She felt brief satisfaction in Paul being alone.

"Estaba muy nervioso," Inés added. "He was sitting, looking around as if watching out for someone. Then he rolled up his white coat and put it inside his backpack. He kept changing from one bench to another."

"How long did he stay at the park?" Adele asked.

"I don't know," the girl said. "Two men walked toward him and he stood to leave, but they ran after him."

"Did he know them?"

"They acted like they were his friends," she said, "one walking on either side of him, holding him by the elbows, and talking and laughing as if they were making jokes. Then they held open the door of a car so he could get inside."

"But you don't think they were his friends, do you?"

"No," Inés asserted. "Eran policías."

"They were in uniform?"

"Not the blue uniform. The white shirts."

"You think some of these people walking by us are policías?" The sidewalk was busy with the morning crowd rushing to work. There were mostly men in suits, not wealthy but still trying their best to look good, with the starched white shirts, nice ties, and shoes polished to a high gloss. The women wore straight skirts and satin blouses and three-inch heels. Unlike the U.S., she thought, no matter how modest their stature as bank tellers or office assistants or government clerks, Mexicans dressed as fine as they could afford.

"No, señorita," the girl squinted. "The policías don't look like they are going anywhere. They're always in pairs. They sit in their cars, staring at doors and windows, or taking siestas. They are together at a café, but not chatting like friends."

Adele noticed for the first time two men sitting at a corner table in front of empty cups and a full ashtray between them, their eyes hooded as if about to doze off. One kept drawing a comb through his glossy hair; the other was intently lighting matches, only to blow them out before the flame reached his fingers. They had newspapers open, the sports *Esto*, the other, *Alarma*, specializing in photos of car wrecks, corpses, and criminals.

119

"Esos son policías?" Adele asked, discretely pointing her chin in the direction of the corner table.

"Pues sí," the girl smiled condescendingly, as if it were obvious that cops were all they could possibly be.

"The ones that took my friend?"

"No, they are others."

More to get away with a surreptitious shot than with any serious artistic intent, Adele took her camera out of her backpack. She asked the girl to stand in a sunny part of the café. She called out to her cheerfully, to move a little to the side, as if she were trying to include the park fountain in the frame.

"Una sonrisa bonita, por favor!"

The girl beamed as Adele nudged her viewfinder to the left and framed the two men as the younger one, perhaps catching a glimpse of the slight motion of the camera or hearing the click of the shutter, looked up scowling. Adele's heart quickened.

"Gracias, chula!" she called out as the girl curtsied.

❧ 14 ❧

A dele had valued the times when she and Paul were alone, preferably at her place because the shower was more reliable—the water always hot, usually abundant. Her bed was wider and she kept her apartment cleaner.

She liked the way he flung himself on her sofa, the ragged upholstery covered by a big sarape, in the red and blue geometric patterns of Oaxacan weavers. She'd make him leave his shoes by the door and he would walk around in socks and rest his feet on the wrought-iron coffee table. Away from his studying, and the steady smoking that kept him in a mellow haze, he was more awake to her. There was always something good in her kitchen, fresh fruit, some tomatoes or an avocado, or a hunk of chihuahua cheese, or a package of pasta that she'd toss with garlic and olive oil.

She felt protective of this nervous, wired guy who invariably needed to make love twice in a row. The first time, he would display an urgency for release that she found unsettling. Then he would fall asleep, holding her so that her head rested in the hollow of his shoulder. When he awoke, they would move slowly toward penetration, their bodies warmed and glowing by the light coming through threadbare curtains.

They made love in other places too—in his room, cluttered with books and beer bottles, and in hotels with sheets that smelled of lye, and once in Victor's black Ford, which they had taken on a drive to the woods along the Toluca highway north of Mexico City. While their friend steered, they nudged and tickled and fondled in the back seat. Finally, giggling like kids, they persuaded Victor to park in a clearing and take a walk. *Por favorcito, Victor. Nomás diez minutos!*

On weekends, Victor, the apex of their triangle, would come by in the big car and they would go for a long Sunday dinner of tacos and guacamole and mariachis at one of the festive restaurants facing the lake in Chapultepec Park. The three would toss down tequilas chased with beer. The green, scummy lake would take on a kind of vibrant sheen, a flotilla of invading dryads glinting on its calm surface. It was during those rare times, when the world seemed to stop in its tension, that Adele knew, without anyone saying anything, that a love so tangible she could almost see and taste its current flowed among the three, circling through them, lighting their skin so that it turned golden in the waning light, burning through their eyes, hers pale blue, Paul's dark brown, Victor's oddly green. She thrilled to the sexual attraction she'd had to each of them. She felt a pull to each other, and she fantasized that Paul and Victor might have had sex with each other, even if only a playful tug or a rub, perhaps during their visit to the steam baths or while visiting the same brothel, a whore cheerfully sandwiched between them. She thought it a kind of communion of the flesh, something physical to anchor their initial inquiries into psychedelics and meditation, their shivers at the possibility of magic and spells to be found in the market, a swallowing of each other's semen to complement their munching of peyote buttons and their licking of LSD-soaked blue squares of blotter paper. She would look from one to the other, from the brown skin and almost delicate nose and sleepy eyes of one to the large ruddy expression, the sensual fullness of lips and earlobes that signaled the other's fleshy nature, and she would shake her head at the images behind her closed lids.

❦ 15 ❦

Adele headed for the center of the city with a renewed sense of purpose to find out what had happened to Paul. The building that served as courthouse and jail had always seemed to her a sad and impregnable place, its stucco façade grown grimy from the constant diesel truck and bus exhaust. The wide entrance led into a cold lobby, its tile floor empty of furnishing or decoration except for a reception desk staffed by a surly guard beside a Mexican flag. A crowd hovered around him, mostly women trying to get his attention, holding up names written large on card paper and pictures of husbands and brothers.

Adele stood out as she nudged her way to the desk. The official looked up at her with small dull eyes. She'd rehearsed in her mind the proper words and the right tone to ask him if, by chance, her friend had been brought here.

"Busca un detenido?" he asked.

Detenido sounded so much kinder than arrestado. Detained meant only that he might have been simply stopped, temporarily kept from going on his way, made to hold still while facts were looked into and the truth was ascertained. "I think he might be here," she said. But due to some mistake, she tried to persuade the guard, for whom looking up a name in a roster was a singularly onerous task.

"Cómo se llama el detenido?" he asked.

"Paul Leander."

"*Leandro . . . Leandro . . . Pol . . . Pol,*" the guard muttered to himself as he ran his finger down the typed list. When he found him, finally, he released a long sigh as if the situation was already visibly hopeless. "Llegó el jueves," he said. Five days ago.

123

"When will he get out?"

"Ay, señorita. That is something I could not know in a hundred years."

She was not cheered by the new sympathetic tone in his voice. "What do you know?"

"If someone is not released after three days, then there is no telling when they will be let go."

"Puedo visitarlo?"

"Hoy, no," the guard said, slipping the list inside a drawer and sliding it shut with a bang.

"Mañana?"

"No sé," he shrugged. "You must ask permission."

"Are you the one I ask?" she said.

The guard burst out laughing. "Ay, señorita. That is a matter for the procuraduría. I only give *no* permission. To get a *sí* you must go to the proper authority." He wrote down an address on a scrap of paper and handed it to her. "Go first thing in the morning."

"Please, tell me if he needs something. Food or money. Or if I can get a letter to him."

"Everybody needs food and money. I can get some food inside for him, if you give me a package. Money, unfortunately, gets lost along the way."

"But food, yes?" She wanted to make sure.

"Yes, tomorrow after eleven when I'm on duty again, I will personally make sure he gets your parcel. I am Sargento Peralta."

"And maybe a note? To let him know I am thinking of him?"

"There may be a way," he nodded as if accepting reluctantly the possibility that he could ease things for the señorita and her unfortunate friend. He made a note of the name on a scrap of paper—*Pol Leandro*.

It had been a warm afternoon when Adele went into the police station, and now, as she left after barely half an hour in the place, and even though the sun was still high and the air warm, the lobby had so chilled her, she felt the cold down to her bones. She walked along the street, uncertain of where to head next. Back in her apartment she could escape into heavy restless slumber for hours, through the night and into the next afternoon. She wouldn't be alert enough to think about this thing happening to Paul, which no longer allowed her the freedom to think and work or hop on a flight back to the U.S. if she felt like it. Paul's detaining had made her a detenida as well, physically as well as mentally. She took a bus toward the neighborhood where Paul used to live. The important thing was to do something, anything.

She got off a few blocks from his apartment and decided to walk the rest of the way, trusting that physical activity would clear her head. As she approached the Coyoacán Square, she felt surrounded by victims. The faces of the women and the children all seemed tinged with a kind of despair that came from living in this dangerous country, this melancholy city where someone could be slammed in jail for five days, and nobody know about it. Occasionally, she met a stranger's eyes, sensing lust and contempt, and she would feel a sudden start, as if the kind of malice and arbitrary cruelty that had suddenly touched Paul could reach her as well. The thought made her feel exhausted.

She reached the building where he used to live and rang the doorman's bell. The portero looked out of the peephole cut into the metal door, careful to keep out vendors, bill collectors, beggars, and strangers whose unannounced presence might disturb the residents. Don Genaro pushed the gate open when he recognized Adele.

"Qué milagro, señorita Adela."

"Buenas tardes, don Genaro," she said. "I'm looking for Paul Leander." She did not let on that she knew he had been arrested.

"Sí," the doorman smiled. "El joven doctor." He shook his head slowly, wondering why the young doctor's girlfriend would not know he'd gone. "He moved, don't you know?"

"Yes, of course. I need to send him something and don't know his new address."

"Ya no son amigos?" The old man sounded concerned. He had always thought they were much more than mere friends, of course. Novios? Amantes? Esposos? Discretion and respect for the young woman would keep him from asking.

"Quién sabe?" she answered sadly. "Yo lo considero mi amigo." She could see the portero was trying to decide whether he should be loyal to his former tenant or break his own rules and reveal the fellow's whereabouts. In the end, gallantry won out. He went into his cramped room by the entrance and brought out Paul's address.

Adele recognized the street as being in a populous residential area far from Coyoacán. Evening was upon her by the time she stood at the courtyard surrounded by two tiers of apartments. There was no good reason to be here since she probably wouldn't be able to get inside Paul's apartment. Still, she felt compelled to understand his movements since returning from Puerto Vallarta. Uncertain as to what to do next, she stepped back out to the sidewalk. She felt as if she were being watched from an apartment on the upper tier. She shook her head as if she had entered the building by mistake. Down the street, at the corner, was a tiny restaurant with a lunch counter and the Cerveza XX logo on the four metal tabletops. She sat at one table and stared blankly at the short menu posted on the wall. A spry old woman, her head at the same level as the seated Adele's, arrived with a notepad. Her face was carved by age so that in a topography of lines and crinkles Adele could read the emotional turbulence of a lifetime of men (surely more than one), some good children, a couple of bad ones, a bunch of deaths in the family, and the tug and pull of about a hundred aunts and uncles, siblings and cousins. Adele would come back with her camera.

The woman looked at her with familiarity, and cheerfully offered soup, enchiladas, tortas, quesadillas. Adele interrupted her with a shake of her head. "No gracias, señora. Just café con leche." The smells of onion and frying beans made her nauseous; she waited for her coffee. She was the only customer in the place, too early for supper. Once Paul picked a café, he became a loyal customer. She looked around and could imagine him coming here for his breakfast, perhaps sitting at this very table. Even now, not having been here with Paul, Adele could not shake off the memory of his presence, the shape and look of his body, the slump of his back, the weight of his arms on the table.

The woman came back with the makings for traditional café con leche, the milk nearly boiling and the syrupy coffee concentrate in a glass beaker. "Le traje pan dulce," she said, putting down a basket with sweet rolls.

"Gracias, pero no tengo hambre," Adele smiled.

The woman pushed the basket closer. "You don't have to be hungry to enjoy pan dulce," she said.

Adele picked at a pastry, working her way through the flaky layers to a jammy center. The woman had gone to her place behind the counter but kept watching her. Adele concentrated on the coffee, the taste of sugar on her tongue, the nicks in the table, and the paper napkin she had been shredding into a linty mound. She had the sensation that she could ask the old woman anything, and that her answers would be true.

"Something else, niña?" she asked from across the room.

"No, gracias. I can't eat much right now."

"You are not hungry because you have your heart full of worries," the woman said.

Adele nodded. Yes, the señora was right.

"You can't eat, you can't sleep."

"I can't keep from thinking." Adele smiled.

"Only because you have questions," the woman said. "When your questions are answered, then your heart will feel lighter."

"I'm not sure I will like the answers."

"Knowing is always better than not knowing."

"You can't be sure of that," Adele said with sudden certainty. The thought of Paul drifting away made her queasy.

The woman reached out and took Adele's wrist. She felt the ache in her heart reveal itself in the thumping of a coded tattoo, its beat heavy and sluggish from the dragging of blood made thick by her sleeplessness. Adele started to pull away, but the woman pressed down on her shoulder. "Espera," she murmured. "Let Madre Mireya tell you the things you want to know."

"I'm scared," Adele said. "I don't want to know what I don't ask."

Mireya took Adele's hand in both of hers and pressed the wrist to her ear. "Ah, I can hear voices from the depths of your soul. Little girl whispers."

"Stop," she pleaded.

"Shhhh. These words are so very faint. These baby murmurs, these quiet night cries, coughs and raspy breaths." She started rocking from her chest to her head still holding Adele's hand to her face, swaying back and forth, and humming a chant, a circular prayer.

"Don't leave her in the night. Mother. Father. It is so dark, she's like la gallina ciega. The blind chicken running after the voices of mamacita and papacito, muffled behind the drapes and walls and locked doors. In the morning one of them will be gone. Poof. Like a cloud of smoke."

She couldn't believe Paul was gone for good, leaving nothing behind in her apartment. Gone from his side of the closet were his jeans, leather jacket, running shoes and white lab coat.

Throughout those first days of his absence, she would crawl inside her bed, under the covers where his presence was so strong, as if at any moment the door would open and he would throw his jacket on a chair, kick his shoes under the bed, coming close, smelling of lab chemicals and the smoggy air of the city and the closeness of the bus.

She didn't want to dredge up history. She wanted to know about the present. "Do you know what is happening to my friend? You know who I'm talking about?"

Madre Mireya sighed with a profound pent-up sadness. "It is the same thing always. The man will always be pulled away and return and then leave again. You will lose him and find him, hold him and release him. He will never go away for good; he needs you to tend to his wounds. He will take your love and bring back his pain. He will never shake off his pain. He is injured to the depths of his heart. His cuts will heal and then bleed again, his scars split, his sutures unravel."

"I need to help him now," Adele said.

"He is waiting," the old woman said.

128

❧ 16 ❧

Leander hadn't been surprised when the two men approached him in the park. He had found a bench situated to catch the early warming sun, and was reviewing a dense biochemistry text. Life felt momentarily normal, even while he had grown increasingly uneasy with Lourdes' frequent visits. He was aware of the sly grins and mocking head shakes from the neighbors. Her kid Fito glared at him. It would not take long for word of her night visits to reach her husband in the city attorney's office.

"Qué pasa?" she would ask, sensing his impulse to withdraw.

"Estoy preocupado," he admitted.

"Well, you are not alone. I am afraid too," she would say, scattering frantic kisses all over his lips, his cheeks, his eyes. "But now you are here," she would add, pulling him into her. "After tonight, I will not return." She sounded determined to let her better judgment win out. He would believe her, and be willing to forgive her recklessness.

But then the next night or the night after that, she would be back. Perhaps she would wait until a later hour before stealing up the steps and letting herself into his room, without so much as a knock or a whisper of warning.

The older of the two cops approached him politely and asked him to kindly show them his documentos. The two policemen wore leather jackets and fastidiously creased beige pants and short boots gleaming with a recent shine. Their nice manners caught him off guard. He thought this might be some opportunistic hassling because a young foreigner could be shaken down to avoid further inconvenience. His wallet contained only about fifty dollars in pesos; the two men had noticed the cash when he pulled out his ID card. He waited while one stared at the card as if he were reading it line by line, pondering the validity of his signature and that of the medical school official, the expiration date stamped on the upper right corner, his address and his enrollment number, the official stamp of the Universidad Nacional.

They in turn showed him their laminated credentials. Even in the formality of the exchange, Leander was unable to look at the men's badges fast enough to read their names.

"We must ask you to accompany us to our office, Doctor," one of them said, as if the whole thing were against his personal wishes.

"Am I involved in some crime?" Leander asked politely. It occurred to him then, that if one of them turned out to be Lourdes' husband, he was ready to offer abject apologies while pleading blind ignorance.

"We are not told everything." The tall one shook his head sadly to indicate that the whole thing was beyond his control.

"Saludos del licenciado Loreto," the smaller one smiled crookedly, giving in to the impulse to let out the reason for the arrest. Paul felt proud that he had intuited the reason for his problem before it had been officially revealed. The cop took another look at Leander's university card and then, with a shrug, slipped it into his pocket. It would serve as proof that the mission had been accomplished.

The three of them, with Leander in the middle, walked briskly to a white car. Leander made it a point to notice the details even though his mind was already reeling with confusion. It was a plain, unmarked Toyota. The taller of the two drove, while the other one sat in back with Leander, like two friends in a taxi.

The police station consisted of a row of desks behind a low wooden barrier with a swinging gate. There did not seem to be much work getting done. A clerk pecked at a clattering typewriter. Bureaucrats in wrinkled suits and shiny ties sat with newspapers spread on their desktops. Some munched on snacks, sipped soft drinks, chatted in tight groups. Leander was told to sit on a long bench behind the barrier. The short cop came by with a paper bag and asked Leander to empty his pockets into it. "Para su seguridad," he said. He took Leander's watch, the ring he had inherited from his father, a couple of pens. He demanded his shoelaces, a nail clipper, and a few coins. He motioned with his fingers for Leander's wallet. The man opened it and took out the folded bills and slipped them inside his jacket before dropping the empty wallet into the sack. He reached out and, before Leander could jerk his head away, plucked off his glasses. "No glass or sharp metal objects are allowed inside."

"I don't see well," Leander said.

"I will deposit your valuables in the main office." He handed the sack to a woman who typed out a form with two carbon copies and gave them to the policeman to sign. He separated one very faint copy and gave it to Leander. "Your receipt," he said.

"El dinero también?" Leander said, gesturing at the man's jacket pocket. He prayed the fifty dollars might buy him some good will.

"You will get everything back when you leave."

"Cuándo?"

"When you leave," the man repeated as if Leander hadn't understood his explanation the first time.

"At what hour?" he insisted.

"Ah, of course," the cop seemed to get the question for the first time. "Sepa la chingada, mi amigo," he said with a clownish mug. Who the fuck knows things like that. The woman looked at him sadly, nodding in agreement with her colleague as she stuffed his belongings inside a drawer. Leander made a point of counting down the desks and remembering it was the third one on the right side. The clerk was about forty years old with a pinched nose and tight, thin lips, her black hair chopped to a man's length. In her black skirt and white blouse she looked as severe as a schoolteacher. Leander attempted a smile, which turned out vaguely simpering, hoping that she might give him back his glasses. He couldn't see whether she smiled back or not. He was aware of a new situation where he would have to rely on the arbitrary good will of clerks.

131

"Wait here." The cop left Leander sitting on the bench. He marveled at the lax security. He was only about twenty feet away from the door which was manned by a sleepy guard sitting on a stool, an old rifle between his knees. He considered the possibility of rushing out the door, but he still believed everything would be resolved with an apology. An hour later he thought that maybe an apology might not be sufficient. He would add voluntary banishment all the way back to the U.S., if it would make things right with the wronged husband.

A couple of hours slipped by; the light outside was waning and some of the clerks had started to shuffle back to their desks, fold their newspapers, close their magazines and put away the files that had sat idly. By then, Leander knew he would be willing to withdraw all his savings and settle whatever fines he might be liable for. It would also help to contact Victor Aruna, who knew his way around and could perhaps negotiate a deal. He feared night would fall with him still stuck in a judicial limbo. He went up to the railing and politely asked if he might be able to use a phone and perhaps consult a directory, because there was a friend he wanted to call, a lawyer who could make it worth everyone's time. The woman with the short hair pointed him to a phone on the wall, and a ragged directory on the floor.

Leander flipped through the pages. Yes, it was there, he realized triumphantly, in clear black and white, Victor's name, his number, his address. Things were looking up. Help was a phone call away. He searched his pockets for a pen until he remembered that his belongings had been locked up. He repeated the number mentally until he memorized it. He went back to the railing and asked if he might have some of his coins from the envelope where they had been put, but which had his name on it and was covered by the receipt in his hand. He could barely see the blurred outlines of the woman's head, but he could tell she was shaking it sadly back and forth. He must've looked puzzled because she added that it was not possible that his belongings be returned to him until he was released from all legal obligations.

"How can I call my abogado?" Leander said.

"After you meet with the judge," she explained, as if the procedure ahead were something quite routine. "The judge allows you to contact your abogado."

"Why not get my lawyer here now, when I really need him?"

"Because first you must appear before the judge, who will decide whether you go free or be tried, and whether you will require the services of a lawyer."

"A judge decides this?"

"Pues, naturalmente," she said. She pointedly stared down at the magazine.

Leander leaned back against the wall and closed his eyes, which smarted from the strain of squinting without his glasses. He kept thinking of Victor Aruna's phone number. Five-seven-eight-four-six-oh-nine. He broke it up into two units: five-seven-eight and then four-six-oh-nine. He bounced the two phrases back and forth. He made a rhythm out of the numbers. He saw little soldiers marching up and down to the cadence. Hands drumming, heels digging in smartly. He pictured a line of chorus dancers kicking up and down. Cheerleaders cheering: Give me a five, give me a seven . . . what do you get? Outta here! No matter how tired or how scared he got, he would recall Victor Aruna's number at will. It was his lifeline.

Other men were brought into the station, their faces bruised, clothes torn, hands balled into a scraped fist. Some were drunk. They were told to wait on the bench. The ones next to Leander inched away as if he were entitled to greater comfort and privacy by virtue of being a foreigner. There was no conversation among them; each seemed reconciled to bearing his situation in isolation. A few were pushed back out, almost apologetically, because they looked like they just wanted a place to spend the night. Others were taken through a black iron door into a hallway beyond the office. The door would open with a whine and close with a metallic clatter. It was secured from the outside with a large sliding bolt that screeched every time it was slid. If anyone wanted to leave, they had to knock in some pre-arranged signal. A guard would peer through a narrow grate and pull open the bolt with a noisy up-and-down motion.

All afternoon into night the rhythms of the station left Leander hanging on the margins, captive to the unresolved mystery of his case. Nobody knew what to do about his situation. His pale skin, American jeans, and a t-shirt with *Yo Amo Puerto Vallarta* and a motif of palm trees and sea shells, oddly festive given the circumstances, made his presence incongruous. Nobody wanted to take responsibility for him. He was not ready for whatever lay beyond the black metal door, but not so blameless that he could be turned out back into the street. He had grown thirsty and eventually hungry in spite of the nervous twitching of his guts. The pressure to urinate had faded with the onset of dehydration. When he stood up to approach the railing and ask for directions to the bathroom where he figured to drink some water, the lethargic motion of the room stopped. A dozen pairs of eyes stared at him. The woman who had received his possessions walked over to the railing.

"Qué se le ofrece?" she asked.

"El baño?"

"No hay," she said.

"There is no bathroom?"

"Only for the employees," she said.

"Where can I get some water?" he asked, his mouth, sticky with thirst, slurring the words.

"You can give some money to the muchacho," she pointed at a boy of about twelve sitting on the steps just outside the door. "He will go get you a refresco."

"Pues sí," Paul nodded patiently. "But you know you have all my cash." He made a show of patting his empty pockets. "I can't pay for a soft drink."

"Lo siento muchísimo," she said.

"You could give me some of the dinero that you are holding for me."

"I can't do that because I already gave you a receipt for it."

"Tengo sed," he pleaded. I'm thirsty.

Leaving his place on the bench and having this discussion at the railing had clearly disturbed the room. The guard who had been dozing by the door now stood poised to block his run out the door. The boy who ran errands was alert to the possibility of some business. At one of the desks, a woman rested her hand on the phone. The clerks had retreated to the end of the room, and one of the functionaries watched vigilantly from just outside his office.

"Adentro hay agua," the woman reassured him. There would be all the water he could drink once he was taken inside.

He found himself nodding stoically. He would wait until he was locked away. "Claro," he said. "Adentro." He realized that's where he was headed. Everyone knew this.

The possibility that he might be released had grown unlikely. The price for a drink of water was jail. And then, when he thought that he was all alone in this awful situation, that nobody, not Adele or Victor or Lourdes could come to his assistance with something as basic as a drink of water, a roly-poly official who had been standing outside his office walked over to him smiling. "Aquí tiene, amigo," he said, handing him a Pepsi bottle half-filled with water. "Now please don't walk around like this, agreed? You can stay there in your place and we will have no problems."

"No hay ningún problema," Leander reassured him. If this little man in his gray wool suit wanted him to sit still for five more hours, he would do so unquestioningly. Still the room was in some kind of expectant silence. The sound of traffic outside came to his attention for the first time, a symphony of horns and exhaust explosions that were so present in the city that he no longer heard them. The room waited while Leander took the bottle and quickly drained it in one long pull. It seemed to breathe a collective sigh when he handed the bottle back to the man. "Gracias," Leander said and plopped down hard on the bench, exhausted by the business of walking to the railing and asking for water and arguing about money.

❖ 17 ❖

E ventually, hours after he was arrested, Leander was escorted down the dark corridor, past a series of black doors to a windowless office, furnished with a desk and a couple of chairs. The room was square with a speckled terrazzo floor, yellow walls with brown stains, cracking plaster, nails where pictures might have hung. There was a calendar on the wall with a picture of a blonde holding up a bottle of Superior beer. He stepped closer and could see the date on the page, November 1973. Over ten years ago, but someone must have liked the blonde too much to replace her with a current calendar. There was also a clock, large and round-faced with big clear numbers and a red second-hand. The clock was stuck at 3:42. AM or PM? He glanced at his wrist, then recalled that his watch had been locked away.

Behind him a lead pipe ran along the wall and culminated in a faucet that looked like it had once poured into a sink, but now simply hung a couple of feet above the floor. A bank of fluorescent tubes flooded the room with a clinical light.

Leander was told to sit on one of the chairs and wait for an important man who spoke English and would explain why he was here. On the desk was a black phone with a rotary dial, and a stack of battered phone books, thick ones from Mexico D.F. and New York City and L.A. Leander thought of DIAL LAWYERS. Dialing a heavy black phone seemed quaint, a touristy kind of thing. "Teléfono antiguo," Leander said.

The man grinned. "It works when it wants to." When he spoke, the gaps of several missing teeth made him look like an overgrown ten-year-old. He wore a blue uniform and a large square gun in a hip holster. He was not unfriendly; he pushed the phone toward him. Leander picked it up and listened to a faint ringing in the distance. If someone answered he would ask for 578-4609, for his friend Victor Aruna.

After a dozen rings, the receiver went dead. He clicked the cradle eagerly, tried dialing O for an operator, but the line remained silent. "Is there a way to talk on the telephone?" Leander asked, sliding the phone back across the top of the desk. The man shook his head and leaned back on his swivel chair. It creaked and whined, and finally tilted back under his weight. He hid his face behind the newspaper.

Leander had learned only that he was to continue to wait in this room, in this building, for señor Cueto, who spoke English and would want to have a conversation with him.

"Pero yo hablo español," he had explained. "We can clear this thing up in a couple of minutes."

"Do not worry," the man behind the desk insisted on reassuring him. "Cueto will understand you perfectly."

Outside the door there was the occasional sound of children running, their laughter echoing up and down the hallway. "There are children in this place?" Leander asked.

"There are children everywhere," the policeman replied. "They are like ants. You can't keep them out."

The man continued studying the newspaper. Leander caught a fuzzy glimpse of a photograph of a woman's body lying on a narrow metal bed. The man turned the page out of his sight. Sometimes, when the cop was reading quietly and not rustling the paper, the only sounds in the room came from inside the pipe on the wall. There was water gurgling, and hammers banging, and occasionally a low tone as if someone were blowing into the tube. At 3:42, according to the dead clock on the wall, the man sighed and handed the paper to Leander. "So you don't get so bored," he said. Leander read the headline: *Extranjeros Involucrados en Narcotráfico*. Foreigners involved in local drug trade. The date on the masthead was from over two weeks ago.

The guard leaned forward and asked solicitously, "Pipí?"

137

Leander looked bewildered until the man made a hissing sound and a swinging motion with his index finger between his legs.

"No." His own laughter surprised him.

"Sandwich? Cigarro? Aspirina?" he added with a weird giggle, as if remembering a joke that only he understood.

Leander nodded toward the case of Tehuacán mineral water at the opposite corner of the room. "Maybe a soda?"

The man smiled and shook his head, as if remembering some private joke. "No," he said. "Es para trabajar." It's for work.

Finally, the guard stood up and stretched, allowing himself a long, sonorous yawn. He glanced up at the wall clock, as if expecting it to be working now. He stepped behind the chair, and with one fluid motion, too quick for Leander to realize what was happening, he snapped one handcuff around his wrist and the other cuff to the water pipe behind him. "Perdón, my friend," he said, ratcheting the cuff so that it bit into his wrist. Then he pointed at the front page of the tabloid for Leander to look at the corpse of a man lying on the floor, his head emerging with a bewildered expression above the edge of a ragged bloody sheet. "The man died in a massacre in Puerto Vallarta. You did not try to help him?" he asked him.

Leander marveled at how efficiently licenciado Loreto had found a way to implicate him in the trouble in Puerto Vallarta. He brought his free hand up hard against his mouth because he was about to vomit. He waited for the nausea to subside, for his breath to regain its normal rhythm. "No. I've never seen him before."

"This man with a bullet hole is known to you?" the man asked. "Someone you met at a party, possibly."

Leander shook his head.

"Bueno," the man sighed. "En un momento comes Mr. Cueto. He will explain to you about your situation." Leander watched him leave, swinging the door shut without bothering to lock it.

A few minutes later a boy carrying a wooden shoeshine box peered inside the room, his eyes traveling all around, and finally stopping on Leander. "Shoeshine, mister." He held up five fingers. "Cinco pesos." His fingernails were stained with polish.

"No tengo dinero," Leander said.

"You pay me later," the boy said.

Leander looked up at the clock, then remembered that it was stuck. He nodded at the kid because he figured it would help pass the time. The boy sat on the stool and lifted Leander's right foot onto the stand. He was starting to wipe the dust off the tops of the loafers when a young girl of around ten looked in. She saw the boy shining Leander's shoes and marched up to Leander carrying three lottery tickets. "Este es el mejor," she said holding one up. "It ends in three, your lucky number."

"Can I pay you later?" he tried to smile.

"No. Veinte pesos each," she said.

Leander tugged at the chain to reach his pockets and turn them inside out.

"I know you are rich," she accused.

"Not tonight," Leander said

"You are waiting for Cueto?" the boy asked, looking up from his stool. "You must be a bad man."

"Why do you say that?"

"Cueto is very important. He only talks to dangerous criminals."

"He is a jefe, right?" Leander asked hopefully.

"He hits people on the head." The girl went to the desk and picked up a phone book. Holding it in both hands she struck the back of the swivel chair with the flat of the book. She hit it over and over again.

"But he won't hit me," Leander said. "Because I am not a criminal. Soy estudiante de medicina."

"Cueto shoots Tehuacán water up people's noses until they scream." The boy picked up a bottle of soda and shook it. "Pshhht!" he hissed.

"You killed the man in the newspaper," the girl pointed at the paper on the chair.

"Who says?"

"Everyone says you are a narco matón," the boy chimed in.

"You put the knife inside him," the girl said, making a rolling cutting motion with her fist. "Blood everywhere," she said. She stood in front of Leander and mimicked sprouting fountains of blood from her chest. "They say you cut out his heart."

The boy started chanting, "El matón, el matón, matarile rile ron, aquí está el matón!" Here is the killer.

Leander looked up at three new brown faces peeking in from around the door. A girl and two boys stepped into the room, their backs hugging the wall. They stared at him with dark, alert eyes. The lottery girl took the front page of the paper and, holding up the picture of the dead man, began to skip around the room, waving the paper from side to side. "Extra, extra," she yelled. "Aquí está el matón." The other children grew bolder and stepped into the center of the room. Silently, they stood about five feet in front of Leander. Now, the shoeshine boy took to hitting the back of the chair with the phone book.

Leander gestured with his free hand for the kids to be quiet. "I am not the killer," he pleaded. "You can just stop with that nonsense now."

"Matarile, rile, rile," the children sang out. "Matarile, rile, ron. El matón."

"Cállense, cabrones," he shouted. "You can shut up right now. This is not a game."

Then the shoeshine boy stabbed Leander in the chest with his finger. The other kids broke into shrill peals of laughter. Leander started to lunge toward him, but his hand was clamped to the pipe, and the boy was able to dance out of reach. Leander roared with pain. "Leave me alone, you little cabrones!" The cry started in the pit of his stomach and surged through his chest and out his throat. He stood up, kicking back the chair, pulling against the chain, as pain snaked into his shoulder.

Giggling nervously at first, then screaming in mock fright, the kids scattered out of the room. Leander pulled the chair upright and sat back, waiting for the pain coursing up his arm to subside. "If I catch you, I will kill you," he added weakly.

A moment later, a moon-faced man in a dark suit walked in and sat on the edge of the desk, like a visitor who knows he will not stay long. "Buenas tardes," he said, glancing reflexively at the clock on the wall. "Yo soy Cueto."

"There is this misunderstanding," Leander rushed to explain his situation. "Hay un malentendido," he repeated in Spanish, looking up eagerly at Cueto.

"I know, I know," he said, with the familiarity that comes from routinely engaging in nearly identical conversations. He seemed sad, as if their respective roles allowed no possibility of variance. "Llaves!" he shouted out the door. The guard who had handcuffed Leander rushed back in with the keys. "I am not going to waste your time or mine, Mr. Leander," Cueto said. "I would like to get rid of you, but I cannot. You will see a judge in a day or two. It's good that you speak Spanish. It can be very complicated communicating with someone who cannot be understood, sabe? Meanwhile, manage to make yourself comfortable inside."

"What do you mean a day or two?"

"Or three," the man nodded. "You will have to wait your turn. We are very democratic about this, unfortunately."

The guard came in, took him by the arm, and led him out the door and down the hallway. Leander felt he was trudging through a swamp, the soft muddy ground pulling at his feet, so that the guard continually had to yank him forward. Night had fallen, and the few light bulbs that had not burnt out provided only the faintest definition of the walls and the approaching gates, then more doors, more bars, and finally, a large square expanse of concrete flooring and the shadowy outlines of two tiers of bunk beds, and the sound of a man protesting that there was no room for anyone else, that they should take this new cabrón some place else. A la casa de la chingada. Anywhere but here.

❖ 18 ❖

After several hours that frightening first night, sleep finally came through the percussive cursing, the clanging metal doors, and the scratching and scurrying sounds along the floor and behind the bunks. Leander had retreated to a corner of the cell when he realized that all the bunks were occupied. He was glad for the ragged blanket which had been discarded in a clump against the wall.

A parching thirst awakened him. Next to the dry sink was a water bucket which one man had dipped in to wash his face. Leander filled his cupped hand and took a tentative sip. From an upper bunk someone broke into a wheezing giggle. "Bebe y caga, bebe y caga," he sang. Drink and shit, drink and shit.

From down the hall a guard approached, dragging a pot of beans and a jug of water on a wobbling cart. It was already morning, judging from the pale light that seeped in through a vent just below the ceiling. Four men jumped off their bunks, elbowed Leander out of the way and hovered by the barred door, each holding out a plastic bowl and cup. In the gloom, their features were dark and indistinct. After the others retreated, softly like shadows, Leander edged his way to the door. The guard held up a ladle waiting for a dish in which to serve the beans.

"Eres nuevo," he said finally.

"Sí," Leander admitted. He was the new guy.

The man made a cone with brown paper and poured a serving of brown beans into it. "Aquí tienes," he said. He made another cone, making sure to fold the bottom a couple of times to create a thicker base, and filled it with water. "Eat before it leaks," he said as he pushed on down the hallway. Leander drank the water quickly, then scooped up mouthfuls of beans with his fingers. They were good, as beans in Mexico always tasted, until a stone chipped one of his teeth in the first bite. After that, he learned to sift through every mouthful and spit out the grit that had made its way into the pot. For years, Leander would recall that experience and feel a shadow of anxiety even as his tongue had, over time, smoothed the small rough indentation in his tooth.

Finally, he unfolded the cone and licked the brown paper clean. The water had tasted fresher than the one in the bucket. He waited for the guard's return trip to see if he would refill the cone.

Most of the day, Leander stayed curled up in his corner. The other men sat up in their bunks, reading newspapers, sleeping, or staring seemingly into space but, Leander later realized, more directly at the patch of blue sky visible through the vent near the ceiling. They spoke softly among themselves, a slurred sing-song punctuated by spells of derisive laughter.

One man started a stream of chingadamadres-cabrones-putos-culeros-mierdas. He cut his rant when he realized Leander was listening. "Qué me ves, pendejo?"

"No, nada," Leander recoiled. "I didn't mean to stare."

"I was not talking to you. Why would I want to talk to you, anyway?"

Leander expected he would be called in front of a judge and allowed to plead his innocence. Just explaining things to the right person would be progress. He prayed that Lourdes' husband would be satisfied after this one scare. There was no way Leander was going to return within a mile of her building.

He asked the guard when he might see the judge. The man frowned as if from the strain of answering such a difficult question. He explained, as kindly as he could, that sometimes it took weeks for a hearing. Leander pleaded with him to call his friend Victor Aruna, and convey the message that he was in the jail. The guard asked him if he had any cash to pay for the service.

"Well, no, not in here." But his friend Victor would bring money.

"That is good," the guard said. "You need your friends and family to take care of you."

"So, call my friend," Leander insisted. "It will be good for the two of us."

"Bueno," the guard said. "But you have to understand, if he doesn't turn out to be a very good friend, then I'm out of the money for the favor I have done you."

"Ah qué la chingada!" Leander blurted. "I tell you, I'm good for it."

"It will cost you double, if I have to wait for payment."

"Fine."

"Twenty pesotes," the guard said. "I will write it in your cuenta." He pulled out a little notebook and flipped to a clean page. "Te llamas?"

"Paul Leander."

"And the friend who I will call, and who will pay for you?"

"Victor Aruna. Cinco-setenta y ocho-cuarenta y seis-cero-nueve."

"Okey maguey," the guard said, slipping the notebook back into his shirt pocket.

The cell was seldom quiet, its momentary silences punctuated by coughs, sniffles, farts. One man in the top left bunk spat frequently, hawking up gobs of phlegm that he would aim at the toilet bowl. Another took frequent turns squatting over the toilet, trying not to touch its rim with his thighs or asscheeks, and letting out explosions of diarrhea. By the second day, Leander's bowels were churning as well. The guard, who had formally introduced himself as Emilio, brought him a thin mattress to shove against the corner. Fifty pesos would be posted in his account.

"Se le ofrece alguna otra cosita?" Something else that I can bring you?

"Hablaste con mi amigo Victor?"

"No, the line is either busy or there is no answer. I will keep trying," he promised.

The mattress felt damp, its gaping tears exuding grayish cotton batting. Its smells of urine and sweat had begun to mix in with those of Leander's own unwashed body so that the resulting blend was growing increasingly familiar, less repellent for its intimacy.

With nightfall came a profound darkness. Most bulbs dangling from wires along the hallway were burnt out. Additionally, the bars on the doors were covered with thick folds of newspaper to block out the cold. By the second night, Leander had memorized the route to the toilet so that he could make it in four steps without bumping his shins on the bunk's iron frame or stumbling over the water bucket.

Leander thought of Adele and of Victor, who must've learned by now what had happened to him. He choked back sobs into hard knots and, instead of crying, shouted out an occasional *fuck*, sounding out its mixture of plea and anger into the ringing chorus of the cell block, joining the chingadas, the putamadres, the carajos, and then, after a moment's hesitation, a series of spirited *fock, fock, focks* in eager response, echoing from as close as the bunks in his cell to voices at the far end of the hallway. He felt comforted. Throughout that night, he would wake up to someone shouting *fock, fock*. And he would answer *chingada madre* in a spontaneous call and response that was reassuring in its unexpected comradeship.

Early the following morning, Emilio came to let him out. The guard looked grim. "Capitán Cueto wants to talk with you again."

"What about?"

"What about?" he echoed. "Pues about your crime."

"I did not commit any crime."

Emilio stopped in his tracks, holding Leander gently back by the arm. He looked around as if about to share some great confidence, and then hissed through tight lips, "You tell Cueto whatever he wants to hear, okay amigo? But not right away. Wait and then scream as loud as you can. If you don't scream, they will think they are not hurting you enough."

When he entered Cueto's office, the man stood up to shake Leander's hand as if he were welcoming a long-expected visitor. "I'm absolutely shocked. I heard of where they put you," he said.

"Yes?"

145

"You do not belong there," he exclaimed with great indignation. "Estos pendejos," he gestured vaguely toward Emilio and other unseen parties down the hall, "have made a grave mistake."

"So, I'm going home."

He raised his eyebrows in wonder, as if that possibility had not occurred to him. "Not home, not yet anyway. Perhaps a bath, yes. You would like the opportunity to clean up? If we are going to have a conversation as equals, you must have the dignity of a clean body and clean clothes." He directed Emilio to take Leander to the shower, and then to bring him back to continue their conversation. "You don't mind cold water, verdad?" the captain said. "Just running water is enough for us in el pinche tercer mundo."

It was not quite a shower. But the spigot coming out of the wall in the cramped brick enclosure provided enough of a flow that Leander could maneuver his body in different positions until he had gotten himself thoroughly lathered and scrubbed until his skin tingled. He stepped out, hugging himself to still the shivering. His rank clothes had been wadded up inside a plastic market bag. The white shirt and pants that he wore on his hospital training days were hanging from a nail on the door. There was even a towel from his apartment. When he asked Emilio how these things had arrived, the guard was noncommittal. "You have friends on the outside," he said. "Even the Capitán seems to be your friend."

"Mucho mejor," said Cueto, offering him a chair in front of the desk. "Now you look like a real doctor. You inspire confidence like that, dressed in white. It is hard to believe that such a serious looking doctorcito would be a delincuente."

"You prefer I look like a gangster?"

"No, no, you would not make a convincing gangster," he laughed. "I propose that you assist me with occasional interpreting. There are foreigners that we need to learn from. They don't understand my questions. I don't understand their answers. We get nowhere."

"I hope to be released. Not given a job."

"And you will be let go. Because I believe you are not a member of any cartel. Meanwhile, as a working prisoner you would be entitled to some amenities. A cell that's like a hotel room. Also, better food, packages from the outside."

"I need my glasses back," Leander said, even while feeling he was pressing his luck.

"Of course, we can't have you not seeing well."

"Great."

"Maybe even a conjugal visit. You have a wife? A novia?" It clearly gave him pleasure to dangle bait. "If you do not have a regular partner, Emilio here can arrange for a visit from the zona de tolerancia." He grinned broadly.

"You just want me to interpret?"

"Yes, and perhaps offer some medical advice. As you have seen, difficulties with intestinal disorders are common here. Especially among los gringuitos."

"I can try," Leander said.

"Good decision, mi joven doctor." Cueto called Emilio back into his office and reached into his desk drawer for a key. "Take our medical friend to privada número cinco."

"Qué suerte," Emilio said, as he led Leander down the corridor. "El capitán must like you. The last man to live in number five was a banker."

The new cell had a working lightbulb, a chair, a bed above the floor. But its toilet was also backed up. The bucket beside it was about a quarter full of cloudy water. The floor was grimy with a coating of gray scum from a previous half-hearted mopping.

"Look," Emilio went on expansively. "After only three days, now you have this."

Leander leaned back on the slab that jutted from the wall. The mattress was much better than the one Emilio had provided in the group cell. It had a generous thickness, there were no holes or tears in its blue and white striped ticking, and it smelled of perfume. He closed his eyes and breathed in the sweet fragrance. It reminded him of the women in the dance clubs, the hip young ones who doused themselves in knock-offs of Shalimar and Ma Griffe. He marveled that there would be a time for conjugal visits. He couldn't begin to guess at the cost.

The rules were structured in basic capitalism. Every comfort, no matter how elementary, required payment. Some prisoners had TV sets while others would not even get messages. Some received pot or mezcal, while many were denied even prescription medications.

Leander enjoyed the rarer luxury of solitude, now able to stretch out on his bunk and notice that the only breathing he heard was his own, that the shouts and curses of others sounded distant and comfortably irrelevant. The first payment for his new accomodations came due around two AM. He was startled awake by the unbolting of his cell door. Two men entered unannounced. One of them kept turning a flashlight beam on and off in Leander's eyes until he had roused himself to a sitting position on the edge of the bunk.

"Andale, doctorcito," the other said, holding his white lab coat. "Capitán Cueto would like you to wear this."

They escorted him along the passageway lined with cells, showing the way with a flashlight, nudging him whenever his pace lagged. From behind the barred doors came a chorus of *Ay, ay, ay, ay*, somewhere between mockery and commiseration. *Canta y no llores*.

The door opened into the room where he had first met Cueto. It took a few seconds for his eyes to adjust to the glare of the overhead fluorescent tubes which flooded the room with a clinical starkness. Cueto and another man stood with their backs to the door. On the table beside them were two bottles of Tehuacán mineral water, and a saucer with chili powder. They spoke to each other in curt monotones. Cueto turned as the door opened, and watched for Leander's reaction once the situation became clear.

Sitting with his wrist cuffed to the water pipe that ran along the wall, a man shivered in his soaked shirt and jeans. Water dripped from his nostrils. His hair hung down the sides of his face in long wet strands.

"Hola doctorcito," Cueto said genially. "I was just telling our friend here—Mister Jones, he says his name is—that you were coming to help him out." The man sat stiffly, head slightly tipped back, eyes shut tight.

"What's the matter with him?" Leander squinted to make out the man's features.

"Quién sabe?" Cueto and his friend exchanged a quizzical look. "Ask him."

Leander took a step toward the foreigner. "Are you hurt?"

The man opened his eyes. "You're from the U.S. too? What are you doing here?"

"Same as you. Some problem, some misunderstanding. I'm in the lockup." Leander stepped closer as the man's apprehension seemed to relax. "I speak some Spanish," he added.

"You look like a doctor."

"Not quite. I'm a med student. Are you injured?"

"No, I'm being treated very well." He wiped the water off his face. The skin was white and nearly translucent, a faint network of bluish veins visible under the light.

"Is there any way I can help?" Leander leaned over and pressed his fingers against the man's wrist. His pulse was racing.

"Help?" The man exploded in a high pitched hysterical laugh, as if getting the full impact of some punch line. "You're going to help me?"

"They want me to translate. That should help everyone."

"Oh, man, fuck you," the man muttered.

"Is that what you want me to tell them?"

"Not a great attitude, right?"

"Give me something to say to them." Leander lowered his ear to the man's mouth.

"Will they leave me alone, if I tell them the name of my Mexican friend?"

"I suppose. Is that what they want?"

"Exactamente," he said, the words now coming in a rush. "Except that I don't have a Mexican friend. They found a handgun in my luggage. A little Beretta that I have for protection. Now they think I'm some kind of gun dealer for the local politicos. It seems they all love Berettas. As presents for their girlfriends."

"Why would you bring a gun into Mexico?" Leander asked with disbelief. "They're rabid about foreigners carrying guns."

"Mexico is a dangerous place. You read about it in the papers and stuff. Even the State Department warns you against robbers."

"They sure as hell don't suggest coming in armed."

Cueto stepped closer and confirmed that Mister Jones was under investigation for trafficking in guns in order to disrupt Mexico's internal order.

"Is your name really Jones?" Leander asked.

"Yeah, they don't even believe that. I tried to show them my passport, but the asshole that arrested me stole everything. My name is Tom Jones. Honest to God."

"Qué dice tu amigo?" Cueto insisted.

"Es un pendejo," Leander nodded. "He brought his gun as protection from bandidos."

"You believe this?" Cueto said.

"Creo que sí," Leander tried to help Jones.

"Then you are a bigger pendejo than he is."

"Are you going to keep asking him the same thing?"

"As long as he gives the same answer," Cueto laughed. "He says he's feeling sick," he pouted. "Do you think he might die?"

Leander reached automatically for the man's wrist. He estimated his pulse at maybe 160. He let the hand fall limply. "His heart is going like crazy. He might have a fever."

"Gracias doctorcito," Cueto said, patting him on the back.

"What did you tell him?" Jones shouted anxiously.

"That your pulse is racing," Leander said. "You want some non medical advice? Give them something they can work with, and get it over with. That seems to be the prevailing wisdom around here."

"Jesus, you're with them, aren't you? The good cop that speaks English. Fucking unbelievable."

❖ 19 ❖

Victor Aruna was glad to hear from Adele. "I'm delighted to be of help to you once again. I am your friend, verdad? And Leander's too, of course." He said there were ways to find Paul inside the judicial system. It was not so impregnable that a man with connections wouldn't be able to figure out what had happened to another hapless foreigner. "They buy dope from the wrong person, they try to leave the brothel without paying, they drink and fight. They end up behind bars."

"None of that is like Paul," Adele insisted.

"Give me until tomorrow morning. After I talk to some people, I should be able to tell you what is happening. Come by the Hotel Regis tomorrow around ten. I'll be in the salón making myself beautiful for you. I treat myself to this small luxury once a month to be ready when our timing is right."

"I don't care what you look like, Victor. This is important."

"Ay, Adele, you don't have to be so sensitive. It's just that I will be getting a haircut at the Regis, and I will make calls, and I will know things. You'll see."

As soon as she entered the barber shop, she spotted Victor's delicate Italian loafers which stuck out from the sheet that covered him all the way down from his neck. An old barber stropped a straight razor; a plump manicurist sat beside the chair snipping the cuticles of his left hand. A steaming white towel was swirled over his face, allowing only a small opening for his nose.

"Hola Adelita," a muffled greeting came from under the towel.

"How did you know I was here?"

"Ah, the radar of a man in love," he said clearly now as the barber removed the towel. "Can I treat you to a hairdo, a manicure, a facial?"

"You were going to find out about Paul," she said, standing by the chair.

The barber was concentrating on shaving him. Every time Victor opened his mouth to speak, the man would lift the razor and sigh impatiently.

"I think it will be better if I don't speak until Gonzalo is done shaving me. His razor is so sharp that the weight of a feather is sufficient to draw blood. Verdad, maestro?"

"Pues sí señor," the barber said. "It will be better to remain silent, especially while I do the neck."

"First, tell me about Paul," Adele insisted, "and then your barber can take his time with your pretty face."

"It's an involved story, this business about Paul," he said. "Sit beside me, and let Conchita do your nails. She's an artist."

Adele glanced at her fingers. She had graceful hands, but her nails were dull and clipped off unevenly. She would have to stick around, knowing that Victor would talk in circles before saying anything of substance.

She climbed onto a chair as the manicurist set a table with a bowl of warm water for her to soak her fingers. "Tell me if he's committed some crime," she insisted.

"No crime," he reassured her. "Only a breach of etiquette."

"That's not so bad, is it?" she said. "It should be possible to get him out of jail if he didn't do something serious."

"I didn't say it wasn't serious. Just not criminal." He sighed and let Gonzalo shave him.

Adele found herself relaxing under Conchita's hands, the shaping of the nails and the filing. She hadn't wanted polish. A vigorous buffing would provide sufficient shine. Victor lay back with his eyes closed while Gonzalo snipped the hair that grew out of his ears and nostrils, trimmed his eyebrows, and was now massaging his scalp with a tonic that smelled of lavender. Victor's breathing was long and regular, as if he'd fallen asleep. But then he let out a contented sigh, and she realized he was awake.

"So, what's with Paul?" she insisted.

"Ay, Adele, it's an involved story."

"You're not going to tell me anything, are you?" she said.

"Of course I am. I'm just trying to sort out the exact implications of what I heard."

"Start at the beginning. Sort later."

"I'd like to," Victor said. "Because you are entitled to know what happened. But the nature of the situation is private, the people involved, the kind of transgression our friend Paul Leander has engaged in. Well, all of that, makes it better not to discuss his problem in a public place."

"Always with your games."

"Ay, Adele. You always doubting my intentions."

After they left the salon, Victor said he was feeling so wonderful that only a fine lunch at Les Mustaches with the beautiful Adele Zarbo would do. They would have red snapper prepared Veracruz style with olives, capers, stewed tomatoes, a bottle of white wine, and their signature chocolate soufflé. During the meal Victor would find the right words to explain to Adele the full consequences of Paul's problem.

The truth was out before the salad course:

"Este muchacho Paul," he began, "is not deserving of your concern and affection."

"Out with it, Victor," she coaxed. "I'm sure you can keep it simple."

"Of course. The short version is that he has earned the jealousy of a prosecutor, licenciado Loreto. This man has decided he likes his wife too much to share her with some gringo student. So he had Paul arrested. He'd put her in jail too, if it wouldn't make him look ridiculous."

"Paul's in jail for carrying on with some married woman?"

"A wife and a mother." Victor nodded solemnly. "His landlady, la señora Lourdes Loreto."

A wave of nausea rose within her as the unblinking fish stared up through the stewed tomatoes. "But that's not a crime," she said, finally coming to his defense.

Victor mocked her with a pout. "It's a crime only insofar as bad manners are a crime. And stupidity, and recklessness, and duplicity. They are all crimes in their small way, verdad, Adele?"

She felt herself sympathizing with him, in spite of her anger. "Poor Paul."

"And poor licenciado Loreto," chuckled Victor.

"His wife must've had her reasons," she said. "When will they let Paul go? It's not like he's done anything criminal."

"Stupidity should be against the law, don't you think?" Victor stared at her. "He's being held on suspicion of something. It doesn't matter what. After keeping him three days, they had to accuse him of a crime. Now he's locked up until the trial, whenever that takes place. In other words, quién sabe?"

"Can't you help get him out, Victor?"

"I will study the situation," he said, loading the fine flaky fish onto his fork and covering it with sauce before bringing it to his mouth. He chewed happily. "If I was rich," he added as if the previous topic had been exhausted, "I would eat at this place every day with beautiful American artists."

"Jesus, Victor." She felt bewildered. "What on earth is there to think about?"

He shook his head as if the problem he faced was too complex for easy explanation. "You see, justice takes contacts."

"And you have plenty." He had, after all, gotten her a working permit with a minimum of red tape.

"Yes, but contacts are like a charge card. Every time you draw on them, you lower your available credit."

"Paul is your friend." She was about to weep.

"Yes," Victor seemed to agree reluctantly. "But he is also my rival. Me entiendes?"

"No, I don't understand you," she said, pushing her chair back. She stood at the table for a moment, as if waiting for some further explanation. Then, she sadly walked away from him, leaving him at his favorite table at Les Mustaches, facing the skeletons of two half-eaten snappers now cooling under their pink sauce.

The truth was that she did understand Victor. The next day she called him and said she was sorry for being angry with him. She swallowed hard and asked him to help her. She wanted to retain his services on a professional basis. He was a lawyer; he knew how to fix problems.

He made his old joke about her needing a lover, not a lawyer.

"No, mi amor," she forced out a light chuckle. "I need to get my boyfriend out of jail."

"Will you be my lover if I get him out?"

"I already love you, Victor," she laughed halfheartedly. "In the finest sense of the word."

"Ah, but I want your love in the worst sense."

"Pues, ya veremos," she said. We'll see.

"My legal fee," he said. "Will be a million pesos. Or one night with you."

Then she offered, so bluntly she could hardly believe her words, "You got it, Victor. I'll have sex with you, if you get Paul out."

"De verdad?" he asked.

"Really," she said, after only a moment's hesitation. "One night. But it needs to remain between us."

"I will not breathe a word to anyone," he said.

In the days following that conversation, whenever she saw Victor, he would wink and smile suggestively. "We are making progress. A friend of my father is pushing for his release. Soon, you will be mine."

❖ 20 ❖

After the first few days, Leander became accustomed to being roused in the night. Grabbing a medical kit that had been put together for him, he'd follow a guard to Cueto's office. Occasionally, a prisoner would see them pass by the row of cells, and yell out, There goes Doctor Cabrón with his bag of tricks.

Some calls came in the middle of the day and the task would be simple. Paraphrase in Spanish some report of a purse-snatching or hotel room break-in. The meeting would take place in the front reception area. Even in cases when someone had been detained, all they needed was some clarification of the procedures by which money could be wired from their family in the U.S., and their release secured, with consequences no more serious than a blister in their memory. In other cases, he could only stand by while Cueto and his buddies complained that detective work was laborious and frustrating. Purposeful interrogation was an art, they explained, and a shortcut to the truth. They went about it as methodically as dentists. Cueto was bringing Leander along slowly.

He was given a new blanket, a fine wool sarape that he could bundle up in when he slept or wear over his shoulders while sitting up. Every three days he could have a bath and a change of underwear. He got a small radio, and then later in the week, the batteries it required. He received some newspapers, a recent *Time* magazine, and a paperback edition of *Don Quijote* that he found absorbing even if the medieval Spanish made it slow going. When the ceiling lightbulb burnt out, it was replaced. He still ate terrible prison food, except for the baskets with fruit, hard-boiled eggs, hunks of cheese, and chocolate that, from time to time, Adele managed to get to him.

156

"Te tengo una sorpresa, doctorcito," Emilio said to him one afternoon.

"Cuánto chingados me va a costar?" Leander smiled ruefully. Every gift from Emilio came at a price.

"Mil pesos," the guard said, as if it were the top figure he could think of. "Did you have a bath today?" he asked.

"Yesterday," Leander said. "You were there, remember?"

"Yesterday is good enough."

"Are you telling me what I think you are?" He had been begging for a visit from Adele, asking Cueto at every opportunity. Other men received intimate visitors. It was one of the few niceties of the Mexican prison system.

Adele sat stiffly in a corner in the receiving room, her hands flat on her thighs, her back straight as if she were trying to have the least possible contact with the chair.

Leander sat in front of her, their knees barely touching, and he put his hands over hers. Her skin was cold, and she looked wan and thin in a white Indian huipil blouse and a plain cotton skirt that came down to her ankles. She kept her head tilted up as if to show him the fullness of her beautiful face, letting his eyes skip around nervously, taking in the melancholy line of her lips, the seriousness of her mouth because there was nothing that she wanted to say immediately, nor much to smile about. He observed the familiar shape of her ear, with the hair tucked behind it. The open expressive look of her eyes, now in this gray dingy room, so transparently blue.

She remained uncomfortably still in this public space, not daring the slightest flutter of her hands, as if she had been warned to contain herself, to keep from touching.

"I really need to get out, Adele," he whispered. "I'm rotting here."

"I don't know what more I can do," she complained weakly. "Nobody tells me anything."

"Talk to Victor."

"I have. He says that the licenciado who got you detained is happy that he has given you a bad time for fucking his wife. He

doesn't care if you are released. He doesn't think you'll go anywhere near his wife anymore."

"Of course I won't. Now, why can't I go home?"

"Victor says that it's now up to the judiciales."

"They can't have anything on me." Paul was confused.

"You had to be accused of a crime. They couldn't hold you
without that. They know you were at Reginio's house the night of
the killings."

"We were there by chance. You were there. Victor was there."

She shook her head as if the matter were so complicated, it
would take hours to unravel it for him. "Anyway, they won't set
bail because you are a foreigner."

"They're right. I would run home."

"Eventually, they will set you free, because there is no evidence that you did anything. But the judge has to wait until your
turn comes to hear your case."

"When?"

"They won't say."

"I'm rotting in here," he repeated.

"I want to help, Paul," she said. "They said you could ask to
bring me inside. That we would be alone for an hour."

"God, Adele, I don't want any part of this place touching you."

"Victor says they're treating you pretty well because you have
a job."

"Victor knows what I'm doing here?"

"He says they like you."

"Do you know what I do, Adele?"

"You help foreigners by interpreting."

"Tell Victor to get me out of here. That I will pay him back
whatever it takes. That I'm rotting in here."

❀ 21 ❀

The call from Victor Aruna, which she had been both dreading and hoping for, came finally, surprisingly, in the middle of the night. "Adele querida, amor mío, corazoncito. I have excellent news."

Victor wanted to make a real date out of their agreement. She took a breath. Yes, she would make good on her offer to thank Victor properly for Paul's freedom. She would be virtuous by trading her virtue for a higher good. She imagined sharing a bottle of wine and some good scampi at La Góndola, and then a drive up the mountains to his house off the Toluca highway. She looked forward to a measure of excitement after the frustrating weeks alone, trying to understand the mess Paul had gotten himself into.

"Bring your camera," he added.

"No, querido. You're not getting pictures too."

"Please, for after we have sex," he said. "I want a photo of my blissful expression after sleeping with La Zarbo."

Years before, Adele had taken stark, nighttime shots of streetwalkers outside the Landry Hotel in Dallas, treating them like an alien life form meant to be studied from a safe distance. She did not think much about what they actually felt. The lens recorded the rituals. Silent cars, their headlights off, would cruise very slowly through the dark neighborhood, would stop for a few words and then suddenly speed away with a woman. Adele was drawn to the body language, more lethargic than seductive, the costumes that tried so hard to promise pleasure, the lamé hot pants, the vinyl thigh-high boots, the rigorously tiny skirts offering with

unembarrassed frankness massive thighs and bowed legs and vari-
cosed ankles. They seemed parodies of real women engaged in real
seduction. She wondered how limits were negotiated. Would there
be different prices for various favors? Would fat and ugly and dirty
men be made to pay more? If she were a whore, Adele would price
herself out of reach of any but the moderately agreeable. The
thought of having sexual intercourse with Victor numbed her.

That morning she lingered in bed, trying to coax a few more
minutes of slumber. It was already after ten when the thought
of the impending evening entered her consciousness with stark
clarity.

The reward for Paul's freedom had been agreed to weeks
before. With all the uncertainty, only Victor had the connections
and wile to help. She would make herself trust him. He would
come by for her at eight. Her first reaction was to rush to the bathroom and wait for the nausea to pass. Now, forces had been set in
motion, for the planets, or God, to properly register what was
about to happen. She could call Victor and cancel their date.
Would she still be able to back down while riding into the hills in
his big boat of a Ford? Once she was inside the house? While on
her back waiting for him?

Adele watched herself make breakfast as if from a distance.
Mindlessly, she squeezed oranges, brewed coffee, and burnt a slice
of bread in her erratic toaster. She felt as if these small routines
were being performed by a more innocent aspect of herself. In the
end, she could only take a few nibbles of toast and drink half a cup
of coffee. She wished she had someone to confide in. She used to
have Paul.

Standing in front of her closet, she felt like a cliché of the girl
on an important date. All her clothes seemed much too personal
for the occasion. The thought of wearing anything she valued
compromised more of herself than she had offered. She didn't
know what Victor would expect her to look like.

In the end she browsed the shops in the Zona Rosa and came
up with a bright Indian-print top with an elastic neckline, a straight
black skirt, new sandals. Unusually showy for her, purple panties
with a lace heart. She would take an extra pair of her plain cotton

160

ones, and leave the purple wonders behind as a souvenir. The blouse and skirt could be given away. No trace of whatever happened between her and Victor would remain, at least not in her wardrobe.

Later that afternoon, she had a steam bath at the Baños Miraflores, the public baths two blocks from her house, with separate areas for men and women. For a few pesos she could sweat in the steam room, the baño turco, then avail herself of the talents of Doña Lupe, a stately Indian woman with large fleshy arms and hands like vises. Adele lay on a tiled massage platform to be lathered with coconut-oil soap and rubbed with loofahs, her feet pumiced and her hair shampooed.

Her body felt lax, the skin still flushed from Doña Lupe's vigorous rubdown. On the walk home, the sense of her body's weightlessness made her light-headed, her feet seeming to dance above the pavement.

Later that evening, by the time Victor came for her in the black Ford with tinted windows, the tension she'd felt in the morning had returned. "We're going straight to my house," he said, once she was seated next to him and the car was speeding out of the city toward the Toluca Highway. "But we're not going to make love right away."

She debated whether she had the right to ask for explanations, or if she should just sit quietly in the car. "You said we were to have a real date," she said "You know, dinner and wine and dancing."

"We need to build up energy before we spend it," he said.

She laughed. "You plan to eat oysters."

"This is serious," he said. "It's not every day that two people are intimate for the first time. This is a night to be experienced with some concentration. We could fuck every day for a year, and no occasion would be like this particular night."

Adele recalled the route to his retreat in the hills above Mexico City, the stone cottage tucked inside a ravine below the highway. She recognized the Zapotec rugs on the red tile floor, their geometric patterns giving the illusion of motion, the equipales, drumlike chairs of stretched cowhide around an armature of sticks and bindings. On the walls hung Victor's prized collection of ritual dance masks. There were dozens of them. Devils with noses like snakes. Dogs with gentle eyes and lolling tongues. Frogs protruding from gaping human mouths, being either swallowed or regurgitated. Bats splayed against startled faces. The red of the devils fighting the green of the frogs, dog breath mingling with the musky odor of guano, wing flutter, snake hiss, and coyote howl. All those eyes looking down on her, not missing a thing.

Once the roar of nearby truck traffic was shut out behind the heavy door, a dense silence magnified the soft rustle of their clothes. A whisper would somehow hang in the air as weightless as a mote of dust, and fall inside her ear.

"Ah, Adele," Victor continued. "This is a night that will last a thousand hours. So much will happen it will feel like we've been here for days and days."

"I'm not smoking your stuff, Victor." Adele tried to sound lighthearted.

"No, mi amor." He squatted to light a fire in the open chimenea. "No drugs tonight." He motioned for her to sit on a pillow close by, so she would enjoy the warmth. "First of all, this is for you." He reached into his pocket and pulled out a typewritten letter with the letterhead of the Policía Judicial. The text signed by a Licenciado Carlos Villazón directed the second district detainment center to release Paul Leander, a U.S. citizen mistakenly held on suspicion of drug trafficking. "Find a way to get it to Paul. He will know who to show it to."

"Thank you," said Adele, making just enough sense of the Spanish legalese to know what it meant. She noticed that it had been dated several days before. "You've had this letter for a while?"

"Well, it took a while to reach me."

"You were keeping it until we had our date tonight," she said.

"Adelita," he scolded gently. "You must not be so distrustful. Things happen when they are meant to happen."

"But now he will get out right away."

Victor nodded. "A few days. They will want to be sure it's real."

"Gracias, Victor," she said, refolding the letter and slipping it back inside the envelope.

Victor stood up to end the conversation. "Even though I've kept my end of the bargain, I'll drive you back to the city right now if you want to go. And no hard feelings. You shouldn't feel that you need to reward me."

Adele put the letter into her bag, safely buried under the condoms, the extra pair of panties, and enough car fare to get her home in case she needed to escape. "I will keep my end," she said.

"You are an honorable woman," Victor said.

"Not at all," she laughed. "I don't want to owe you any favors."

"That means we don't have much of a future." He said with genuine disappointment.

"I am here tonight," she said. "A promise is a promise."

The fire was now blazing, the ocote kindling, sticky with resin, hissing and spitting sparks into the room. "I'd like to think that now you're here because you want to be," he said.

"We made a date, Victor," she said. Then she added quickly as a look of disappointment veiled his eyes. "I wouldn't be here if I didn't want to."

"But which is it?" he insisted.

"It's both," she said.

"Aha, so I do own you for the night."

"I didn't say that."

"No, you didn't. But there is a possibility that I do. Right? Either because you want me to own you, or because you are bound to our deal." He sounded so proper, almost prissy, as if he were splitting the fine points of some philosophical riddle.

"So, what difference does it make?"

"I can't really own you, unless you allow it," he smiled weakly. "Otherwise, I'm just renting you."

"And you want to own me."

"Correct." They sat crosslegged on the big cushions before each other, the fire lighting half their faces, the other side hidden like the dark side of the moon.

"People don't really own each other," she argued weakly.

"They do, querida," he said. And because there didn't seem to be any question about this in his mind, because he seemed so absolutely sure of himself, she felt at that moment, that if she

163

conceded an inch of her being to him, a fraction of her soul would be lost beyond the possibility of ever regaining it.

"Even if you owned me for one night, I would not let you know it." She was enjoying some small spark of power as they sat with their faces inches apart.

"You're right, Adele," he said, appearing to give the matter weighty consideration. "There's the question of what I will own. Your body. Your sexual response. The whole of your mind. Your soul, whatever that is. But *you* will know. The knowledge will follow you."

"Is this what you want to do?" she asked brusquely. "Talk."

"Talk scares you?" His gaze was fixed on her.

She looked away. His eyes seemed to have grown brighter even as the the big blaze dwindled and the house grew darker. She had expected a simple physical act, measurable in its arc from arousal to satisfaction, inevitably curtailed by the limitations of time and physiology. The talking was making her nauseous again.

"You're toying with me."

"Fine." He mimicked the zipping up of his lips.

"Actually, Victor," she said, wanting to reassure him, "we can do whatever you want. Talk is fine. Not talking is fine too."

"Spoken like a true whore," he laughed.

"I'm doing my best, querido," she said.

The turn of the conversation had suddenly filled him with sadness. "Let's just be quiet for a while," he said. He straightened his posture, pulled his shoulders back, and closed his eyes. "We can meditate."

"I don't know how."

"Sometimes we mediate without realizing it."

Victor was no longer sitting across from her. She heard rattling pans, chopping knives, sizzling oil from the adjacent kitchen. She found it hard to imagine Victor Aruna whipping up a gourmet meal. Cooking was not something Mexican boys were encouraged to learn. She marveled at how silently he had crept away, and wondered how much time had passed since he had pushed at her with his soft murmuring questions. She might have drifted asleep. The room had grown very warm in that time; Victor had stoked the fire and a fine blaze now hissed and popped in the fireplace. The air smelled of pine cones and copal incense.

She rose unsteadily; her legs and arms had the muscle tone of a rubber doll. A sudden gust could tip her over. The smoke from the kitchen suddenly overpowered the sweet scents from the hearth. Whatever Victor was cooking gave off a pungent smell of secret fluids and alien flesh. Billows of oily smoke rose from a large iron pan.

"Hungry?" He flashed an eager grin at her. He leaned back from the spattering oil, and shook the skillet back and forth to sift a mass of assembled meats in various shapes and sizes, their colors ranging from a dark brown to shiny red chunks of oddly shaped, vaguely recognizable organs. There were several little round chicken livers and sliced kidneys, a whole identifiable heart the size of a golf ball, a length of tongue, a pair of sheep's eyes, three testicles, a stirring of brains.

"That's dinner?" she winced.

"Power organs," he said. "Energy to get us through the night."

"I think I will have plenty of energy, Victor," she said, leaning back from the smell.

"Well, that may be true for you," he laughed. "You are not a man. You can just lie on your back and smile."

"If that's all you think I'll do," she said, "that's what I'll do."

"Ay, Adelita," he whined. "Perdóname. Just have a little of this supper with me. For social purposes."

They sat at a low table in front of the fire. Victor spooned out some pieces of meat onto her plate, ladling out the thick brown sauce. He poured wine into heavy goblets. Adele recoiled as Victor speared a large piece of meat on a knife, and studied its fissures, crevices, tendrils of skin and nubs of fat with a kind of scientific detachment. He blew on it, impatient for it to cool, and finally stuffed the chunk into his mouth, chewing with noisy enthusiasm. "You should have at least a bite from each organ," he counseled. "For good eyesight, muscle tone, vigor."

Adele laughed, finally, as the ludicrous nature of the advice struck her with sudden clarity. The idea that nibbling on the

165

gonads of a distant species would somehow affect her libido, rather than her digestion, recalled to her some bizarre, surrealist cookbook—*La Gioia de la Cucina* by Federico Fellini's mom. But Victor was not laughing, was in fact turning away from her so he could chew in peace, stuffing his mouth until it would barely close, and then trying to flush the whole mass down his throat with more of the wine he'd poured all over the sizzling pan. He ate with singular absorption, relishing every bite and smiling as he swallowed, as if he'd set out to prove to some squeamish child that this home-cooked dish was delicious and that only a picky, ungracious guest would pass on its delights.

"Adele, you don't know what you're missing." He smacked his lips with showy abandon.

"You're disgusting," she said.

"I am not disgusting," he said. "My mouth is disgusting. My stomach is disgusting. My fingers are smeared with this meat and they are disgusting."

"Yes, and you are disgusting."

"Am I a mouth, a tongue, a nose, a stomach, a rectum?"

"You're playing games."

"And you haven't learned anything."

Victor finished the wine left over from his cooking and opened a new bottle. He kept stuffing himself with meat until all that was left were a few scraps and the muddy gravy covering the bottom of the pan. "What would you say were your favorite organs, dear Adele?"

She forced herself to look away from the grease glistening around his lips and trailing down to his chin. He positioned his head below the line of her gaze so that he was looking up at her, grinning impishly.

"I personally enjoyed the brains because they were like butter, in texture if not in flavor," he said. "The kidneys were nice too, even though they had an air of urine, more sensed by the nose than the tongue. But clearly pipí, all the same."

"Now, I'm even happier to have passed on the pleasure." She realized, even before the sentence was completed, how prissy she sounded.

166

"I am not going to let you pass on any more pleasures tonight." He mimicked her, his voice carrying a small forced chuckle meant to mask the sudden tension between them.

Adele felt queasy again at the anticipated intimacy. It made her inch away from Victor who was leaning across the table to her, reaching her hand with his oily fingers. She resisted the impulse to run out the door.

❖ 22 ❖

On his eighty-second day in the cárcel, Leander's release came as a surprise to him. Emilio walked into the cell, but instead of leading him down the passageway to Cueto's oficina, he told him to pick up his stuff. He handed Leander a grocery bag for his books and extra shirt, plus his watch and wallet, which had been locked in the office for safekeeping.

"Cueto says to go away before you become a problem. And that you are to keep away from women with husbands. If you say to anybody where you have been, he promises to bring you here again."

He followed the guard along the corridor through the reception lobby and into the sunny street. The glare gave him a headache. About two blocks from the prison his legs started to buckle. For nearly three months he had not walked more than the few steps between his cell and Cueto's office.

His wallet had been emptied of even the last few pesos for the bus. The familiar streets were barely recognizable, as if he'd returned from a long absence to find the habitual routes scrambled. It took hours to walk to Adele's apartment. He lost track of where he was at any given moment, concentrating only on keeping his footing along the uneven sidewalks, reeling with the occasional shove or bump from someone walking too close to him. When he did pause in front of some remembered building, the gate to the secondary school or the edge of Chapultepec park, he marveled at the rediscovered beauty of these places.

Hours later, he stood before Adele's building, the familiar green paint flaking off the wooden door, his hand pulling on the string that rang the bell inside. There was no answer, so he waited until a tenant in the building recognized him and let him in. He sat in front of Adele's apartment, leaning his back against the wall, and stared at the door as if by force of his gaze he could unlatch the bolt. He'd been dozing on and off for hours when Adele showed up around midnight.

"I hope you don't mind," he said when he awoke to her touching his shoulder gingerly, as if he were hurt and the lightest motion might bring him pain. "I didn't know where else to go. I didn't think I should even try my old room. Chances are they've locked me out and thrown my stuff away."

"God, Paul," she sighed over and over.

"I tried to get them to call Victor, but he let me down, like he didn't know me."

"Can you get up?" she tugged at his hand.

"Sure enough, I can get up. I wish I had as much money as I can get up for you. Get it up for you, more like it." He tried a lop-sided grin as he held on to Adele's hand and pushed himself up from the floor with the other. "I'm just tired from walking."

Once inside her apartment he was desperate for a bath. He felt himself to be dirty beyond the skin, contaminated internally, his muscles and organs and bloodstream as cruddy as sewer water. He stepped under the spray while it was still cold and marveled at the luxury of a shower, and then at the nearly scalding water and pink soap that lathered up with a flowery scent.

"I thought you'd fallen asleep in there," Adele said when he came out. She could see how thin he had grown, the wide span of his collarbone stretching the skin.

"It's the cleanest I've been in months," he said. "I will remember this bath forever."

He sat on her bed and she draped him in a sheet so that only his head stuck out. Eventually, cupping a mug of coffee, letting his body steam under the damp sheet, feeling a new weight of content-ment, he grew drowsy in Adele's big generous bed. As he lay back, she took the empty mug from his hands and pushed a pillow under his head. It wasn't until he awoke sometime around four, to a night mercifully silent, that for the first time in nearly three months that he dared reach for and pull himself close to her, his belly and groin hugging her hips.

That first morning they rose late, Paul awakening only when the sound of traffic outside became a kind of raucous, sweet reminder that he was no longer in the cárcel. He walked around wearing the sheet like a toga, because he didn't want his skin to touch anything that he'd worn in the jail, as if the very fibers were tainted with ill luck. She found him a pair of her jeans which, because he had lost about twenty pounds, now fit him around the waist even if they stopped a couple of inches short of his ankles. He found a baggy t-shirt that she wore for sleeping with a big image of Coatlicue with her head of snakes.

He started some eggs, waiting for Adele to come back with fresh bolillos and milk and a couple of ripe mangos, delighting in chopping the sharp green chilies and mixing in the tender green onions, tomato and cilantro. He stood over her two-burner stove slowly stirring the mixture in a cast-iron pan. It was all so good, the onion so sharp in his eyes and the chilies like fire, the fresh bread warm and yeasty from the bakery, and the mango smooth and sweet in his mouth, that he couldn't keep his eyes from tearing.

For about an hour after eating they sat around, drinking coffee, not talking much, letting the injuries of the past few weeks start to heal. After making love, she reached to touch his cheek where once again tears were rolling. He took her hand and kissed her fingers, tasting his salt on them. He hadn't cried like this since he was ten.

He didn't leave Adele's apartment for three days. He lazed on her bed and dozed and didn't feel at all restless, because he knew he was free to step outside anytime he wanted. When she asked him if he was ever going to go out in the world, to the university even, he said it was not something he felt up to doing just yet. He wasn't all that eager to be a doctor anymore.

Adele asked him what he meant. She said she wanted to know what had happened to him, that he should get things off his chest, that it would help him get over stuff.

"Prison is destructive," he said. "If you're lucky, you go numb before serious damage is done."

He wanted to ask her about Victor. If she knew why he had dropped him, forgotten him inside the jail.

170

"Have you seen him?"

"A couple of times," she said. "He was trying to help you."

"Did you have to talk him into getting me out of jail?"

"Not exactly," she said. "It just took him a while to get around to it."

He waited for her to go on, but she would not elaborate. "You should call him. Ask him."

Leander had not seen Victor Aruna since they had returned from Puerto Vallarta months ago. Victor had suggested a drink in the airport lounge. He said they needed something to steady the nerves, and a few moments to assimilate the events of the previous night.

"We are still friends, no?" he had reminded them, and they had all nodded emphatically. But Adele said she was not sure she could hold down a beer without getting sick, and Leander had pleaded a need to prepare for a biochemistry exam. Victor kept insisting: They should make an effort to get together soon.

When he and Adele made love, he imagined he tasted Victor Aruna on her skin, perhaps the faint smell of cigarettes and of Brut or English Leather or some other cloying scent that Mexican guys were wearing. He buried his face in her hair to shut off the presence of the other man. Sometimes he would lose sight of Victor, when Adele had been developing pictures, and chemical smells clung to her skin and clothes, and he could picture her alone, bathed in red light inside the darkroom.

On warm afternoons, Paul liked to pull a chair onto the narrow balcony overlooking the park across the street and hold one of his heavy textbooks on his lap while the sun warmed his face, casting a pink glow through his eyelids, making bluish spots dance in front of his eyes, beams boring their way through his skull and warming his brain. It had been a month since he'd left the prison. He no longer wore the white coat which he now found embarrassing.

In the morning, on his way to a modest lonchería for his café con leche and pan dulce, he stopped and bought the daily newspapers and occasionally *Alarma*, the weekly crime tabloid. Then, sitting by himself at the table with a glass of strong milky coffee, he would scan the headlines, making his way to the inside crime

171

sections. There were items he knew might be related to his experiences in the jail, the routine discoveries of men killed in the drug
lords' traditional style, perhaps ordered by Reginio himself, a
bullet through the head, genitals stuffed into the victim's mouth.
The occasional photos showed bruised faces, eyes swollen, lips
torn, noses broken, a weary stillness under the morgue's fluorescent lamps. Sometimes, the photo would linger in Leander's
memory and a wave of nausea would make him push away the
half-eaten sweet rolls. Journalists did not make much of the bodies
that were found day after day because the wars among traffickers
turned up casualties that were deemed a welcome weeding-out of
characters who would otherwise disturb the peace. Paul would try
to reconstruct the features of the dead men to match the faces that
he'd seen in Cueto's office.

Some days, when he thought he recognized a victim in the
newspaper, he could barely muster the stamina to move out of the
closed world encompassing the café and the apartment. His class
attendance became erratic. Instead of going on to the university
after breakfast, he would retrace his steps to the apartment and clip
out the pictures of the murdered men, hoping to reassure himself
through prolonged study of their features that they were in fact the
same men that he had seen in the jail. Leander grew indifferent to
the cruelty, the impersonal nature of the photos, no details about
them given beyond their name and alias. No mention of wives and
children, parents, cousins or uncles to mourn them and remember
them, to celebrate them. Leander would scrutinize the photos for
some revelation of a personality. The alligator logo on a knit shirt,
a gold-capped tooth glinting between parted lips, a Dallas Cowboys cap still jammed on a man's head, a hole above the bill, about
the size of a quarter, ringed black with powder burn.

He was torn between dread and relief. If they were dead, then
he would not meet them again. Never before had the life and death
of strangers mattered so much to him.

Unwilling to consign the faces of the dead to the oblivion of
the garbage can, he would tuck the photos between the pages of
books. He would feel depleted then, his energy sapped by the confrontation with these anonymous faces. He anticipated that the

172

consequences of his involvement in the pain of strangers would come while he slept. So he stayed awake as late as he could, reading textbooks to keep up with the lectures he had missed, but mostly talking with a sleepy Adele or watching Spanish dubs of sitcoms. He became acutely aware of the creaking floors, doors opening or closing, and steps on the stairs. He would eventually crawl into bed, still dressed in case he had to run toward the balcony two stories above the street.

He would wake before dawn and lay in uneasy stillness, feeling a reprieve when daylight brought the routine sounds of the neighborhood stirring, the roar of bus traffic, the familiar murmur of families squabbling, children being coaxed to school. Then he would resolve to rejoin the normal rhythm of life. He would have his café con leche and pan dulce.

As the weeks passed, Leander no longer bothered to check the newspapers every day; the swollen faces of murdered men started to blend one into the other, so that on any given morning, there was hardly any difference from the victims of previous days. It was as if the same man died over and over again in a prescribed ritual manner, the photographs always showing the unfocused milky glaze between half-closed lids, the nose broken, the skin bruised and split, the head misshapen from the bullet's impact.

Finally, Adele asked him not to bring the newspapers to the apartment. He had built a stack on the floor by his side of the bed, and she thought they were poisoning the room. "Are you looking for someone you know?" she asked.

"Sometimes I see a face that looks familiar."

"You're like an old man checking for the obituaries of his friends."

"No," he said. "It's not like I met any of them formally."

"You're never going to tell me about all this, are you?"

"I'm starting to forget stuff," he said. "That's the best part of being here with you."

173

❖ 23 ❖

Leander's plunge into the sweet rhythms of romance was occasionally chilled by the suspicion that Adele and Victor had been together while he was gone. The thought, which earlier in their relationship might not have mattered much, now churned inside him. He grew protective of his time with Adele. He could not get enough of the tilt of her head when he said something that amused her, of the unexpected touch of her fingers when she turned his wrist to look at his watch because she never wore one of her own, or the easy way she would plop her feet on his lap when they were sitting on the couch.

One day he had felt so afraid he might lose her that he proposed marriage while they were riding a bus to the centro. A momentary, small panic had gripped his heart and for an instant he'd felt such profound loss that he knew if they didn't marry he would carry that regret for the rest of his life. It was Sunday and Adele wanted to take pictures of the old buildings downtown— carved doors and wrought-iron window bars and stucco lintel angels. Leander remembers the very spot along the route, the intersection of Reforma and Insurgentes Avenues, while the bus was circling the monument to Cuahutemoc. He and Adele had squeezed close in their seat, to avoid the press of people standing in the aisle. They had been gazing out the window and Adele had pointed out how the sun lit up the leaves of the ancient elms, the light fragmenting on the ground in a dappled mosaic. He felt a surge of gratitude that she could so easily make him see the world with her eyes. During a lurching stop, he turned to her and, without knowing what he was going to say, said, "Adele, I want to marry you more than anything."

Having blurted out his confession, the corresponding relief enveloped him in a cloud of well-being. His declaration of love seemed to have caused a rush through his system. He found himself loving the moment he was living; people's faces glowed with a golden light. An old woman turned toward him as if he had spoken to her, and looked at him with the kindest, most luminous eyes that had ever met his.

Adele looked at him blankly, and his heart sank at the blandness of her response. "Why?" she asked.

He hadn't a reason beyond the panic he had felt at the imagined prospect of losing her. The picture he had of himself as a kind of encrusted barnacle would do little to seduce her or win her commitment. While he could honestly say he wanted to marry her because he loved her, he knew there had to be more to his answer. The longer he waited before explaining himself, the weaker his proposal.

"I don't have one reason," he said, unable to meet her gaze. "There are many reasons."

She seemed to be waiting for him to continue, to list the various justifications for his proposal. In the end he remained silent.

"It will never work." She added before he could argue with her, "Us getting married would be one of those asinine acts that would screw up our lives for all time. We would eventually become a cold, passive, indifferent couple that gets along only because it's too painful not to."

"Are you saying no?"

"No."

"Why aren't you saying yes?"

"Jesus, Paul, let's get off this bus. I can hardly breathe."

His sense of profound happiness was clouded; the bus felt crowded and stuffy. He stood up and shoved his way out of the seat, pulling Adele behind him. He squeezed through the massed bodies standing in the aisle. The bus had slowed to a crawl around the fountain sculpted with all those Indians standing around looking heroic for no reason that he could fathom. He reached out and kept yanking the bell cord until the driver swerved toward the sidewalk and opened the back door for them to jump off.

"I can't believe you proposed on the bus," she said later. "So original." They were sitting under the shade of a dark elm, on an iron bench that felt pleasantly cool through the thin fabric of his t-shirt.

"Why aren't you saying yes?" he repeated.

"For the same reason you're not telling me why you want to marry me."

"Adele, don't complicate things."

"You're right," she said. "It will be much simpler if we keep our secrets."

"Is there something you want to tell me?"

"No, of course not," she said. She reached for his hand and held it in both of hers.

"We'll never know everything there is to know about each other, will we?"

"Is there something you want to ask me?"

"No, Adele," he said, and he wondered if she could hear the sadness edge its way into his voice.

"Okay," she said letting go of his hand. "We're starting from scratch."

"Clean slate."

"Tabula rasa."

"Blank page."

"With this lie detector I thee wed."

"So you will marry me?" He had to raise his voice above the clatter of traffic, the crackle of a nearby radio playing cumbias, a newsboy hawking the Ultimas Noticias.

"Yes," she said. "Let's not ask each other any more questions."

"We'll be happy, you'll see." He wanted her to believe.

"Yes," she echoed.

❖ 24 ❖

"So, amigo, tell me about dying," Victor said one night in California, when he and Paul and Adele were sitting out on the terrace of their home, listening to the distant surf below, sipping brandy. They had poured a little for Victor, because Paul and Adele felt they all needed the gentle dulling of alcohol to digest their unexpected reunion. In the past week the visit had grown awkward. There was no clear end in sight, no set departure. Meanwhile, Victor's moods became increasingly variable; he could go from a frothy ebullience, finding giddy delight in even ordinary experiences such as red Texas grapefruit in the morning or little Fauré piano pieces on the stereo, to a dense sort of despair that the sun would not come out the next morning or that he would never regain the trust of his old friends.

"But we do trust you," Paul insisted.

"Nice of you to say it," he smiled. "Tell me you don't wonder if I'm not trying again, with the last breath of my life, to have a sexual adventure with your Adele. Don't you wonder if I'm thinking of her when I masturbate? There are no boundaries in private pleasures. In the night, when the fear comes, it is the only escape that I still have. I think I will eventually die with an erection."

"One could do worse," Leander said.

"You're humoring me, doctorcito."

When Victor's mood darkened, he would not bathe or change his clothes for days, but would stay curled up in his dark room, with the laptop that Leander had taught him to use. He'd grown tired of looking at diseased livers on sites such as WebMD. He liked reading *La Jornada*, *Proceso*, *Siempre* and other Mexican journals. "I have to keep up with my countrymen," he said.

177

Adele complained that it was boring for her to listen to him carry on about Mexican politics. She did not go into Victor's room for any reason, because she did not like its stifling air as he sat in front of the cheerless screen feeling sorry for himself. Leander explained to Victor that they had no problem with his viewing matter, but that he could maybe open the windows once in a while.

"You will not stop a dying man from staying in touch with his country, will you?"

"This talk of dying is not helpful to you."

"Will it be like falling asleep?" Victor pushed, "Or more like falling apart?"

The men had lit up cigars and were idly watching the puffs of smoke rise and gradually disappear into the black sky. Adele had gone inside because, when Victor asked that question, she felt like a bystander. The problem of his dying was Leander's responsibility.

"Nobody knows what it's like to die," Leander ventured.

"But you have seen people go." It sounded like an accusation.

"I saw my father die. But I'm not sure I learned much about the experience. He was old. He got pneumonia. His lungs were filling with water, so the nurses kept propping him up to help him breathe."

"How did it happen?"

"He drowned while sitting on the bed as straight as a judge. His breaths became shallower as he struggled for air."

"Did he say anything to you?"

"He was in a coma."

"So he didn't suffer."

Leander shrugged. "He wasn't able to talk about it, beyond an occasional whimper, soft as the peep of a small bird."

"Is that how I'm going to go?"

"Maybe pneumonia. More likely, you'll go into septic shock. Your liver will stop filtering toxins. You'll basically be poisoned with your own blood." He paused. "Are you sure you want to hear this?"

"I asked, didn't I?"

"You'll be disoriented. Weak. Yellow. Smelly. Exhausted. Hallucinatory."

"When will it start?"

"It's already happening, Victor. Your liver is gradually failing."

"Why are you doing this to me, doctorcito?"

"Doing what? You don't want the truth, after all?"

"I have seen all those pills in your bathroom," Victor said, as if bragging that he was in fact in control of things. "I took a few to sample later."

"I noticed."

"I could just swallow them all."

"It wouldn't be the Buddhist thing to do, Victor. The experience of dying is not to be missed."

"I'm not much of a Buddhist anymore," he sighed. "Or a Catholic for that matter."

"Then suicide is in fact an ethical option, isn't it?"

"Why are you doing this to me?" he asked again.

"You wanted to talk. We're talking."

"You'd like me to go away, hide and fold up like a dog."

"Of course not."

"You want to be here when I die?"

"I want to help."

"You and Adele? You can each hold one hand. Read from the *Bardo Thodol*."

"Give you pain medication."

"Help me pull the trigger."

"You're being melodramatic now, Victor."

"Perdón, doctorcito," he said. "I think the occasion calls for melodrama."

"Maybe you should give me the pills back."

"Don't worry," he said. "I haven't taken any yet."

"I prefer that you don't."

Victor smiled. "That I don't use *your* pills to kill myself?"

"Go to bed, Victor," Leander said, stifling a yawn.

"But we haven't finished our cigars."

179

❧ 25 ❧

Adele was not sure what was going on between Victor and her husband. It had been a couple of weeks since Leander had invited their old friend to stay with them. It made for a curiously unsettling visit. Victor continued to swing from the depths of dark despair to a kind of random exuberance. Some days he stayed in his room with the curtains drawn and news about Mexico on the screen. He claimed he wanted to keep up with his enemies.

After Leander brought him Klonopin to ease his anxiety, he would sleep for hours, regardless of the time. When he grew depressed, Leander came up with some Zanax and Prozac to be taken together. It occurred to Adele that her husband was gradually stoning Victor into a kind of ambiguity about the prospect of his imminent crisis. Victor called them his valemadrina pills, from *me vale madres*—I don't give a fuck. She had expressed her worry to Paul, but he said it was the kind thing to do. It helped Victor if he knew that he could escape. Still, a depressed, doped-up terminal in their house was a disturbing presence.

On occasion, Victor would take a long shower and come out beaming. One day, he wanted to buy new clothes. He was tired of wearing Leander's sweatsuit around the house. He wanted to go on a spree, max out his credit cards and not worry about the bill because he would be dead. The joke would be on Saks, Neiman's and Nordstrom's. And on his third wife back in the Lomas district of Mexico City. They could all squabble over his estate, have an international incident. For now, he was going to concentrate on looking good. "Help me shop," he begged Adele.

"You don't need me," she said. "You can borrow my car. Or go with Paul."

"Adele, querida," he said. "You're the one with taste."

In the end, Paul urged her to go with Victor because it would not do to have a guest so depressed that he cast a pall over every moment they were together.

"Go with him," he said. "You'll be his fashion consultant. You can help him spend money."

Shopping with Victor was a prolonged, tedious exercise. Once he'd decided to shuck off his dull clothes, nothing was too extravagant. He wanted bright colors and silky textures and precious details in shoes and belts. He told salespeople that he was embarking on the ultimate journey, and that he had to look his best; you only live once. He laughed at the price tag of $200 for an Italian shirt with a print of gold clock faces on a sapphire background. And time is running out, he grinned.

"Well, it's a perfect shirt for that Adriatic cruise," the salesman smiled, as he handed him a pair of shorts, in complementary robin's-egg blue.

"How do I look?" Victor asked, stepping out of the dressing room.

Adele thought that he looked like an Easter egg, with his round belly over skinny legs like sticks below the droopy shorts. "Very dashing," she said.

Victor stood in front of the full-length mirror and frowned. "Qué ridículo," he said. "Like one of those old guys that drool after beach bimbos."

"The light's too bright here," Adele tried to be helpful. "You need sunglasses."

Later, sitting amidst several shopping bags at a café near the mall's fountain plaza, Victor wanted to talk about their friendship. About Paul and Adele and him and how he hoped they had recovered from the bad times in Mexico.

"Let it rest, Victor," she said. "It's been twenty years."

"Yes, but I don't think you and Paul have stopped blaming me."

"I certainly can't speak for Paul."

"And you?"

"You acted like a jerk, Victor," she said.

"I was crazy for you."

"All you Mexican guys, the juniors, were jerks. At least when it came to American women."

"Well, it's important that you forgive me. I don't think I'll be able to die at ease if you don't."

"Okay, you're forgiven."

"You don't mean it."

"You're right, you are not forgiven," she said. "Does anything change what happened? None of us will ever be the same. Especially not Paul."

"He hates me?"

"I don't know."

"He hasn't spoken about me to you?"

"Not really," she said. "Anyway, you're here. He invited you. We're taking good care of you, aren't we?"

"I think he must hate me. He thinks I put him in jail back then, in some strange way."

"I thought you took him out of jail."

"That too," Victor sighed. "Nobody knows the whole story. I would be in trouble if anyone did besides me."

"You're the one that didn't have to pay a price for those horrible weeks."

"Just the loss of your friendship."

"Paul still considers you his friend, doesn't he?"

"I do wonder what he thinks."

"Ask him."

"Yes, that would be the easiest thing, wouldn't it."

"Yes."

"I don't have the guts."

That night Victor emerged from his room wearing a sampling of his thousand-dollar shopping spree. Linen trousers, a silk batik shirt, expensive sandals. "I've decided I'm not dying after all," he announced.

"It's the right attitude," Leander said. "And you look marvelous."

"I'm not just acting positive," Victor insisted. "There are cures out there that you and your white-coat friends haven't even heard about."

"Out where?"

"Well, I know what your reaction is going to be. But I'm still looking into some of the clinics in Tijuana. People all over the world go there, you know. From Europe and Canada, and the U.S., of course."

Leander sighed. "Ozone radiation, blood chelation, laetrile, insulin. All very scientific."

"Ay, doctorcito," Victor smiled. "Your skepticism is cruel to a desperate man."

They had been sitting together at the dinner table. Paul and Adele made it a point to give their guest a semblance of normalcy; she had made a simple pasta, and he had tossed some baby greens with his signature balsamic vinaigrette. She had bought Mexican cajeta to reward Victor's sweet tooth, and this declaration of immortality had occurred just as he stared in delight at the steaming brown confection running down the sides of a mountain of the richest vanilla ice cream money could buy. "Precisely what a diseased liver requires," Leander had prescribed, "butterfat and sugar in generous quantities. Cholesterol be damned."

❧ 26 ❧

Victor had been staying with them for close to a month when Adele found herself working later at the office, lingering over designs, postponing the anxious drive home. She was glad when she'd get there close to ten PM, and Paul and Victor had already eaten dinner and were sitting on the terrace sipping brandy, talking quietly. Even with the breeze from the ocean, the air felt heavy with the lingering smell of grilled meat, the last stale puffs from Victor's cigar, and the abrupt silence that greeted her presence.

One night she called Paul to say she'd be working late again. It was after six and he was getting ready to leave the lab and pick up some salmon fillets for dinner.

"How late?" he asked.

"All night, unless I had somewhere else to go," she blurted out. Then, she added softly, "Let's walk the beach at Del Mar. See stars."

"Victor thinks we're having dinner together."

"So, we're taking the night off. Lean Cuisine in the microwave will be good for him."

They met in a parking area along Paseo Del Mar. Adele arrived first. She was leaning back in the seat with the top down, Bill Frisell guitar music playing. Paul parked next to her. As soon as he got in her car, Adele turned off the music. "Amazing, isn't it?" she said. "Parking by the ocean for the first time in who knows how many years."

"A neglected pleasure," he agreed.

Adele rummaged around in the grocery bag she'd stashed in the back and pulled out a bottle of fifty dollar cabernet and two nice glasses.

"Are we celebrating something?" he said.

"Just taking good care of ourselves, darling."

Paul searched inside the glove box until he found her Swiss army knife. He dug the screw into the cork and, grunting theatrically, pulled it out with a faint pop. He poured the wine. "Like old times."

"We keep saying that," Adele said. "Even our recent times, not so old at all, were better than our present times."

"Okay, then," he said, "to normal times."

"Why are we whispering?" Adele wondered, as if hearing their voices for the first time, gentle against the murmur of the surf. "It's as if were still at the house, being careful. We can yell if we want to." She stood up from her seat, her head above the windshield, and shouted, "Help, our house has been taken over by an evil spirit!"

"Even really good friends feel that way after they've stayed with you for three weeks."

"No, Paul," Adele insisted. "We like our friends. Friends we trust. Victor Aruna is in a different category. He is really an ornery spirit rummaging around in our things. I see signs of his fingers in our medicine cabinet, my desk, my lingerie drawer. What is he looking for?"

"He finds us interesting."

"Oh, Paul. He already knows more about us than we know about each other."

"That is our doing, isn't it?" He drank quickly now, and refilled their glasses.

"We need a good long talk," she said.

"We haven't played True Confessions in quite some time."

"We will," she said. "After Victor leaves or dies or whatever. Meanwhile, I intend to spend as much time as I can out of the way."

"I want to know something right now," he said. "I was in prison for eighty-two days. Victor had me released with a call to his father's friends. What took him so long?"

"We've been through all that," she said. "He claimed that those things took time. There was this man whose wife you were seeing. He wanted to punish you. Then, word got out that you'd been at Reginio's party. Finally, the judiciales liked having you around. Victor said you all became friends."

"That's a joke. As bad as Victor claiming he was my friend, " Paul said.

"With Victor friendship was always more complicated than what appeared on the surface. He said he was your friend. But that he was my special friend."

"Not all friendships are created equal."

"He said you would understand," Adele said.

"Understand what?"

"That he would help you get out as a favor to me."

"Were you supposed to return the favor?"

"Not exactly. I kept stalling him. I gave in when he pointed out that my refusing him was prolonging your time in jail. That the sooner I agreed to be with him, the sooner you would be released. You see, in a way it was my fault that you were stuck in jail so long."

"I figured he left me in there so he could get to you. That seemed awful enough."

"He was always vain," she smiled. "He felt that once he and I were lovers, you would not be able to reclaim me."

"But we got together again."

"He was wrong. We did not become lovers."

"In the end, I should be grateful to you. You fucked him in order to get me out of jail."

"No, Paul," she said sadly. "I also fucked him because I was curious. I mean, we all had a crush on Victor Aruna."

"I should feel flattered that you ended up choosing me."

"He was terrible at the physical part," she said. "With Victor, sex has always been a thing in his head. The reality of it just couldn't measure up."

The night with Victor seemed to have gone on forever. The air inside the cabin had been stuffy, heavy with the vaporous smells of the organ meats, the copal incense burning in a corner of the

186

room, the smoke seeping out from the dying embers in the chimenea.

"You will accept pleasure from me, won't you, Adele?" Victor sat back and drank more wine. His speech had taken a slurred, impatient tone.

"Of course." She stood up and briskly unbuttoned her blouse. "You want me to stand here? Maybe the bed would be better?" She nodded toward the mattress covered by a red and black sarape.

"Just so I can see you."

She wriggled out of her clothes and stood quite still, arms folded across her chest, her skin starting to feel the chill as the fire dwindled. "I'm not going to stand here forever," she said with an unintended edge.

"So, come closer." He clasped her arm. His fingers felt still oily and she tried to pull away. "A dónde vas, chulita?" he said.

"You could wash your hands," she said. "They're greasy."

He dismissed her comment with a shake of his head and pressed his fingers to her face, drawing spirals around her mouth, to her chin, and on to her cheeks. She could smell the meat barely masked by the wine and rosemary sauce. Victor pulled her down to the rug. Instinctively, she tried to turn on her side, draw her legs up against her belly, but he pulled her knees down so that she lay prone, still except for the panting motion of her midriff. He reached inside his shorts and slipped the elastic band under his scrotum. He stared down like a boy marveling at the sight of his pubic hair, the weight of his testicles. The utter seriousness of his desire and her unabashed response struck her as funny.

Victor did not slow his graceless rhythm, a pants leg dangling from one ankle, his white jockey shorts pulled down below his balls and buttocks, his brown socks drooping. He pressed his face against hers, his ear next to her mouth, so that her laughter must have gone past the twists of the ear canal, finally exploding at the core of his brain. There might never have been such laughter, so close and so penetrating in his life.

"It was that funny?" Paul frowned.

"No, more like relief." She added, "I think he was embarrassed. Neither of us saw him after that night."

"And now here he is, twenty years later."

"Suffering amnesia, it seems," she said. "I wish he'd leave. Or go ahead and die."

"For my part, I wish it wasn't so hard to make peace with him," Paul said.

❖ 27 ❖

Adele had flown back to New York with new ArtoFilm lay-outs and Victor decided that he and Paul should go out for the evening. It took some persuading, because Leander had settled into a kind of domestic torpor. He was tired from work. All he wanted was take-out Chinese and an early night.

"You're the one that's being a viejito," Victor laughed.

"Not old," he argued. "Overworked."

"The less fun you have the duller you will be."

"So you're giving me medical advice now?"

"Yes, with an invitation to go look at some chichis."

They sat at a bar while dancers in sequined G-strings and pasties bumped and shook to a tenacious beat, occasionally pushing their crotches in Victor's face. He thought the place was charming. Leander was grateful for the numbing noise because it inhibited their increasingly awkward conversations.

The outing had come at a good time; Victor had resurfaced from walking around looking unshaven and rumpled, and had gotten his new clothes out of their store boxes. He looked like he was out on some kind of celebration. He gave the dancers big tips and drank until he was silly.

As soon as they went back inside the house, Leander resented that Adele was not around to help him deal with Victor. The lights on his answering machine and pager were blinking urgently. There were messages from the clinic asking why he wasn't responding to earlier messages and pages, and one from Beth Moreau, wanting to talk about some tests she had been asked to redo, also about getting away maybe, about having a talk. That last annoyed him. There was enough going on between them that he didn't want to weigh down their relationship further with talk. He clicked her off in mid-sentence. As for the rest of the messages in his machine, he marveled that he had cut himself off for only four hours and the world around him was agitating for his attention.

"Quién es esa Beth," Victor grinned. "I like that deep voice, you know, from her chest. Es tu novia?"

"Some matters are private, Victor."

"I have other questions, doctorcito," he said. "You know, ones that you have to answer." He was standing in the middle of the foyer, as if trying to decide whether to go further into the house.

"Sure," Leander said. "We can talk later. Take a bath first. We'll both take baths. We smell of beer and Shalimar."

"We want to be presentable for our Adele," he snickered. "Whenever she shows up, verdad?"

"Give me your clothes. I'll dump everything in the washer." Leander was already unbuttoning his shirt and unzipping his pants. Victor followed suit and within seconds they were both standing naked, their dirty clothes in a mound between them. They caught themselves glancing at each other, as if for the first time taking the measure of the time that had passed, the erosion of muscle and skin, the sag and bulge of idle flesh. Victor had soft enlarged breasts and a small pot belly, his cylindrical torso supported by a pair of thin legs. Leander had grown increasingly pear-shaped, a firm chest expanding down to accommodate the soft, almost feminine contours of an expanding waist and a fleshy rump.

"Nos vemos de la chingada, doctorcito," Victor laughed finally.

"The worst is yet to come."

"I can't wait," Victor said.

"I'm sorry, amigo," Leander said, cutting into the awkwardness that swelled between them.

"It's all a falling apart, isn't it. The outside gets ugly, and the inside rots. I don't see how you can stand being a doctor."

"I stay in my lab, far from sick people," he said.

"You're making an exception with me."

"That's right," Leander sighed. "Get in the shower. You will look better."

190

Leander showered quickly and changed into soft khakis and a pocket t-shirt. He paused outside the closed bathroom door and listened for signs of Victor inside. He could hear the water spray against the shower's glass door. He went into the kitchen and opened the freezer. An exhalation of chill air greeted him. He sifted through the various lumps of foil and plastic made mysteriously opaque by frost. He found a baguette and a plastic container of lentil soup, a perfect meal waiting for such an occasion. He also took out a hunk of gouda cheese and uncorked a bottle of pinot. He left the soup heating on the stove and walked down the hallway until he was outside the bathroom. He was relieved to hear the shower stop suddenly. A moment later, the door swung open and Victor appeared wearing Leander's terrycloth robe.

"Were you waiting for me, doctorcito?"

"I wanted to make sure you were okay."

"I looked for a razor blade, but people don't use them anymore. Not to shave anyway."

"You found everything else you needed?"

Victor smiled. "You have wonderful shampoos and soaps and lotions. I smell like a fucking English garden."

"Actually, you smell like Adele. It's her stuff."

"Ah, Adele," he sighed, bringing his arm up to his nose. "Did you know I was in love with your wife?"

"It never crossed my mind, Victor."

"Ay doctorcito, what a cabrón you are."

While Victor dressed, Paul served two steaming bowls of the thick lentil soup, fragrant with bay leaf and garlic. They sat at the kitchen table and cracked the toasty baguette. Leander poured wine.

"You know," Victor said. "This is the reason I hate having to die. To no longer have soup and bread and enjoy a nice wine with a friend."

"You can only have one glass, you know."

"How much more wine can I have before it kills me?"

"Don't think about that."

"Why not? The terminal process could be so much more enjoyable. Instead of saying you have some number of weeks left to live, they should say you have a thousand glasses of wine left.

This could be particularly accurate for conditions such as mine, don't you think? I mean, every sip of alcohol pushes the clock a tick further along, another white dot on the liver, another cell rotting. Heart patients would get so many pats of butter. Emphysemiacs would leave the hospital with a set number of cigarettes, an armful of cartons, perhaps. They'd live out their life one inhalation after another, thousands of them. That final puff would be like the guy in front of the firing squad. Dead even as the last plume of smoke was exhaled from his leathery old lungs."

"You're a poet, Victor. More soup?"

"More wine," he said sliding his glass across the table.

"It's your body," he said, pushing first the glass, and then the bottle back toward Victor.

Victor seemed taken aback by the challenge. He tried to steady the tremor in his hand as he filled his glass. He offered to pour some for Leander.

"No, gracias," he said placing his hand over the glass.

"I don't want to drink alone."

"I'm not going anywhere," Leander sighed. "More soup?"

"No."

"I'll keep it on the stove for Adele."

"Ah, sí, la hermosa Adele. When is she coming in?"

"It could be after eleven. There's an 8:50 flight out of La Guardia that she sometimes takes." He stood up and stretched. "You don't have to wait up."

"I want to, of course," he said. "I have hardly seen her."

"She's a busy woman these days," Leander said. "I don't see much of her myself."

They sat in the living room, Victor on a large velvet sofa, sinking into mushy pillows, his feet resting on the marble-topped table before him. Leander watched him from an overstuffed arm chair at the opposite end of the room. Victor stared into the wine glass as if to glean some truth from within it.

"You're complaining," Victor said. "Things between you two are not happy."

"We've had better times."

"You took her away from me," Victor chuckled.

"You had your chance. I was in jail for eleven weeks."

"She loved you more while you were in jail than when you were out."

"That must've been frustrating for you."

"Everything about Adele Zarbo was frustrating to me," he smiled sadly.

"And now, here you are." Leander leaned back on the chair and folded his hands across his belly, watching Victor, trying to discern his emotions.

"But we had our moments," Victor added. "She must've told you, verdad?"

"Why would she tell me anything about you and her?"

"Americans do that." Victor shook his head as if contemplating some great folly. "They think confession is good."

"Do you think confession is good, Victor? You're dying, though not tonight or even tomorrow."

"So you're telling me that I can take my time getting it all out."

"I don't even know if you have anything to confess."

"Is there any point in confessing stuff you already know?"

"Try it. See how it feels."

"But I don't know what you know."

"God knows your sins and you confess to him."

"You doctors like to play God, don't you? You know my sins. You've decided I'm dying."

"What's going on inside your body is not my decision."

Leander was torn between the original friendship and the rivalry that had resulted in a few weeks of his life turning into years seeded with resentment.

"I'm trying not to die too soon. Maybe I can have chemo."

Leander shook his head. "Chemo will make you sicker."

"How about a transplant? I could buy a liver just like that." He snapped his fingers. "Write a check or put it on my Visa."

"Did you discuss it with your oncologist?"

"He said he would put me on the list. He didn't say how long a list it was."

"Believe me, they will do for you whatever they can."

"But you can help me with the pain, right? Americans don't put up with pain. It goes against their values."

193

"You have the same drugs in Mexico. And cheaper."

"So why am I still here?"

"You tell me. You ended up at our hospital by chance. Am I right?"

Victor sighed. "It was fated that we meet after twenty years."

"I didn't have to see you."

"Of course you did," he said. "We were friends." Victor shrugged and seemed to doze off. Leander went to the phone to check his pages. There was a new one from Adele back in her hotel. She was exhausted. Her meetings had not gone well. She would get a decent night's sleep and fly home the next day. He played back all three messages from Beth Moreau. He called her even though it was past eleven. She sounded as if he'd awakened her, but he asked her to meet him for a drink anyway. Suddenly, he had to get out of the house, and away from Victor.

❖ 28 ❖

Victor Aruna feared a shadow would continue to follow him wherever he went. He could not forget that he was dying. Even though the ghost never went away, not even while he was asleep, occasionally, when his attention was caught up in the details of Paul and Adele's life, Victor was glad to let the fear recede into the background of his awareness. He'd been intrigued by the full chronology of their life after Mexico, their tentative courtship and casual marriage, and now their odd autonomy.

He resumed his Buddhist practice. When he wasn't watching TV or surfing for porn, he diligently maintained the awareness of death. He practiced shutting off his senses, from the darkness of the blind to the oblivion of the deaf to the stillness of the breath. In a way, if he looked at it from the proper angle, the knowledge of impending death had given him a measure of freedom, because he had problems back in Mexico that he no longer needed to live with. The strained relationship with at least two of his wives and five of his children was beyond repair. Let them deal with him in the best way they saw fit. If they chose to spit on his grave, that was fine. If they forgave him before he died, that would be far better. He knew himself to be soiled with guilt, and no amount of perfume could disguise the stink.

In the evenings he might shut himself in his room and tie up the phone for hours. Adele and Paul would cook or pick up a meal on the way from work. They'd knock on Victor's door; he would say he'd be right out, but then it could be an hour before he finally emerged. He had been talking with someone in Mexico. Some old friend whose forgiveness he would want before dying. He called people he hadn't spoken to in years, short-lived loves he had betrayed and childhood classmates he had bullied. Some had no recollections of him at all. He would beg forgiveness and they would hang up, thinking it was some crank. Others were eager to end the call, not particularly happy to hear from him. Yes, forgiveness would be granted, and wishes for good luck expressed, but there would be the request not to call again, because there was a husband nearby, or a child, or the hour was late and there was no time to talk. And if forgiveness was withheld, if the person on the other end of the line who had not talked to Victor in years reached for the opportunity to insult him, then Victor would accept all manner of vituperation as his due. He was called traitor, hypocrite, thief, liar. Insults and recriminations were simply another way of wiping the slate clean. It was impossible to be forgiven for every sin. Every prostitute he had ever hired, every beggar he had refused, every single evil, envious thought he had harbored could not be expiated. He grew to understand the weight of his sins, as the glutton acknowledges the dead weight of excessive body mass. He knew himself to be obese with guilt.

The insistent ringing of the phone shook him from his reverie. As he had on other occasions, he picked up and listened in on the answering machine as it went through its recorded formula. He enjoyed the voyeuristic thrill of wondering what lay behind the casual, often cryptic messages that came for his friends. Meetings cancelled, lunches arranged, often the hot pursuit of the crisis at the office or at the lab. Call right away. This is urgent. Confirming your haircut, your massage, your teeth cleaning.

"Hello, this is Dr. Manning from Oncology at Scripps Memorial, calling for Mr. Victor Aruna. I have excellent news for you, Mr. Aruna. Please call me . . ."

Victor wrote down the number and pressed 7 to erase the message.

"You two are an inspiration to me," Victor said one time to Paul and Adele. They were on the terrace early in the evening. "So steadfast."

"How else would you expect us to be?" Adele asked.

196

"You had the right to cut me off." Victor sighed. "We did not part on good terms. You had every reason in the world to reject me now. Even after all this time. Twenty years does not change the differences we had. You trusted me. It didn't help that I was in love with Adelita. I wanted to feed on her, breathe her in, hold her until she melted against me. I'm still in love, but in a good way, you know. I'm in love with you both."

"Everything gets worked out over time," Leander said. "We're not the same as we used to be," he added, without much conviction.

Victor stood up and yawned. Paul and Adele stood next to him, looking out toward the ocean, which was dense and black under the shimmering starry night. "Amigos," he said, opening his arms to draw them in a close embrace. "I can't think of any other reason to live. To have friends like you two."

❖ 29 ❖

When Adele got home from New York the next morning, she sensed Victor watching her through the living room window while she paid the driver. She walked self-consciously up the walk, clutching her presentation case and dragging behind her the rolling overnighter that seemed to follow her everywhere. Her dress was wrinkled from the long day's wear, hair flat from trying to snooze in coach class, middle seat, full plane. Victor greeted her at the front door, looking clownish in Leander's oversized sweats. "Adele, bienvenida!" He smiled broadly like a genial host welcoming a long-awaited guest.

"Hola Victor," she sighed. It sounded like the preface to a longer greeting, but she smiled and walked past him into her house, sending the suitcase skidding into a corner of the foyer. She marveled that he had made himself quite at home, the stereo tuned to a Mexican station playing obnoxious norteño music.

Victor announced that Leander had left for work early that morning—actually, before daylight, was the way he put it. "Por fin solitos," he said after she had kicked off her tight pumps and collapsed on the sofa. It was like Victor, after all these years, his every word loaded with seduction. She coolly ignored his flirtations. He offered her some coffee he had brewing in the kitchen. "I made it stronger than your husband," he bragged.

She had read his intentions. He would pour them both big comforting mugs, hand her one while she was splayed on the couch, and sit beside her. They would be all cozy and warm, sinking into the sofa's blue velvet folds. "Gracias," she said, rising from the couch with some effort and following him into the kitchen.

"I hear from Paul that you are a very successful art director."

"I'm a vice president, and I make two hundred thousand a year, and I haven't taken a photograph in fifteen years."

"Caray!" He tilted back his head as if to dodge a punch. "I don't know whether to offer congratulations or condolences."

"Figure it out, Victor."

"Okay, you have my condolences. But only temporarily. You can always shoot pictures again."

"So, how are you feeling?" she asked earnestly once they were both seated at the kitchen table, the morning's newspaper spread between them, the radio now tuned to a bland mix of new age and instrumental versions of sixties hits.

"Fine, great." He struck his chest Tarzan style. "Your Paul and I have even gotten drunk twice since you left on your trip."

"You must've had a lot of talking to do."

"Well, yes, we talked," he chuckled. "Between dances."

That afternoon, Adele tried Paul's number at work and heard the call roll over to another phone. "You're not at the clinic," she said as soon as he answered.

"I'm in a presentation at San Diego General. Very boring."

"I think you're fibbing," she said. "But I appreciate the effort."

"How did you find Victor?"

"Feeling abandoned," she said. "He says you spent the night away from home."

"He's very mixed up. He's been getting stupid on wine and dilarude."

"Sounds like our Victor."

"He means to go with a bang."

"Is he taking us with him?"

"Don't let him hear you asking that."

"What do you want me to do with him?"

"Try to cheer him up," he said. "I mean, he was your friend too."

He added after a pause, "He's like a time bomb. Now that he knows he's going to die."

"When, for Christ's sake?"

"Nobody knows that. I've known of people hanging in a coma for weeks. Then they wake up as if nothing had happened. They get sent home and they gasp their last breath in the minivan while sitting in traffic."

"Kind of makes you crazy to think about it," she said.

He was quick to change the subject. "How did your presentation go?"

"Fine," she said. "I showed them ethnic weddings, silly grandpas, tropical sunsets, soccer moms and flag wavers. They're going with kids and dogs."

"Not frogs," he sympathized.

"What was I thinking? I go back to New York tonight," she said. "Again."

"Yes. Enjoy your conference."

Leander folded the phone shut with a sigh. He was certain that he would eventually die from deception, as a lifetime of secrecy ended up exploding around him. He knew enough about the heart, its map of veins and arteries and capillaries, to realize that he was planting the seeds of his own dissolution: secrecy from his wife, his workmates, from the woman coming out of the shower with a towel tucked above her breasts.

"It's rude to talk on the phone while you're with someone else," Beth Moreau had said in a tone as neutral as if she were communicating a routine test result.

"I know," he said. "You have no idea how important it is to me that we're here."

"It's been a while," she said.

"Yes."

"Has something come up?" she asked.

"I'm on call," he said. "But I just found Dr. Larson to do a pancreas. I told him I was out at sea. He owed me a favor."

"What a liar," she said from the edge of the bed. She pulled off the towel and briskly rubbed her hair.

"I tell you the truth. It makes me very happy to see your beautiful body without clothes."

She blushed and slipped into a sun dress. He liked that he could make her self-conscious. "Not everyone inhabits their bodies with such ease," he added.

"Except when you're ogling."

200

"It's an honor to be allowed to ogle," he said. "It makes all this," he gestured vaguely at the rumpled bed and at their clothes piled together on the room's single easy chair, "so natural."

"Messing around is complicated," she said. "How can that be natural for men?"

He hoped she didn't sense him squirming. "I wouldn't be with you if it was that difficult."

"Good, let's take all this out into the world." She smiled at him with great innocence. "I get hungry, you know. With physical activity."

"I'll call down for lunch," he offered.

"We've spent enough time inside this room," she said quickly. "I want to feel the sun on my skin, before we go back to work."

The night before he'd had the impulse in the middle of the night to get away from Victor's presence and had run away with Beth Moreau to the Hotel Barcelona. It had been her idea the following morning to have brunch in this outdoor café facing the wide expanse of lawn that led to the sheltered cove of La Jolla. For his part, these episodes, more of the brain than the genitals, meant to ease the superego more than appease the flesh.

Out on the terrace of the Café Pacifica, she had asked where his wife was calling from.

"How did you know that was my wife?"

"All your lying," she sighed. "To her and to me. Such hard work, this being a married man. I don't know how you can handle it."

"I like you even when you're sarcastic."

"I'm being truthful," she said. "I don't think I could live with myself doing all the fibbing men need to do."

"You have much experience with married guys?"

"I've known two," she said. "I mean, known them well."

"And they both lied?"

"All the time."

"It doesn't bother you?"

"I'm flattered," she said. "That a man would risk burning in hell on my account."

Paul sighed. His pager was beeping. He glanced at the screen and clicked off. "Sorry about this. We were having a nice time."

201

"Don't worry about it," she said, eagerly dipping a chunk of baguette into her eggs, yolks running now and mingling with the thick hollandaise. "Your wife again," Beth said.

"No. One of our liver guys last month; turns out he was a friend of my wife's. And mine. Years ago. He's staying with me. I'm following his progress. Unofficially."

"He's one of the tests we had to redo."

Paul took a breath, forked up a potato, and chewed thoughtfully for a few seconds. "When did that happen?"

"Over the weekend. You can set your friend's mind at ease."

"What do you mean?

"The results came back from Rochester. His liver is tough and lumpy, but not yet malignant. Just hepatitis B edging into cirrhosis."

"I didn't misread, Beth. You saw the slide."

"Apparently there was a mix-up with the samples. The patient that didn't have cancer has it. The one that did, doesn't. It's been known to happen."

"Not to me."

"Of course not. Not to you, Dr. Leander." She softened her tone with a smile.

Paul made an effort to treat the revelation lightly. "Next thing, you'll be telling me we're all human."

"We're all human," she nodded. "Anyway, your friend will be glad for the news."

"It will be my pleasure to tell him. He thinks he's going to die within the next twelve weeks."

"They're mailing a revised oncology report to him. With apologies." Beth pushed away her empty plate. "That was delicious," she said. "You haven't touched yours."

❦ 30 ❦

Leander had been edging toward telling his friend that the biopsy had, after all, turned out negative. That while his liver might eventually kill him, the moment was not imminent. He had worked out a tableau for the sudden emergence of the truth. He'd broach the topic while they were having their customary cognacs in the evening. He might say: Victor, I have good news and bad news for you. The good news is that you don't have cancer, so you are not going to die right away. The bad news is that you have to cut out alcohol, otherwise you will die sooner rather than later from a degenerating liver caused by hepatitis B.

Before the right opportunity presented itself to set things straight, Paul Leander came home to find that Victor had packed up and left. The house had been unnaturally silent when he first let himself in. A scattering of mail lay on the floor of the foyer. The TV, which normally blared Univision's Spanish language talk shows, was off. The plum-colored drapes in the main room were drawn, sinking the normally bright room into a somber gloom, leaving only a fine line of brilliant sunlight glinting like fire along the edges.

Leander felt a sense of foreboding as he walked along the hallway, pausing first outside the bathroom and listening for sounds, then moving down to face the closed door of Victor's room. He listened for his voice. The last phone bill had climbed to a couple of hundred dollars with numbers in Tijuana, Mexico City, Puerto Vallarta, and 1-900-MAMACITA.

Leander inhaled deeply; the room had grown unnaturally stuffy, as if Victor's departure had left some kind of vacuum. He walked around, opening windows. There was a note propped on the nightstand, in Victor's neat hand, it read. "Gone south for a miracle cure."

He'd only been home a few minutes when phones beeped throughout the silent house and Victor's shrill voice proclaimed that he had decided to drink and fuck himself to death at Mi Casita, the famous brothel in Tijuana. That Leander should come and watch. And to bring eight hundred dollars because that was the amount of the bill he had run up. They wouldn't take promises, checks, credit cards, or anything that wasn't U.S. dollars in cash.

"Come keep me company," he whispered now, as if afraid he might be overheard. "I want to share this final adventure with my oldest, dearest gringo friend."

Then someone took the phone away from Victor and said that if he was a friend of Señor Aruna he should come for him and bring lots of money, because the man had been going through the señoritas one after another, sometimes twice with the same one, and buying drinks for everyone, and now he was drunk and had been crying, saying he wanted to kill himself, and the house was nervous because if Señor Aruna succeeded in killing himself then the account would remain unpaid. "No checks, no plastic," the man reiterated.

Leander asked him to hand the phone back to Victor.

"Help me out, doctorcito. Hit the cash machines. Then come for me."

Leander hung up and called Adele at her hotel in New York.

"You don't have to go get him," she said. "Do you?"

"I'm feeling kind of responsible. He's on a bender to end his life."

"You were taking care of him," she reminded him. "I'd say you're not responsible for his suicidal inclinations."

"It's not that simple. We've been friends for twenty years."

"You don't really believe that."

"It's enough that Victor thinks it."

"Look, Paul," she said. "I have to run, and meet with this jerk that either gets pictures of babies and puppies, or he feeds me to his fish."

"Good luck, Adele."

"So, go get Victor," she relented. "We have to deal with the friendships we claim."

Adele was right. He could have simply processed the biopsy sample as one more anonymous number in the stream that crossed his laboratory table. But, he'd had to see how the past twenty years had left their mark on him. Then, he'd needed to feel the power of his knowledge over the other. Just as a man becomes responsible for the life he saves, the death he predicts becomes an even greater attraction. Victor was dying in his own mind. Leander would watch him fall apart, and then, when the time was right, put him back together again.

Leander approached the border with a growing sense of apprehension. He had for years avoided the ravines, parched in winter, flooded in summer, that served to separate rich from poor, clean from polluted, sane from crazy. Since leaving the D.F. twenty years before, Mexico had become for him a dark, dangerous territory. The cadence of its language riddled with ambiguity. Every guarded gaze sullen and resentful. The line between the two countries was no more than a crease on the earth, a hair's width and a thousand miles long. Murky, shallow, slow, sometimes motionless, the network of drainage ditches appeared uncertain of where to take its flow, swathed with brown film from the sewers and the iridescent green and yellow from the manufacture of cathode tubes, adhesives, plastics. Separated by miles of chain link and barbed wire, the two sides were nevertheless joined by an eight-lane highway.

Leander parked on the U.S. side and walked past the immigration booths and onto the main avenue choked with lumbering semis. He turned onto a side street, into a section of the market with groups of long tables in front of open kitchens fragrant with burbling beans in clay pots, frying onions, roasting chilies, their charred seeds filling the air with a caustic vapor that made Leander's eyes smart. From the back of a stalled pickup, pulque spilled white and slimy out of ribbed wooden kegs and collected in muddy puddles in his path.

He hailed a taxi and showed him the address for Club Mi Casita. "Está lejos," the driver explained. "Not in Tijuana actually, but towards Santa Catalina."

"How far is it?"

"Maybe an hour," he said. "They are having their fiesta today. There is a lot of traffic going into the town."

One moment, they'd been crossing through the peninsula, dun brown and desert scrub everywhere he looked, and the next they were turning off onto the paved parking area of a squat two-story cinderblock building that seemed to have been transported whole from some strip mall in Encinitas or Chula Vista. The Mi Casita club, done up in turquoise with purple cornices above a row of narrow windows, tried to appear festive under its flaking stucco.

Leander told the driver to wait, then walked in from the heat through a plate glass doorway flanked by two planters with dead flowers into a cool lobby. Standing behind a reception counter, a man with bleached hair and sleepy blue eyes looked up from under heavy lashes.

"Hey, amigo," he said. "You're looking for a good time, I bet."

"Are you the manager?"

"Are you a customer?"

"That's funny," Leander said. "No, the customer is Victor Aruna. A friend of mine. I'm taking him home."

"I think he's asleep. Exhausted," he added with a snigger.

"So, go wake him," Leander said.

"It will take a minute to add up your buddy's charges."

"Add away."

It took over half an hour for Victor to come through the lobby, walking unsteadily and almost stumbling on his way to give Leander an abrazo. "Let's get out of here," he said. "The whores sit in their rooms like at a hospital; they have sex until they die. Only the living walk out. That's how I know I'm still alive, doctorcito."

"It's time to go home, Victor." He returned the embrace reluctantly.

"Let's have a little fun, doctorcito," Victor said as he got in the car. "I'm up for a tequilita."

"Not the best thing for the liver."

"But you keep saying I'm dying anyway."

"We all are, Victor, sooner or later."

"Is that the official pathology report?"

Leander hesitated, searching for the proper course of the conversation. "It's not an exact science, predicting a patient's remaining time on earth."

"Me estás bulshiteando," he laughed. "But that is perfectly all right." He patted the driver on the shoulder. "Llévanos a una cantina, amigo."

The car stopped suddenly and the driver did a U-turn away from Tijuana, toward the town of Santa Catalina. It crept onto the main street where the traffic had slowed to a standstill. Buses and pickups and cars sounded their horns, the drivers yelling out the windows and the people on truck beds laughing and shouting. The roads were festooned with streamers of crêpe paper and strands of colored lights. Victor jumped out of the car as Leander was paying the driver, weaving through the crowd toward the fiesta.

Ahead, there was the blare of trumpets and the thump of bass, the hiss and pop of firecrackers. A clanging bell led out of the bustling center of town into a maze of rutted streets crisscrossing a dusty basin. Along the way, fragile dwellings squatted side by side, their fronts of scrap lumber and brown brick shuttered in the afternoon swelter, their rooms empty during the fiesta.

Leander tried to follow Victor but, turning a corner off the main avenue, soon lost him in the crowd. He surrendered to the web of streets, turning haphazardly with the flow, always toward the tolling bell. Bursts of fireworks rained down sparks on the small square in front of the church. Its façade had been girdled with lights that gave the dun stucco a golden patina. Underneath the urgent ringing, a restless murmur started with a whisper. *Santa Cata, Santa Catita, Santa Catarinita . . . Allá viene mi santita.* The church's shuttered doors were flanked by two pairs of tall brass candlesticks. There was a hush as a boy in a cassock that swamped him in its folds of white lace and red flannel emerged with a burning taper.

The kid kept reaching up to light the candles, which were new, their wicks buried in wax. The crowd followed his progress with

207

shouts and groans. As soon as he'd lit one candle and moved on the next, an errant gust would blow out the first so that he had to keep going back again and again. Finally, as scattered applause celebrated that all the candles were lit, the church doors opened barely wide enough to allow his thin body to squeeze back inside. On the other side of the square Leander thought he caught a glimpse of Victor elbowing his way out of the crowd. He called out but his voice was lost in the din.

A moment later the bell stopped ringing and the loudspeakers crackled: *Santa Catarina . . . reza por nosotros.* Pray for us. The drone rose and fell in waves. Santa Catita, our little sister, intercede for us. "Es la fiesta de Santa Cata," a woman in a plain gray dress explained to Leander. She spoke to him slowly, anticipating the hesitation in his Spanish. "Are you a religious person?" He felt her take hold of his sleeve and pull him down to his knees. The crowd sang their response to the loudspeaker. *Santa Cata, hermana de Jesús, hermana de María, hermanita nuestra.*

His knees burned from the hard ground; he started to get up. He needed to find Victor. "Ya viene," the woman scolded. "Ahorita viene la santita." She took hold of his arm again to help herself up.

The crowd stood quietly now. The amplified voice told the true story of how little Catarina became an official saint of the church which Leander half understood and half imagined through the distorted crackle of the loudspeakers. She was just fourteen, had been a woman less than a year, when it happened. She lived in a village in Andalucia which was overrun by Moors in the eighth century. One day a mob of Saracen infidels tramped toward the village, cutting a swathe through the countryside with their scimitars. No one dared stand in their way, except for little Catarina, the pride of her parents, the angel of her village.

Quick as the wind, the girl raced through the back streets and alleys of the town. "See her run. Her golden hair streams behind her like a comet's tail. Nothing can stop her faith," the voice intoned. She reached the town's church just ahead of the infidel rabble. Alone in the silent nave, she barred the doors and hid the chalice and the holy oils. The Moors burned the doors down and faced a slight girl who blocked their path with arms outstretched. Gazing up as if at some distant light, she spoke clearly to their leader, Ali ben Hassim. These were her words: "I command you, in the name of the Holy Mother Mary, to stop your sinful march." This is the way it happened: Catarina was stabbed with swords and knives and lances one hundred and twenty times from head to toe, front and back. While a breath of life lingered, she was defiled by Ali ben Hassim, who mounted her from behind as easily as he would a lamb. Two hundred years later she was canonized by Pope Sylvester III.

The church doors creaked open to let out the altar boy swinging a brass incense burner, his feet tripping over the hem of the red cassock. He was followed by two priests. One was old and gaunt with a neck like an ostrich. The younger one, short and pudgy with a red face and a bemused smile, struggled under the weight of a steamer trunk on his shoulder.

Four men in black suits bore on a wooden palanquin ringed with votive candles the life-sized plaster image of Santa Catarina, draped in purple velvet. Her lips were frozen in a smile, hair painted yellow, cheeks a bright crimson as if her last reaction to the Moor's assault had been a blush. People touched the cool velvet of her robes and crossed themselves.

One man pulled off Santa Cata's vestments, allowing them to fall at her feet. The figure had small breasts with painted rosy nipples; a hint of a womanly curve at the waist flared outward along her hips. The plaster had yellowed with the years, the body criss-crossed with fine cracks and pocked with several chinks and breaks. One of her hands was raised like a schoolgirl reciting a poem. The other hid her sex.

The fat priest let the trunk clatter to the ground, and men shuffled toward the statue. Leander felt a finger poking him in the back. "Andale," the woman whispered loudly. "It's what the men do." People made way for him to step toward the saint.

The trunk was piled with knives of all kinds—butcher cleavers, bayonets, machetes, their edges dulled and pitted with rust. One by one, the men picked out a knife or a sword. They kneeled and crossed themselves, and then stepped up to the saint and pushed their knife through one of the breaks in the plaster body.

A dozen knife-handles were already sticking out from the middle of her chest, from her stomach, hips, and breasts, when the old priest motioned for Leander to choose a bone-handled dagger. The deep silence of the crowd made him feel alone, his breath coming fast and shallow. "It will be for your good." The priest touched his shoulder and pushed him to his knees. Leander felt as if he were being dunked in a dark warm pool. "The saint forgave her killer. She will forgive you for all your life's cruelties."

The figure swam in and out of focus. Leander rose forward. The knife was heavy and unwieldy in his hand. The plaster saint loomed before him and filled the whole of his vision. Her crystal blue eyes fixed him in an unblinking stare, her painted lips smiling vacantly. He searched across her body until his eyes finally rested on her lower abdomen, where her appendix would have been, he thought to himself.

It surprised him how easily the knife sank into her belly as if the blade were new and sharp, the plaster softened, yielding to its edge. He lifted his eyes and, for an instant, saw the saint looking down on him, her eyes gaping in bewilderment, mouth open as if she were about to speak. A puddle of blood welled up at the hilt. It flowed down the groin, then narrowed to a trickle and ran along her cupped hand and down the inside of her thigh in a stream that was thin and winding like the rivers drawn on maps.

After the ceremony, groups of men meandered down the dusty streets, no longer possessed by the urgency of the fiesta, but shuffling away from the church square, clinging to the walls. Leander followed some through the red louvered doors of El Nuevo Bar Nueva York.

He stood just inside the cantina, waiting for his eyes to adjust to the dark. The Nueva York teemed with men hunkered at metal tables or standing lined up against the back wall like targets for a firing squad. Through the smoky shadows, he made out Victor Aruna pressed shoulder to shoulder among the men along the counter. He looked out of place in his crisp plaid shirt tucked into tan slacks, the shiny loafers, the sunglasses dangling from a buttonhole. The men stared down at the sweating bottles, at their own fists resting on the concrete slab of the bar. One cleared his throat and hawked noisily into the tiled trough that abutted the base of the counter.

Leander shoved his way toward Victor. "Hola, amigo, what will you drink with us?" Victor tugged at his shirtsleeve. "A ver, háganle cancha a mi cuate. Make room for my friend," he called out.

"Gracias, Victor, but we should be going." Leander forced a smile and raised his palms. "Esto no te conviene." This is not good for you.

"Oh, choor. Joo speakete espanich?" Victor put his face close to Leander's as if to read his expression. Apparently satisfied with his inspection, he leaned his head back and roared with laughter, "Una cerveza y un tequila para mi amigo."

Leander took a deep breath and forced a grin. "Okay, sí. Gracias."

Victor turned with his arm around Leander's shoulders. "Es mi mejor amigo en los United States," he announced, embracing him tighter. My very best friend.

"Mucho gusto," said a large man with an oval belt buckle cutting into the overhanging belly. He wore a cap with the legend *Jefe de Jefes* flanked by two .45's with crossed barrels. "I am The King of Santa Cata. El Rey." He waited a moment, then asked, "What is your name?"

"Paul Leander." He pronounced his name distinctly.

"*Le-anda*," the man repeated. "Ya le anda por hacer pipí? *Pol . . . Pol favol, tenk you very moch.*" The man laughed uproariously.

A Carta Blanca and a pony of tequila appeared on the counter. "I will show you how to make a submarino," the man said. "You know what is a submarino?"

Leander laughed. He mimicked a boat diving beneath the ocean.

"Yes, yes. But this submarine is better." He placed an empty mug in front of Leander. He took the slender glass of tequila between his index and middle fingers and carefully stood it inside the mug. He poured the beer around the small glass, finally letting the foamy head overflow. "Salud."

211

Leander raised the mug. "Salud."

"From all my good friends," the man said, with an expansive wave of his arm. "Not too many turistas come to Santa Cata."

"My friend Victor here loves a fiesta," Leander explained. He drank slowly until the smaller glass emptied and the burning tequila mingled with the cool, yeasty beer.

"Do you like, my submarino?" The man insisted.

"It's good," Leander said, even as another drink was placed before him.

"What else can we do for you?" the man asked.

"Nada más, gracias." Leander put up his hands. "We need to get going, verdad Victor?"

Victor shrugged. He was in no hurry.

"A smoke?" the man offered.

"No, thank you." Leander shook his head emphatically.

"A woman?" The man gripped his wrist and breathed moistly into his ear. "I can get you anything you want. Do you believe I am the King?" he insisted.

"Of course," Leander said, reading the cap. "Tú eres El Jefe de Jefes."

"Pues claro," the man nodded. "Traigan a la Niña," El Rey shouted toward the back of the room, eliciting a surge of hoots and snickers from the tight circle around the two.

Some men shifted out of the way as a confused girl, looking barely thirteen, was pushed through toward the counter. The Jefe de Jefes reached out and pulled her forward, his arm around her waist so that she was wedged between Leander and Victor.

Purple mascara shadowed her eyes, thick lipstick caked her lips, and blush spots the size of poker chips lit up her cheeks. She wore a black skirt and a red blouse with the elastic top pulled down below her shoulders. Her high-heeled shoes kept buckling under her ankles.

The man caught Leander's expression of disbelief and roared with laughter. "So what do you think of our Niña?" he demanded to know. "Very developed, verdad?"

He took the girl by the shoulders and made her turn slowly. "See, she is brand new. Say 'how are you' to the señor, niña." Victor took her hand and put it in Leander's; it was limp in his grasp.

"You want to be el primero?" he grinned at Leander.

"No," he said, finally understanding. He dropped her hand and edged away, careful not to touch her.

"She's not going to bite you," Victor coaxed. "She wants to play, that's all. See?" He embraced the girl from the back, burrowing his fingers inside the blouse's elastic neckline. Chuckling softly, as if remembering some private joke, he felt around with his fingers and finally pulled out two small balloons filled with water. "Here, for you, a fine pair of chichis!"

Leander held the quivering balloons as if they were delicate things and quickly handed them back to the girl who took them with a look of bewilderment. The Jefe took Leander's hand and pressed it flat against the girl's chest. He started to pull back, but then, feeling the gently sloping breast, he hesitated for a moment, and felt the warm skin through the thin fabric of the blouse, his fingers grazing a nipple as hard as a pebble, and underneath, the pounding of a heartbeat gone haywire. As the girl raised her hands to fend off his, the balloons rolled off and burst at her feet. A second later she was shoving her way through the crowded room; then, kicking off her high heels, she ran out through the swinging doors.

"You see what you do?" Victor pouted. "You scared away the Niña."

Leander elbowed his way through the crowd. "Jesus, Victor, she was a kid," he murmured.

Victor turned to the group and said, his voice breaking with mock sadness, "Dice que sólo es una pequeña." He made some clucking noises with his tongue that made the other men laugh again, and started out the door.

Leander was edging his way after him when the Jefe de Jefes clasped his wrist. "Qué pasó, amigo. You are not going to buy your new friends a drink?"

Nodding, he slapped down some peso bills on the counter. "I am going now, okay?" he announced. "I have to take my friend home. He is very sick."

"Adiós, Señor Le-anda." There was scattered applause as the crowd opened a path for him.

213

Leander spotted Victor down the road, sitting on the curb, knees apart, shoulders slumped, his head hanging inches from the ground. He stood off to the side and waited while Victor struggled to empty his stomach with a series of heaves.

The town seemed deserted, the bells and music having ceased, leaving only the lingering smell of gunpowder. Victor wiped the corner of his mouth with his sleeve and pushed himself up. Leander stepped in to steady him. They started down the street, its packed dirt rutted from the day's heavy traffic.

"Ya estamos borrachos, doctorcito," Victor said, his words slurring together. "Like in the old days."

Leander did not answer. He was concentrating on keeping Victor from sliding and stumbling over every bump and pothole. The central plaza in front of the church beckoned with the strand of lights still twinkling around the kiosk.

"Mira," Victor said, stumbling toward a bench. "We can take a rest, no?"

"We need to get home," Leander said. "There may still be a bus to Tijuana."

"Ay, doctorcito, all I want to do is sit down and take a siestecita."

"You can sleep on the bus, Victor."

"But I am so tired," he said. "Please, we can sit for a minute, no? I am sure the bus comes through here, the center of the town."

Leander looked down the deserted streets converging on the square, one of them leading south, the other north to Tijuana. There was not much to do but sit and wait. A bus seemed unlikely until daybreak; he would flag a ride from the first vehicle that rolled by. Beside him, Victor was nodding off, deep snores blowing into his throat and out of his open mouth. His face, normally so animated, had settled into a gaping passivity, soft and pale like tortilla dough. Dead to the world, Leander thought. He marveled that an ordinary drunken slumber could so easily mirror death and poked him in the shoulder. The sudden motion invaded a dream. Victor's eyelids flickered as if the context of his inner landscape had shifted with the simple jab in the shoulders. It took very little to change the course of consciousness. A pebble on the

214

road could cause a stumble, a change in direction, a derailing of the day's anticipated trajectory.

Leander expected Santa Catalina would have an unofficial taxi. He rummaged around Victor's pockets and pulled out a few loose bills. He had the impulse to walk away and leave him to fend for himself. He would leave him money. Victor would come to and catch a bus in the morning. He looked down on Victor's placid face, and marveled that for a drunk who knows he's under a death sentence, he seemed to be sleeping peacefully. Even if his death was not imminent, Leander did not want to give up the power which that knowledge gave him over his former friend.

"No me dejes morir aquí, doctorcito." Victor awoke suddenly, startled by Leander's pacing.

"Why not, Victor?" he said. "Isn't it the same to die in one place as another? Isn't death merely a change of skin?"

"Ay, manito," he sighed. "Cómo eres cabrón. I'm not a yogi anymore, you know."

"You were never a yogi," Leander said. "Go back to sleep. It may be hours before we see a bus."

"I dreamt that you took all my money," Victor pouted.

"That was no dream. I put most of it back in your pocket. I was trying to see whether we had enough to get a ride back to the border."

"And do we?"

"Barely. I spent most of what I had at Mi Casita paying for your fun."

Victor sighed as if enjoying the recollection of the previous night's excesses. "The party is over. Verdad? When do we go home?"

Leander checked his watch. "It's after midnight. We'll have to sit here all night."

"You were going to leave without me." He clutched Leander's sleeve.

"I thought about it," Paul said, jerking his arm back.

"Because you think I'm going to die?"

"No, because you are drunk, and I thought I could walk to the highway and catch a ride easier than if I have to drag a borrachito around." He gazed down the road, hoping to somehow cause a bus or a taxi to emerge from behind the hill.

"So you don't think I'm going to die." He seemed to be daring Leander to contradict him.

"I don't know what you're going to do, amigo."

"But the tests don't lie, verdad?"

"Well, you haven't died. You woke up."

"You sound angry with me," Victor sighed. "It's not the first time we get drunk together."

"We are not drunk together," Leander said. "But you are lucky. The only way to deal with this weird night is by getting drunk."

"Ah, yes, you could be sitting at home with your little wife, your mujercita, giving each other tongue and sipping Chardonnay."

"It doesn't help for you to bring up Adele. Makes me want to leave you here, amigo."

"Ah, you are still jealous."

"No. She slept with you to get you to help me."

"So she had to make a big sacrifice to go with me?"

"Maybe she wondered what it would be like to fuck you. That's all."

"People don't have sex out of curiosity."

"You flatter yourself. You never had any hold on her."

"I can tell you things about Adele that only you and I might know. Her lips get puffy, and that little vein on the side of her neck swells and throbs." He grinned. "Where to begin?"

"She dumped you after that night. That says something."

"I stopped seeing her because of you. I cared for you both, and I knew that I should get out of the way."

"That's unlike you, Victor. You are basically a bad person."

"I think it's an open question as to who is the worst of us."

"Go back to sleep, Victor."

"Yes. Wake me up when the bus comes. Or I die. Whichever comes first. Because, if I really, really start to die, you will be the first to know. Verdad?"

The night would not stay quiet for long. Some of the men who had been drinking at the Nueva York finally trooped out onto the street and staggered toward the plaza, vague apparitions emerging out of the fog, weaving in and out of the shadows. Two men paused in front of the bench and stared at Leander and at the motionless Victor, who had curled himself up against the night's chill. The strangers sitting on a park bench in the middle of the night in the middle of this village were an object of speculation. Everything about them—their shirttails blousing out above the waist, pants rumpled and stained with vomit and spilled drink, the fragile city shoes covered in dust—gave off the impression of tourists left behind by the sightseeing bus.

"Qué chingados hacen aquí?" the oldest asked.

"Nada," Leander shook his head sadly. "Just sitting here, waiting for a taxi. Or the bus. Whatever comes first."

"Claro, el camión," the man nodded sagely. "The bus will come before any taxi."

"Good," said Leander. "When does the camión come by here?"

"You want the bus to Tijuana. Or the bus to La Paz. They come at different times."

"We want to cross the border."

"There are two buses a day to Tijuana," the man explained patiently.

"There must be one in the morning."

"Choor," he nodded. "Always, it's late."

"Looks like we have a long wait."

"Maybe you will not have to wait so long," the man said after a long pause.

"Because the bus will come soon?"

"Ay, no, the pinche camión may not come until noon." The man thought for a moment. "If you don't mind riding in the back of my truck with these pelados here, we can take you to Tijuana."

"That's great," Leander said. "We can pay you."

"No charge. I don't want you to go back home and say to everyone that the people of Santa Catalina are all a bunch of cabrones. You think that, I know, because you saw us getting drunk. It was only for the fiesta."

"I will not say that," Leander promised.

"You will say that we are cuates, real amigos, verdad?"

217

"Amigos," Leander stood and reached out for the man's hand, which was dry and rough in his own soft palm.

When the old man arrived with his truck, they all climbed in back. Leander had to wake Victor and then, with the help of a couple of the younger men, pull him onto the truckbed. Victor tried to steady himself by leaning against the slats. He seemed confused, as if through some twilight of consciousness he could hardly understand where he was going. A damp layer of straw that smelled of livestock helped cushion the hard bounce along the road.

The truck made several stops, dropping off men at the junction of paths and dirt tracks to then disappear into the night fog.

It was morning when they reached the main highway. Its eight lanes were already backed up with traffic for half a mile leading to the inspection points, where Leander and Victor could cross on foot, then get a taxi to the parking lot on the U.S. side. Leander jumped off first and helped the still groggy Victor clamber down from the truck bed. They walked along the sidewalk until they joined the line of maids, gardeners, janitors and cooks who crossed the border every day.

An official with a jowly face punctuated by a thin mustache greeted Leander and Victor, and his expression went from unhappy boredom to a coiled hostility. These fellows, weary after a night of partying, were too old to be servicemen or frat boys.

"Ah, amigos!" the officer said with fake cheerfulness. "And where have you fellows been?"

"Just Tijuana," said Leander.

"Both U.S. citizens, I take it."

"I'm Dr. Leander." He placed his driver's license and a business card on the counter, DR. PAUL LEANDER, PATHOLOGY. "My friend Victor Aruna has been a patient at Scripps."

"Purpose of the trip?"

"He got homesick for his country. We stayed to celebrate the fiesta of Santa Cata."

"You bringing any souvenirs?"

"Just hangovers."

The man shook his head. "What's wrong with your friend?"

Victor showed a glimmer of interest in the conversation. "My friend here assures me I have advanced hepatocellular carcinoma." He said it, as someone might claim to have run a marathon or gone on a hunger strike or climbed Popocatépetl. "But as you can see, I'm not being a maricón about it."

The official stared at Leander. "So you're the guy's doctor. And you've both been on a drunk."

"A sentimental drunk," Victor added. "Somos amigos del alma." He grinned and put his arm around Leander's shoulders.

"Actually," Leander said. "I can't take all the blame for my friend's condition. We started out together. We got drunk separately. And then we joined up for the trip home."

"Is your friend going back to the hospital?"

"No. He's coming home with me."

"You've been hitting the drugstores for OxyContin?"

"No drugstores. Just bars."

"Do you mind if I bring out my dog to smell you guys? I know it's animal cruelty, but it will help me send you on your way."

"I don't mind," Leander said. "Y tú, Victor?"

"Claro que no," he said. "I am a friend of many sons of dogs."

"Good. Now if you'll step aside so I can help the people behind you move along, Grizzly will be here to get a whiff of you."

"Can I have my ID now?" Leander said.

"Come back after Grizzly sniffs you out."

In the end, the dog, a friendly grinning shepherd, was not at all interested in the two, except for some nosing around Victor's rear end, which caused them to break into laughter.

The official tapped the edge of Leander's license on the counter. "Could I see your friend's visa?"

Leander looked at Victor inquiringly.

"Ay, my passport is back in your house."

"Driver's license?"

Victor patted his pockets. "I don't know where my wallet ended up."

"Do you have anything that says you are who you say you are?" The official looked pained. "It will take thirty seconds to check through the system, as long as I have the name that goes with the guy."

"His name is Victor Aruna," Leander said. "I vouch for him."

"Welcome to the U.S., Dr. Leander," The man said, bringing the discussion to an end. "Your friend stays in Mexico."

"No, sir," Leander said. "I am this man's doctor. He needs chemo, pain management, counseling."

"Okay, you both stay in Mexico."

He slid Leander's license across the counter and waved him along impatiently. "These good people behind you have clocks to punch." He held his arm out in front of Victor. "I'm sorry, señor. Maybe your doctor friend can get your passport and come back for you."

Victor looked up at him in disbelief. "Qué la chingada, where the hell am I to go?"

The official seemed to take pains to explain the obvious, "You are Mexican. You're in Mexico."

It was already late morning and the crowd crossing into California pushed Leander past the INS inspection desks and toward the arched entrance that marked official American territory. Leander called to Victor, "Nos vemos en Sanborns. Tonight, around 7:00." That part was like old days. Sanborns with its ubiquitous locations and decent coffee had been a natural meeting place in Mexico City. The one in Tijuana was a convenient place to store Victor until he decided what to do with him.

"It's okay, amigo," Victor called out as Leander was swept forward in the line. "You know I'm not going to die before we meet again." It was the last thing he heard him say.

❖ 31 ❖

As Leander left behind the congestion of trucks and buses at the border, he felt a growing relief from a weight dating back twenty years. He believed that the bad current between him and Victor had, to some extent, been neutralized. A retribution of nearly mathematical balance had been exacted. He expected that, as the realization settled in his mind, he would find some small satisfaction in its curious justice. The past, while not expunged, could be distanced to hover motionless like film frozen in mid-frame.

By the time he pulled off the freeway and started toward the winding road that climbed the fresh green hills overlooking the ocean, he'd decided he wouldn't make his date with Victor. He pictured him waiting for hours at the Sanborns lunch counter, stirring a cold cup of coffee, glancing at the clock on the wall, a vigilant eye on the entrance to the restaurant. Eventually, he'd know that Leander would not show up.

He dismissed a pang of remorse at having misled Victor by reassuring himself that he had actually done the man a good turn: The prospect of imminent death, a measure of pain and fear would make his friend a better human being, all the more sincere a transformation because Victor had never realized he was being punished. How long would it take before he figured out that he'd been the unwitting player in a one-sided game of Leander's devising? Victor would curse him for lying to him and leading him so close to death that the only thing separating his cranked-up mind from his body's final breath was a small lie. The international border and a cadre of INS officials lay reassuringly between them.

It's not given to every man to experience imminent death without having to go through it. Fear was a small price for the ecstasy of life reclaimed. There was something cathartic in the mock execution, the empty pistol's click. Leander believed himself off the karmic hook, the means redeemed by the end. He had fulfilled a higher function, and therefore, he would in turn be forgiven as well. He had played inquisitor for the good of Victor's soul. The deception would be another shared secret that bound them to each other, locked in their minds along with the weeks Leander spent in the Mexican prison. Only Victor could fathom the cruelty that Leander was capable of. It was a gift he had managed to inhibit for most of his life. Such an odd talent, he realized, of dubious benefit to the world. However, in the case of Victor Aruna, the pain artist had helped cleanse the man's soul. With any luck, there would be repentance, reconciliation, restitution: the three Rs of salvation. And none of that would have happened without Leander's elegant mischief.

By the time Paul let himself into his house, Victor Aruna was already four hours in the past. Leander wouldn't mind if another twenty-five years went by before he saw him again. The house breathed a new freedom. The weight of the awkward, unhappy visitor had been lifted.

He kicked through the pile of mail that lay scattered by the door, pushing out of the way the catalogs and commercial pitches that had spilled in through the mail slot. His eye was drawn to two identical white envelopes, pristine in their institutional gravity with the muted Scripps Memorial logo, one addressed to him, the other to Victor Aruna. He slit one open and stared, initially uncomprehending, at a letter directed to Victor and stamped Copy. As he read it quickly, gradually guessing its contents, he folded the other envelope into thirds and stuffed it into his pocket. He felt momentary relief at having intercepted the letter:

Dear Mr. Aruna,

In confirmation of our phone conversation of two days ago, this letter contains an apology. It also bears good news. As I said to you, during the pathology analysis following your liver biopsy of May 16, an error occurred in the identification of the various samples. We don't understand how this happened, but

222

the net result is that a false positive showing advanced hepato-
cellular carcinoma was mistakenly attributed to your case. You
don't have cancer. A subsequent analysis of your sample liver
tissue exhibits a definite hardening of the organ which gives cause
for concern. Blood analysis does show evidence of hepatitis B,
which accounts for the symptoms that originally brought you
under our care. In any case, accept my apology for the stress and
anxiety this mixup has caused you. Please call for an appointment
at your earliest convenience so that we may further discuss your
options and determine a course of treatment.

> *Sincerely,*
> *Mark Manning, M.D.*

cc: Dr. Paul Leander, Pathology
> *Patient file*

Leander had a sense of foreboding as he walked along the hallway
pausing before the closed door of Victor's room. He nearly
expected to hear the sound of his voice on the phone. The letter in
his hand caused the house to swell again with Victor's presence.
He sensed that in the days and months and years ahead Victor
would continue to disrupt his fragile hold on the predictable
career, the stable marriage, the occasional desperate adventure. All
the time, throughout their escapade in Mexico, Victor had known
that he was not the hopeless terminal case Leander had made him
out to be. His expected response had been to celebrate in a brothel
until his money had run out. Leander marveled that Victor had
been able to hide his knowledge of Leander's deception, had probably found humor in Leander's posturing.

The room was as Victor had left it, his clothes neatly folded in
the drawer Adele had cleared for him. Leander reached under the
bed and pulled out the candy box full of photos that Victor had
been sorting through. Occasionally he had plucked one out to
show to Paul and Adele, the three of them sitting at a café table or
at the beach, Adele peering from behind her huge sunglasses.
"Miren," he would rush in exclaiming. "Weren't we the fine-
looking ones." Now, Paul sifted through the hundreds of slippery
snapshots until his fingers, as if drawn by a kind of heat, picked

out several he had noted during his previous search through Victor's memory trove. He pocketed them with barely a glance, and slid the box back into its hiding place.

He walked into the study and quickly checked the answering machine, his pager, the caller ID screen on his phone. A number he didn't recognize with a 212 area code appeared half a dozen times on the tiny screen. He guessed Adele was in a hotel in New York, but she hadn't left a message. There were no other calls, no work emergencies, no calls from Beth Moreau. After often besieging him with calls and e-mails, in less than twenty-four hours the world was eerily revolving without him.

His laptop was on sleep, its pilot light pulsing softly. He raised the screen and clicked on the mail icon. He expected the blinking to signal a message from Adele with some idea of her plans. Instead, the solitary note was from the head of pathology at Scripps Memorial:

—Subject: My First Patient—

—a weird joke? please explain . . . —

—BF—

Bob Fletcher was nominally his manager, but the two had little interaction, except for occasionally abrasive department meetings. Leander didn't recollect having sent any messages to him, much less jokes. He opened his mail log and there, at the top of the list, dated two nights before, was a message sent from his account, under the subject heading *My First Patient*. The distribution list showed that it had gone to about a hundred names in his directory, ranging from his Christmas card list to most of the senior medical staff at Scripps to various publishers and professional associations in his field. Included in the distribution were Adele at work, Beth Moreau at her personal address, and, of course, Fletcher.

Leander opened his message. There was the slow downward scrolling of a color photo, which Victor had scanned onto the e-mail, revealing first a wall with peeling plaster, then the top of Leander's head, and soon his face, and finally the full shot of him standing next to a naked man, arms and chest strapped to a metal chair. Leander was wearing the white coat from his University days. His hands were on the man's head and face, tilting it toward him as if to examine it. The burst of the flash had caught Leander looking up startled. There was no text beyond the odd subject heading—*my first patient*. Leander felt a sour thread burn up his throat and fill his mouth. The picture had been taken twenty years ago during his stay in the prison.

❧ 32 ❧

When Leander walked into the room they called La Oficina he'd felt like an actor onstage joining a scene he had not rehearsed. The guard who'd been sitting outside the door stood up, leaving on his chair the scattered pages of a newspaper. "Aquí está el doctor." He knocked and waited for someone to acknowledge their presence.

The door opened a crack and a slight man in tan slacks and a bomber jacket stepped out. He made sure to shut the door behind him. He was sweating but seemed to take pride in the leather coat. "Good to see you again," he said, reaching out to shake Leander's hand. He removed his sunglasses and tightened his grip as if to reassure Leander.

Leander mumbled the obligatory, "Sí, mucho gusto," then pulled his hand back.

"It is unfortunate that you have become mixed up in this situation, doctor. We did not mean to frighten you back in Puerto Vallarta, but the operation was very delicate, and then it turned unpleasant. The problem is we are not finished."

"I am here because I was invited to some party?" Leander asked.

"Qué pinche suerte, verdad?" Such luck.

"My friend Victor Aruna will assure you that we did not know anything beyond that there was a party going on."

"Licenciado Aruna is of little use." He put his sunglasses back on. "But you can help us, doctor."

"I'm here to translate?"

"We are at this moment talking to a man who knows where Reginio is. You see, it's very important that we find him, because

226

it is our duty to eradicate the traffic of narcotics between our two countries. We must resort to all means to end these evil drugs that hurt your American children in the very schools and playgrounds where their parents think they are safe." He took a breath as if pausing from a well prepared speech. "It seems that the man we are talking to may need the attention of a doctor." Cueto attempted a dry, tight-lipped smile.

"I don't know what you're asking."

"You have taken your oath of Hippocrates, have you not?" He did not wait for an answer. "So, doctor, come inside with me."

Leander had learned in the past few days not to question authority. He felt the captain's fingers digging into his back as he ushered him into the room. A half-dozen men in the unofficial judicial uniform of leather jackets and tan slacks lounged around, perched on the edge of a table or on stools leaning against the wall. The air was heavy with the smells of a body losing control. The men, appearing to stand randomly, were actually surrounding a slumping, naked figure sitting on a chair made of iron pipes, its tubular back and armrests joined with globs of hardened solder.

"Your patient, doctor." The captain introduced the nude man with a flick of his fingers. He was soaking wet, his head slumped forward, hair plastered down, pinkish mucus dripping from his nose and chin, water puddling up around the chair. His skin was brown, the flesh underneath loose and flabby, and a protruding belly as big as a soccer ball fell over his genitals and seemed about to roll over onto his lap. His forearms were pressed flat on the armrests, bound at the wrist with electrical cord. A leather belt was strapped around his forehead, the end dangling down to his shoulders.

Leander stood stiffly. "What happened to him?"

The captain shook his head sadly. "It is most unusual. We were having a conversation and then he just seemed to go to sleep."

"You've been hurting him."

"No, señor," the captain said, putting his hand over his heart. "I assure you, we have taken great care to avoid any injury."

"What do you want me to do?"

The man laughed suddenly. "You are the doctor, joven. Take his pulse or something. Wake him up. We have not finished our conversation with him."

"I'm sorry," he muttered so that only the captain could hear. "I can't be a part of this."

"I thought we had an agreement, that you help us out. Until your case gets resolved, of course," the captain said, shaking his head in confusion. "Really, you are enjoying your privacy, no?"

Leander almost laughed as a refrain rang in his head: *Dance with who brought you, or you don't dance at all.* He yielded to the captain's grip on his arm guiding him firmly to the center of the room. A heavy stink surrounded the seated man's every breath. "Con confianza," the captain said. "He is not going to bite." He prodded the slumped figure as if to jar him awake. "Here is your doctor, Panchito. To take care of you."

Leander stepped closer; an empty Tehuacán bottle clattered along the floor. He looked down and sidestepped several bottles half-filled with mineral water near the chair. On a table nearby were a portable cassette recorder and some Tabasco sauce. "Loosen his arm so I can take his blood pressure," he said.

"I can't do that," the captain said. "He is extremely aggressive. Twice he has attempted to kill us."

Leander tipped the man's head back and pulled open one of his eyelids. The face felt cold and clammy. "I need his arm free."

"He is a criminal," the captain explained.

"He's probably in shock," Leander said. "He's not going anywhere."

The captain nodded to another man who stepped closer, gingerly, as if dealing with someone who could explode in a sudden rage. He undid the knots. The man's right arm dropped limply to his side. Leander knelt beside him and pulled the cuff snug around the biceps.

"Somebody bring a chair for the doctor," the captain ordered. A man got off his stool and pushed it toward Leander.

"How about a little light?" Leander snapped. He squeezed the bulb to inflate the cuff. "I can't see the numbers." He watched the gauge move as the cuff swelled, then loosened with the released air.

He heard the first click, the unmistakable snap of a camera shutter, and the instant of a bright light. First once, then a pause,

228

then twice more, flashing at him in quick succession. Leander found himself staring dumbly into Adele's little Minolta. The captain lowered the camera and smiled. "Don't let me distract you, doctorcito. Continue."

"Why did you take my picture?"

"For the album of your girlfriend." He continued snapping pictures in the windowless room, hardly pointing, blinding everyone with the repeated flash bursts. He aimed the camera again at Leander while he was bending over the naked man; he held the camera steady for a moment, then clicked the shutter. At the moment of the photo, Leander had been holding up the man's head, pulling down his lower eyelid and shining a penlight into the iris. The man's eyes bulged with fear.

"No more. No fucking more."

Leander stood to one side until the captain nodded contritely and handed the camera to a guard hovering nearby. "Shall we get back to work?" he said.

After that first time, there was always the black medical bag on the table in the interrogation room. It contained a stethoscope and a blood pressure gauge, and Leander was asked if there was anything else he might need—an assortment of bandages, popper inhalants, a disposable hypodermic, a vial of adrenaline.

"What am I supposed to do with all this?"

"You may want to give them a little help."

"I'm sure the judicial can call an ambulance if someone's hurt," Leander said.

"We don't expect to need an ambulance, doctorcito," Cueto laughed. "How serious that would be."

"So this equipment is not for a medical emergency."

"More like reassurance," Cueto said. "The white coat helps."

"You want me in a white coat?"

"Yes, we like the white coat very much," he said.

Leander pumped up the cuff again. The man's pulse was racing at 140 and his blood pressure was 204/118. He had opened his eyes and stared at Leander, smiling tentatively, as if believing that he'd been somehow delivered into the hands of a medical savior.

"Look," said the captain. "Your patient is glad to see you. He feels better already, verdad, Panchito?"

Leander loosened the cuff. "He's under stress."

"Is he having a medical problem?" the captain asked.

Leander shrugged. "His blood pressure will go back to normal once you lay off him."

"Do you have something to give him?"

"He needs to rest."

"I mean if he starts to die."

"He probably won't die."

"You hear that, Panchito?" the captain smiled. "Good news from the doctor. We don't want you to die. We want to continue our conversation." Then he turned toward Leander as he stepped back from the man in the chair. "You can sit outside and we'll call you when we need you to take another look."

"I can't be part of torture," he blurted.

"You are insulting me," the captain said blandly. "You are insulting my men. We do not practice torture. Do you see bruises or burns on Panchito?" He raised the man's head for Leander to see. "His face is as smooth as a girl's. Do you see any cattle prods or electrodes around? No. I will show you our method. And then you can tell me whether it's torture or not."

"I don't want to see," Leander insisted. "Please."

"My friend, you have offended the Mexican Judicial Police. Torture is what Secretaría de Gobernación, the interior ministry, does with political subversives. They use electroshock and beatings. They are brutes," the captain explained, as if exercising great patience with a slow student. "You will see how we ask our questions of Panchito. Then you will apologize to me and my men. Entendido?"

He paused and stared at Leander, silently pressing for an answer to his question until Cueto forced him to nod reluctantly.

"Very well, then," the captain continued. "We are in a contest here, Panchito and me. I want him to tell me dates, places, names that he knows. Mainly, I want to know where his jefe Reginio is. He does not want to tell me this information, for many logical reasons. For one, if he tells me, and we let him go with our thanks, then Reginio will have him killed. If he refuses to say anything, then he will end up in prison. So, he will lie and hope that I believe him long enough for him to get away. See? It's a contest. This contest is part of his profession as a drug trafficker and part of my profession as a judicial. We are two professionals in a contest. Right now, I have the upper hand. But other times, he has earned millions of dollars by outsmarting me. When I retire in thirty years I will not have earned one hundredth of what he gets in a year. You see that life is not fair."

Leander removed the cuff from the man's arm and stuffed it back into the bag. He stood, waiting for Cueto to finish his speech. The captain continued lecturing him. "The method we use is carefully measured to provide some pain but to cause no injury. Pain is useful. We use not too much and not too little. Panchito knows that he is not being damaged in a physical way; verdad, Panchito?" Then, turning toward Leander, he added softly, "His head will feel like it's on fire, and his lungs like he's breathing needles. But that is not the reality. No fire, no needles or electric shocks, only a spray of fizzy water with chile sauce. Very innocent, el tehuacanazo, no?"

A man wearing a Texas Rangers baseball cap and a thin mustache, well trimmed and delicate within the large puffy face, stepped up to the table, interlaced his fingers, and stretched lazily.

"This is Teniente Julio, our técnico en interrogación. He is a graduate of the School of the Americas in Fort Benning, Georgia, U.S. of A." Julio acknowledged the introduction with a modest nod; he would not be distracted by social niceties. He popped open the cap from a new bottle of mineral water to make sure the carbonation was at full power. He shook some Tabasco, turning the mixture a faint red.

"Panchito," the captain began formally. "I know you want to tell us where Reginio is. But first I must let you have a little Tehuacán. Not to hurt you, but to remind you that we know how to use it. And that we recognize lies when we hear them. And to give our doctorcito a demonstration of our technique. So, you don't mind taking part in a demonstration?"

"Por favorcito, mi capitán," the man in the chair pleaded. "Ya no quiero Tehuacán."

"Poquito nada más," the captain smiled. "With a little chile. After all, we Mexicans like our chilitos, verdad? You're a macho,

231

not a marica. You must show the doctorcito how macho we mexicanos are."

"No, mi capitán," the man sobbed. "No soy macho. Soy marica. I've already told you the pure truth."

"That Reginio is in the ranch of his mother in La Primavera? That he is holed up with some putas in the penthouse of the Hotel Presidente? That he was having lunch at El Caballo Bayo, but left twenty minutes before we arrived?" The captain sighed. "I need today's truth. Not yesterday's. In which bed will Reginio wake up in the morning?"

"Mi capitán, I am not so important that Reginio would tell me where he was going. I think he might be with his mamacita. Or with his novia. O quién sabe . . ."

The captain appeared distracted, as if absently considering what the man in the chair was saying. He began to whistle softly. It was the sinuous musical theme rising in a spiral that Leander had heard outside his room in Puerto Vallarta. The Lark Ascending. He nodded a signal to the man in the baseball cap who quickly stepped behind the chair. He pulled on the strap around Panchito's forehead and wrapped it around the top of the chairback so that the face was raised and held rigid. He put his thumb over the bottle's mouth and shook it. He pushed it under Panchito's nostrils and shifted his thumb so that the carbonated water exploded high up into the sinuses. The initial searing pain would be followed by the sensation of drowning. The man struggled against his bindings; he stamped his feet and let out a high wailing cry. He kept gasping and trying to cough up the water that was gushing down his windpipe.

Leander slinked toward the door and walked out into the hallway. The guard, hardly glancing up from his newspaper, raised his foot. "Capitán says you wait here." He pointed at a chair opposite him.

Leander sat stiffly as a chastened schoolboy. He was attentive to the sounds coming from the other side of the door. Sometimes the questioning would rest for several minutes and there would be scattered conversation among the men. Someone would make a joke, and the others would laugh.

232

After a period without screams, Leander was brought back in. The judiciales drifted about. They drank coffee, smoked cigarettes, munched on potato chips. The man in the chair had been granted a rest. Though still tied up, the binds were loosened and he was allowed a couple of sips of brandy Presidente. Cueto personally lifted a glass to the man's lips. He blotted the dripping head and face with a towel, like a manager at a fighter's corner, whispering advice, encouragement, and always whistling, sometimes a cheerful melody, but usually coming back to the melancholy refrain of the Lark. He stood back, his lips pursed silently, while Leander pressed a stethoscope to the man's chest.

"This is not the same guy as before," Leander said. He peered into the eyes under the beam of a penlight.

"They are different men," the captain admitted. "But they are also all the same. Basura. Garbage."

"What happened to the other fellow?"

The captain looked puzzled, as if he had long forgotten about him. "We sent him home."

"You are not worried about him telling what happened here?"

The captain gazed at Leander with bemusement. "*What* happened here?"

"Me for one," Leander murmured. The description of a young American doctor helping out the judiciales spreading through the narco world chilled him.

"Yes, we've all had to work very hard to complete our investigation."

"He told you what you wanted?"

The captain dismissed any thought of him with a wave of his fingers. "He did not know anything. Just a pendejo."

"Is this new guy telling you anything?"

The captain did his customary slow raising of the shoulders, indicating that the world was complicated. "We won't know until we ask, verdad?"

The interrogations went on through the night. After a couple of sessions, Leander no longer bothered to wait in the hallway. He stood in a corner of the room, picking at the snacks they kept bringing in. Occasionally, the onlookers would borrow the bottle of Tabasco to splash it directly into a bag of chips. Sometimes the chair would be in darkness and the screams would take on a disembodied quality. They would turn the lights on long enough for Leander to do his examination. He would listen intently for the smallest breath. The blood pressure was high. The pulse racing. He went through the motions, pressing the scope against the man's dripping chest, inflating and releasing the air in the cuff with hardly a glance at the gauge. Leander realized his presence was unsettling the fellow being interrogated, to have his long systematic misery under medical supervision. The guy in the chair would not be allowed to die, but be released and left to explain that he was not a snitch. Reginio would be skeptical; the judiciales would not readily free someone, except as a reward.

Leander wanted to shut up the men's whimpers as he was examining them. Surely there would be an end to guys in the iron chair, to be the star of the show, as the captain put it. El heroe de la aventura. El muchacho chicho de la película gacha. When he wasn't whistling, Cueto was making little jokes for his men. They passed around the Sabritas chips, and drank brandy and Coke to stay awake. The carbonated water was reserved for work.

Toward dawn, the captain shouted "el que sigue" for the next candidate, and the guard announced that there was no one left. The long night of questioning had yielded little information. The process had become a numbing chore, the screams from the hot seat hardly more than an irritation. Cueto asked the time and someone said it was nearly six in the morning. He allowed himself a wide open yawn.

A couple of judiciales had been entrusted by their colleagues to fill a paper bag with wallets, watches, heavy gold chains and big rings confiscated from the suspects. One of them emptied the paper sack on the table for the captain to distribute. Leander was heading for the door when Cueto called him back. "Doctorcito," he said. "You should have a souvenir of your contribution to the war on drugs."

"No, I don't need anything," Leander said, lifting both hands, continuing to back out of the room.

The captain smiled. "You will not show contempt for my gift, will you?" The captain ran his fingers through the pile and chose a heavy gold medallion of the Virgen de Guadalupe on a thick chain. "Here you are," he said. "The holiest saint for Mexicans. She will protect you."

"Like she took care of the previous owner?"

"Aha!" The captain went along with the irony. "Good question. Maybe he was colombiano."

"Then I don't think she will help me."

"She protects the deserving. Take it," he ordered.

The captain held Leander's wrist as he was about to put the medallion inside his pocket. "Wear it, like you're proud of it. Como los narcos." Leander slipped the chain over his head, and tucked the heavy medallion inside his shirt where it rested warmly against his skin.

Now, staring dumbly at pictures on the computer screen, Leander realized that a hundred details of those sessions remained lodged in his memory, even though he'd seldom known more about the man in the chair than a first name and a vague sense of the questioning. After that first night, he was called to assist with increasing frequency. He would be brought out from his cell, still dazed from the sudden awakening, his white jacket draped over his shoulder and marched to La Oficina. The man being interrogated never got any medical care, but the medical bag would be on the small table beside the chair. Leander's presence, and the props in his hands, reassured the subject that the pain would not get out of control.

⚜ 33 ⚜

This particular moment on the screen took on a sharp focus in his memory. He had marveled that a grown man could whimper like an infant or yelp like a small dog. He recalled him being about fifty, dripping wet from the latticework of hair on top of his skull to the undershirt clinging to his breasts and protruding belly.

In the three pictures Leander was clearly identifiable, even with his hair long, needing a shave, his clothes disheveled under the wrinkled white coat. With the press of a *Send* button, the image had metastasized into a hundred cancerous cells, its devastation simultaneous, irretrievable, unexplainable.

He stared at the pictures, unable to allow himself the double-click that would vanish the whole thing, as if this revelation of the real Paul Leander had never happened. It had sprung up on its own, out of some rare ether, and found its way in equal measure to some nearly forgotten acquaintances from a Caribbean cruise eight years ago, to his colleagues in the State Association of Pathologists, to an editor at the *AMA Journal* and even to some one-time poker buddies in San Francisco.

He imagined the quizzical frowns at the familiar name as the sender of the e-mail, and then recognition of the young doctor's face, and finally, the slow confusion, the wondering and then the revulsion, realizing that all the sympathy one could feel for the shamed colleague did not erase the awful reality being brought to light after so many years.

Leander scrambled for an appropriate response. He wanted to believe that there were things he could do to minimize the damage.

Truth alert. Explanations. Exculpations. Rationalizations. There was a reason for everything. Things were not as they seemed. The photos had been staged, altered, concocted by some insidious prankster. Threats and blackmail and lies were being wielded against him. He could erase the original file and claim to have known nothing of the message, feign ignorance at Bob Fletcher's request for an explanation, at Adele's shock when she finally confronted him, at Beth's distance when he showed up at the lab the next day.

The smartest thing might be to do nothing. Wait a few days, then assert that he'd been the victim of some hacker's invasion of his e-mail list, his face singled out by some elaborate virus. Even if not widely believed, his denials would let everyone move on.

Bob Fletcher would charitably accept any coherent explanation and not pursue professional censure; they would continue to be wary and cool toward each other. Adele would be understanding. Even without knowing the details of his imprisonment, she had sensed how disturbing the experience had been. She had offered to listen if he ever felt like talking. Some day, he said, once he had figured out what exactly had made him do the things he had done. What things? Things to help him get by. You look out for yourself in places like that, he had explained. You are turned into a different person.

He wondered how much he'd changed once he was free from the threats and pressures of the situation. He brightened the screen and tried to understand the odds of his being the same man as the youth in the photos. He'd been startled by the flash, but not foreseeing the ramifications of the moment, his face showed irritation rather than concern. He searched for the resolve to erase the evidence; dragging the document toward the trash felt like self-destruction. Even now, he was aware of the connection that had remained in force through time. He would always be guilty of the surprising cruelty he had discovered in himself. Through some wrinkle in his soul he derived pleasure at the sight of pain. There was nothing erotic in what he felt. A surge of energy rose from deep within his mind and transformed itself into a physical tremor that began in his breath and found its way to the tips of his fingers.

During the interrogation sessions, he had wanted to touch the men in the chair, to lay his hands on their head or their shoulders, perhaps flat on their torso. Not to ease the pain, but to understand it. As if the suffering itself could only be appreciated by touching it. This was not an impulse he would encourage in himself. After medical school he had avoided contact with actual, suffering patients. The agitation had to be stilled as too shameful to be indulged.

The pain and fear he had so directly caused Victor Aruna in the past few days had been empty of emotion. Watching Victor face his imminent rotting with cancer had been a cool, dispassionate exercise. Victor's retribution was his just due. Their destinies had been locked over time, an exchange of cruelties that seemed predetermined.

Knowing that Victor now realized how skillfully he'd been tormented was a bonus. Hour after hour, Paul had managed to guide the flow of conversation, the innocent question, the vague non sequitur, in such a way that Victor would be constantly reminded that he was dying. Three weeks of measured anguish had been abruptly resolved. Deliverance had come for Victor in a brief phone chat with his oncologist. He was free to live.

Leander wondered if anyone could be so detached from life that they were free to die. He lay down on the bed, hands folded over his belly, letting the exhaustion of the past two days seep out of his skin and trickle down his groin and legs and escape through his toes. As his body settled, his mind anticipated facing the following morning as a pariah physician, torturer of helpless drug traffickers and gun smugglers. In truth, it had not been so difficult to stand by while arrogant thugs were turned into whining victims of systematic interrogation techniques. There was something satisfying, he realized, in seeing the typical drug dandy in his lizardskin boots, leather pants and silk shirts start out with curses and threats and end up yowling, naked and steaming in his own piss. In ninety percent of the cases, the Capitán took great effort to reassure him that the timely collection of names and places resulted in fewer lives lost, in the containment of the drug dealing that was devastating America's neighborhoods. He had accepted Cueto's reasoning that pain, for these men, was the price of doing business. Telling what they knew was a way to set things aright against the bosses who put them at risk.

Leander punched the password in his voice mail and heard Adele's voice, somewhat muffled as if careful not to be overheard.

"My God, Paul," she said, her voice choked from weeping. "What have you gone through? Are you okay? Why would Victor do this to you?" She added, "To us?"

He thought of calling the Plaza. With the time difference it would be past midnight in New York but Adele would still be awake. He would say to her that he was tired, exhausted actually. Not up to having much of a conversation. Yet he wanted her to know that he was fine, back in the house, alone, coming to terms with what had happened.

The earlier rage had dissolved into lethargy; he could put off the call till morning, when talking would not seem such a big effort. He yawned as he set the phone down.

The ordinary sounds of the house seemed louder in the night. The air conditioning blew on and off, rattling the ducts, making the vents vibrate. He switched off the thermostat; the fan stopped. Then his ears picked out a variety of hums and buzzes that swirled about him like mosquitoes. The room soon felt warm; he threw off his shirt and pants and lay back with a sigh. The windows were open, but there was only the faintest breeze to cool his skin.

Feeling restless, he padded to the kitchen and pulled the plugs on the refrigerator and the electric wall clock. For good measure he went on a purge of electrical devices, disconnecting radios, the TV, the toaster, the stove, every phone and pager, and the computer.

Yearning for the deliverance that would come with sleep, he searched his bathroom for the proper supply of Klonopin to put him away until the stark morning. Then he remembered that Victor had been gobbling sleep meds every night, in the process clearing out his and Adele's supply. One last nasty trick.

A nightcap might do the job as well. He emerged from the living room with a crystal snifter and a bottle of cognac and went out to the terrace. He poured generously, admiring the liquor's silky tracks inside the glass and the starry sky glinting gold through the brandy. He leaned back in the recliner and let the night air evaporate the sheen of perspiration on his skin.

He closed his eyes and sharpened the resolve that was taking hold in his mind. He would not get drunk. The numbness that had dulled his soul for twenty years was to be thawed. He would stay awake, all night if necessary, and with the cognac's help, search out the thickness in his heart and soften it through his attention. He would rummage through the cobwebs and the forgotten crannies of his mind until the reality of his character became so familiar that he would examine its pain. He watched as the moon rose to cast a silvery glow on the flat stone of the patio, painting his body in a cool light, his thighs and belly lax and heavy on the recliner. From the first sensation of warmth there was a pounding in his chest, a kind of anticipation, as if he were lighting up a hidden corner for the first time in his life, feeling both agitated and deeply calm at the same time, reconciled to a fate that he had avoided for the better part of his life. The confusion of the past few hours was giving way and the thoughts that had crowded his mind were dimming, the screams quieting down, so that the only thing that seemed to exist then was the brandy soothing the knot in his chest.

The snap of the front door latch, sharp and metallic in the silent house, startled him. He hardly dared to imagine that Victor had been able to walk across the border and then taken the commuter bus to San Ysidro. There was still a suitcase with his new clothes, an attaché case, the candy box full of snapshots scattered over the bed in the guest room. The other reason for Victor to return would be for him to get a close look at the effects of Leander's exposure. He would want to gloat.

Leander steeled himself for a confrontation. He would tell Victor to leave. He could push him out the door, yell for the neighbor's attention, even use the bottle of expensive liquor as a club. At the sound of footsteps across the foyer, his fingers clenched around the cusp of the brandy glass and its thin walls shattered in his hand. He tightened his fist and felt as if he were holding hot cinders.

He waited for the rustle of clothes, the sound of labored breathing which would signal the intruder's approach. His hearing quickened to where he could make out the distant rumble of traffic, the chatter from a neighbor's TV, the music from some boombox down by the breakers. He felt oddly disconnected from the rest of the world. The cuts were stinging now in frantic alarm. Blood seeped out from between his fingers and dripped on the tile floor. He opened his hand and poured brandy over the splinters that had dug into the palm.

He had been waiting for Victor to appear on the terrace, for the heavy steps, the familiar voice. He was surprised to feel from out of the stillness a cool hand resting firmly on his shoulder. Adele was standing behind him, her familiar scent reassuring him.

"My God, what have you done to yourself?" She walked around him and held up his hand to the faint light from the adjacent room.

"Adele."

"You're bleeding."

"I don't know my own strength." The relief he felt at hearing her voice helped him try to laugh off his predicament. "The glass broke in my hand." He pushed himself up from the recliner, and stood a few inches from her as if too shy to touch her. "God, yes, Adele," he finally breathed out. She started to reach for his arm, but he held her still. "Just stay like that for a bit. I can't get enough of looking at you."

"We need to take care of your hand," she said briskly, holding it up by the wrist to the faint light from inside the house. "Let me clean out the mess."

A moment later they were in the kitchen, Adele holding Leander's hand over the sink. She parted his fingers so that the palm was stretched under the hard spray from the faucet. She shook dish soap from a detergent bottle and rubbed a stiff brush hard on the tender skin, the water running pink at first until the hand was clean. "Am I doing this right?" she asked. "You can supervise, you know. You're the doctor.

"It burns," he said with a tight smile.

"It's a good way to dislodge all these bits of glass. They're so tiny, I can hardly see them."

"I can feel every one."

When she had dried his hand and wrapped it in a clean white towel, and they were sitting now facing each other in the brightly lit living room, she tried to joke about her nursing talents.

"You're the tough-love kind of nurse," he smiled, pressing the towel against his hand. "They're the best."

"It's the first time you've let me get close enough to give you any kind of love. We haven't talked much during our whole life together. Are we going to, finally?"

"God, Adele, it's what we need to do."

"Why didn't you ever tell me what you had gone through in Mexico?"

"You've seen the photos."

"Yes, God, yes," she sighed. "For a couple of seconds, anyway."

"Look at them for a bit longer," he said. "You'll know why I never wanted to think about that time."

"I can't believe Victor knew about all this," she said. "You must hate him."

"That's the problem. I've been wanting to see him dead for years." He paused, as if considering the shame of yet another confession. "I finally got my chance."

"You're not responsible for the state of his liver."

"Oh," he started in lazily. "His liver is not in such bad shape. Not in good shape, but not so sick that he was going to die anytime soon."

"You've been telling him he's dying for weeks."

"Yes, well, I was going to tell him that he was all right, you know," he paused again, "until his oncologist beat me with the good news."

She nodded as if finally coming to some understanding that had been eluding her. "You were eager to let him stay with us."

"Not at first," he said. "But in time I grew to enjoy watching him squirm. It became a game. I didn't realize how badly I had wanted to get back at him."

He waited for Adele to say something, but he found himself facing a dense silence from her. He was relieved that she continued to meet his gaze, that she had not yet judged him. The full weight of his retribution seemed to be dawning on her only gradually. He could not guess what her ultimate judgement would be. After all, she had in the past few weeks expressed her distaste for Victor's presence in their home, had made a point of traveling, staying late at the agency, finding excuses to be away. He gave her a chance to collect her thoughts. He would hold on to the contact as long as she didn't look away.

He broke the silence. "You see," he said, finally. "I'm not so far from the guy in the pictures. Seeing a thug brought to a state of abject gratitude at the sight of a guy in a white coat gave me a taste of power that grew alluring with repetition. You didn't know that about me."

"I knew you," she said impatiently. "I was in love with you."

"I'm not the man you think you know."

"I haven't known you for years, then."

"This is the part where you say you love me anyway."

"Will you feel better if I say that?"

"I'm not sure I'm entitled to love."

"Darling, I'm here with you. We're talking."

"It's a start."

"You will carry on with your life." She said in a tone that brooked no disagreement.

"I've been numb, Adele. Not a healthy response, but numb has been quite the bearable condition." He said this with some satisfaction. To be numb was to hold remorse at bay, to intercept and neutralize it and take off its edge. He'd had a knack for numbness, a talent for blotting out memory, a myopia for self observation, a deafness for the inner screams of conscience. He could die numb and not even know it. The numbness allowed the corruption to continue eating at his soul. "I never thought I'd have to let you into this particular warp in my character. I shouldn't expect you carry on as before, can I?"

They lay together finally on the bed, naked over the covers, feeling the pleasant chill from air conditioning starting to blow through the room. He was curled up on to himself, and she had curved her body to hold him against her breast and belly and thighs. He found himself feeling profoundly happy, as if the floodgates of his love for Adele had suddenly opened up, and the whole of his body shuddered with relief. She felt the tremor of his muscles under the skin and tightened her embrace. The renewed strength of her love was like a wall surrounding his newly acknowledged fragility.

Early the following morning he would take a long soak in the bathtub and lather up with sage soap and massage lotion on himself and comb his hair with sweet lavender tonic. He would pat his hand dry with a soft towel, protect it under a clean bandage, and drive to work with the top down, letting the crisp morning air buffet his face into a serene expression. With each look and uttered word, the practice of equanimity would take on the gravity of a higher calling. He would walk calmly into a wall of silence at the lab. He would learn to conduct himself with composure through the silent chorus of shame and derision from his colleagues. He would own his punishment, and understand it, and cherish it. And every day, he would be poised for Victor to return. Victor would not die until he had seen the proof of his triumph. What he would face instead would be the fortress he and Adele had begun to build around themselves.

* * *

❧ ACKNOWLEDGEMENTS ❧

From the start, the writing of this novel led me into hidden corners of the human spirit. As questions arose, I'm grateful to those who offered answers, often painful and unsettling. David Weissbrodt at the University of Minnesota Law School generously made available his rich resources on human rights abuse. John Conroy's *Unspeakable Acts, Ordinary People*, is a landmark study, now achieving frightening relevance, on how readily humans can justify inhumanity. Amnesty International and the Center for the Victims of Torture provide ongoing education and support. To all, thank you for the work you do.

Friends and colleagues volunteered insightful criticism and counsel through various manscript drafts: Joe Helgerson, Greg Hewett, José Jessurun, Jeff Kellogg, Marly Rusoff, Bart Schneider, H.K. Stefan.

Jim Cihlar, with resolve and insight, was instrumental in positioning and editing the manuscript for consideration by publishers.

Juanita Garciagodoy continues to read my work with an eye on the page and the other on my soul.

I'm grateful to you all.